THE FORMIDABLE MISS CASSIDY

'Miss Cassidy is a tremendous protagonist—
witty and clever, with just a hint of her own secrets.
Singaporean horror is juxtaposed against a pitch-perfect
Victorian tone: this is a captivating and clever novel
you won't want to put down until the final page'

Helen Corcoran, author of *Queen of Coin and Whispers*
and *Daughter of Winter and Twilight*

'A page-turner, exuding the daylight smells and colours, and the cicada-singing nights of Old Singapore'

Nuraliah Norasid, award-winning author of
The Gatekeeper

'A stunning blend of history, myth and magic from Singapore and beyond'

Ng Yi-Sheng, multi-award-winning author of
Lion City

'An utter delight… A charming adventure, a competent heroine and a middle-aged romance you find yourself rooting for'

The Straits Times

'Completely immersive and bursting with characters who leap off the page. A debut as impressive as Miss Cassidy herself!'

Amie Kaufman, internationally bestselling author of
The Other Side of the Sky

'A rollicking good ride!'

Time Out

'Quirky, charming and with a gorgeous heart of gold… A feminist tale, ghost story and period piece wrapped up in one fascinating book'

Suffian Hakim, bestselling author of
The Keepers of Stories

THE
FORMIDABLE
MISS
CASSIDY

MEIHAN BOEY

AN IMPRINT OF PUSHKIN PRESS

ONE, an imprint of
Pushkin Press
Somerset House, Strand
London WC2R 1LA

The Formidable Miss Cassidy was first published
by Epigram Books in Singapore, 2021

First published by Pushkin Press in 2024 by
arrangement with Astier-Pécher Literary Agency

1 3 5 7 9 8 6 4 2

ISBN 13: 978-1-80533-755-3

Designed and typeset by Tetragon, London
Printed and bound in the United Kingdom by Clays Ltd, Elcograf S.p.A.

www.pushkinpress.com

For my husband Steven, always a "kilty" pleasure

CONTENTS

PART THREE (1904)
THE SCHOOLHOUSE SEANCE

PART ONE

1895

THE BENDEMEER HOUSE PONTIANAK

I

Miss Cassidy Arrives

"I'M sure we will be very good friends," said Miss Cassidy brightly.

Sarah Jane Bendemeer attempted a faint, polite smile. To be quite fair, it was very, very hot on Collyer Quay, and they were both looking terribly bedraggled. Miss Cassidy was seldom put out by long journeys, but it was an inhuman distance between Scotland and British Malaya, and even she was feeling somewhat less than all there.

Miss Cassidy jumped back, startled, as a small, grey, wizened man seized her trunk and loaded it onto his back, and scurried off without a word. "I say, should I be worried about that?" she asked as Sarah Jane listlessly fanned herself.

"What? Oh, no, no. That was Ah Kio."

Miss Cassidy waited for further explanation, but Sarah Jane seemed to believe this was sufficient in itself, and began to drift away, muttering vague sounds of gratitude. So Miss Cassidy lifted her skirts and pursued her. Several eyes followed her passage, but Miss Cassidy was not put out—apart from being tall and, well, of healthy build, she was also blessed with a head of brilliant flame-red hair, which seemed to glow under the tropical sun. She was used to being stared at.

Her surroundings were very interesting, and if she had not been so hot she would have felt an urgent need for her sketchbook. The quay was crowded and noisy. Around them surged the Chinese coolies, skinny, incredibly strong; unloading and loading sacks and crates and boxes as though they weighed nothing, though they certainly weighed more than the men carrying them.

"What do these fellows eat?" murmured Miss Cassidy as Sarah Jane, herself and her large poplar-wood trunk were loaded into a rickshaw, which was then dragged at a furious rate through the dusty, noisy streets by another skinny man whose waist was surely of less substance than Miss Cassidy's thigh (admittedly, Miss Cassidy was a well-fed lass).

"Oh, rice and that sort of thing," said Sarah Jane, unperturbed.

"They're terribly strong."

"Are they? I suppose it is what they are like."

It was clear Sarah Jane was not of a descriptive bent, so Miss Cassidy, with neither sketchbook nor notebook to hand, tried her best to memorise what she was seeing, the better to write a nice juicy letter for poor Anna later on. The noise and bustle of the quay gave way now to a panoply of conflicting aromas: spices, mingled with dust and the perspiration off both bullocks and people. The faces had become more varied in colour, shape and dimension, as had the clothing; small women with very large voices lined the streets, bearing on their backs children, fresh produce, bricks and dirt, tiffins of food, buckets of water—sometimes all at the same time. It was most marvellous.

The squat little buildings with indecipherable Chinese characters over the doors began to dwindle away by and by. Sarah Jane did not know the names of the large European-looking buildings they passed, but Miss Cassidy recognised churches, mission schools and what were probably government buildings, not so very different from the ones she'd seen in London.

Her family had been horrified to hear that she had accepted a post as a lady's companion in British Malaya. "You will die of cholera within a year," her sister Anna had exclaimed furiously, and nothing would convince her otherwise. It was no use telling her that Singapore was not the wilds of India or Africa, that she was not forging through the jungles (though that would have been a splendid option, had it come round), that the Bendemeers seemed a perfectly respectable family. Sarah Jane was said to have a docile and manageable temperament, and would not at all be a difficult charge.

Miss Cassidy had not told her own family that Sarah Jane was the last surviving child of Captain James Bendemeer, the rest of the family having perished from an unfortunate tropical fever. None of the other children had survived, and when Mrs Bendemeer herself was taken, Captain James had offered a considerable salary to any "decent, well-bred, good-tempered lady of middle age, widow or spinster" to sail to

British Malaya and give "company and guidance" to a "poor forlorn child of fourteen".

Sarah Jane was certainly docile, thought Miss Cassidy. Docile was too lively a word, even. Sarah Jane was…was…

The rickshaw stopped at the iron gates of a large compound. The grass around the gates was overgrown, and though there was a fine black-and-white bungalow visible beyond the path, raised up from the ground about seven feet, Miss Cassidy could see it had not been well-kept for a while. The view of the house was much obscured by a large rain tree with enormous spreading branches, some so heavy they hung nearly to the ground. Speckled here and there, in no particular sense of order, were trees and plants Miss Cassidy would later come to learn were largely banana, papaya and frangipani. The fragrance of frangipani flowers was thick in the hot heavy air, an odd, cloying, sugary scent.

Sarah Jane was getting out. "Will he not take us to the door?" asked Miss Cassidy in dismay, as Ah Kio—who had been clinging on to the back of the rickshaw—again shouldered Miss Cassidy's trunk. The rickshaw driver accepted coins in a rough palm, turned and left at high speed.

Sarah Jane shook her head. "They do not like our house."

"Eh? What do you mean?"

But once again Sarah Jane did not answer, silently drifting in through the old iron gates, leaving Miss Cassidy no option again but to follow. Ah Kio, despite his load, was running on ahead of them with the trunk.

An elderly Chinese lady in a white Chinese blouse and black trousers stood at the steps. She had a long grey braid, a gold tooth and a welcoming smile. "Ah Nai," said Sarah Jane, with the first genuine joy Miss Cassidy had seen her produce. "This is Miss Cassidy, from Scotland. Miss Cassidy, Ah Nai was my nanny, and is our family's bondservant. She'll take care of you."

"Bondservant?" No—it was no use. Sarah Jane had already entered the house without a further word of explanation.

"The Captain will see you tonight," said Ah Nai, in carefully enunciated syllables. "I will show you to your room. Hoi!" The last strident holler was not directed at Miss Cassidy, but at Ah Kio, followed by a fiery stream of hard consonants that, Miss Cassidy assumed, were instructions to bring her trunk.

The house was like nothing Miss Cassidy had ever seen. She had some experience of the tropics, having been a governess in India briefly (before that family perished from a combination of malaria and the Sepoy Mutiny), but this was something entirely different. The floors were polished wood, the ceilings were high and the windows were numerous and large, allowing for a little much-needed ventilation. The furniture was of some kind of dark woven wood, upholstered in plain cotton. There were no heavy draperies and deep carpets and brilliant bejewelled knick-knacks here. Perhaps the Bendemeers couldn't afford to maintain the upkeep of unnecessary decorations. Or perhaps, reflected Miss Cassidy, it was just too hot to do so.

Every room was big, bright and well-aired, and Miss Cassidy was pleased to find that her little annexe was no different: a small cosy room with a large window whose wooden shutters had been propped open all day for air. A white netting hung over her bed, a mosquito net; she'd had one in India as well. Fragrant leaves had been bound to the window frame.

"Pandan leaves," explained Ah Nai. "To keep insects away."

"Lovely! I do like how that smells. Tell me, Ah Nai—where can I buy some cloth? Cotton or muslin…" Miss Cassidy thought a while, as Ah Nai looked faintly puzzled. "Well…you see, I need to make another dress. I brought along the dress I usually wore in India, but even that will not be cool enough."

"Ah! You can make Western dresses!"

Miss Cassidy blinked, then laughed. "Oh, I forget! Most of the white ladies here are wealthy, aren't they? They have dressmakers. I make my own clothes, Ah Nai. We all do, back home. I can make men's shirts as well, and bake bread, and kill a pig, and roast a fowl."

Ah Nai grinned, her gold tooth gleaming. "Perhaps you can teach Miss Sarah Jane."

"Goodness gracious, no. I will teach her embroidery, dancing, and French or German."

Miss Cassidy and Ah Nai looked at each other a moment. Then they both began to giggle. Then they were boisterously laughing. Miss Cassidy couldn't think why it was so funny, all of a sudden. It was quite literally true that these were the skills she had been hired to educate young ladies in. She had never found it funny before.

The sun set.

Miss Cassidy had changed into her India frock, which was of pale grey poplin; she had left out the petticoat. She did not have corsetry—ever since India, she had done without them. Nobody looked at a middle-aged governess anyway, and corsets were wildly uncomfortable in hot climates.

Sarah Jane had drifted in to the annexe. "You are well-settled?" she asked politely.

"Indeed, yes, I am very comfortable," was the cheerful reply. "It is hot, but I am used to that from India. Have you ever been there?"

"To India? No."

"You would find it fascinating. Tell me, is Singapore an Indian name? It is very similar to the names of many Indian cities."

"It is in some old language," said Sarah Jane without interest. "I think the 'pore' means 'city'."

"Ah! So it is also Sanskrit. And the Singa?"

"Means lion."

"Well! But there are no lions here—why is this place called Lion City?"

"I suppose lions are important in some way," was the vague response. Before Miss Cassidy could continue the conversation (which she personally found quite interesting), Sarah Jane had drifted back out the door again.

"I think she might not be keen on having a companion," Miss Cassidy remarked to Ah Nai when the old lady later brought her tea and biscuits. It was the finest Lapsang tea, and the alien-looking biscuits speckled with little black seeds turned out to be most delicious.

"Oh, no, it is not that," said Ah Nai. "You see, Miss Cassidy, this house is haunted."

Miss Cassidy sipped her tea, put down her biscuit and said, "Eh?"

Ah Nai nodded in a matter-of-fact way. "There are many mok-mok in this area. We stay indoors at night. If you smell frangipani, don't step outside. If you see a beautiful woman standing under a banana tree, don't speak to her. We are safe, for they haunt menfolk, mostly, but do not tread on her ground."

"Her ground? Whose ground?"

"The pontianak." Ah Nai smiled warmly at her. "I am glad you have come, Miss Cassidy. Miss Sarah Jane has been very lonely."

"Hmm," said Miss Cassidy, but Ah Nai had hurried off to some other task.

Miss Cassidy carefully finished her tea, then peered with interest into the grounds. "Hmm," she said again, more sharply, to herself.

The house was very dark after sunset. Ah Nai lit the way to Captain Bendemeer's study with a kerosene lamp; Ah Kio was busy burning what Miss Cassidy at first thought was some fancy form of incense, but turned out to be mosquito coils. It was a strong scent, but not unpleasant.

The study was surely the darkest room in the house. Sarah Jane sat in a low woven rattan chair, reading a small Bible by the light of a gas lamp. Seated beside her, but slightly turned away, was Captain Bendemeer.

Miss Cassidy's immediate impression was that Captain Bendemeer was not long for this world. Sallow, with bruises under his eyes, he barely filled out the shoulders of his coat, and he seemed to shiver even in the oppressive heat. He must have once had sandy thick hair and lush whiskers, but everything was now in patches and knots.

"Miss Cassidy, I am pleased to meet you," he said slowly, his voice hoarse. "I hope you have had a comfortable journey. It is a long way to travel, and I am grateful you have undertaken such a passage for the sake of my dear Sarah Jane."

His dear Sarah Jane turned her face away from the light, as if she might have spoken, but didn't.

"I am pleased to make your acquaintance, Captain Bendemeer, and anxious to know how I might best be of service to you and Miss Sarah."

"I should think that plain. As you can see, we are rather isolated here. There is no one to keep Sarah Jane company except old Ah Nai, and that will not do for a girl of fourteen. She has not had a respectable chaperone since her Mama died. Now, with you, she may go out visiting again, and to dances, and whatever it is girls must do these days."

"I should be quite satisfied to stay home with you, Papa," said Sarah Jane.

"Now, I cannot allow that," said Miss Cassidy briskly. "A girl may be close to her Papa without being a nun. You are terribly low of spirits as it is, Miss Sarah Jane. I will undertake to remedy that. We will have walks, and picnics, and visits to friends."

"Excellent," murmured Captain Bendemeer, interrupting Sarah Jane's faint protest. "Miss Cassidy—pardon me, your first name is...?"

"Leda, Captain Bendemeer."

"Unusual name. Is it Irish? Cassidy is an Irish name, is it not?"

Miss Cassidy raised one eyebrow just a touch. "Cassidy is, indeed, of Gaelic origin, Captain. You have an unusual family name yourself, I think. I have never heard it before."

"It was a different name two generations ago, Miss Cassidy. There were...difficult circumstances."

"I see. Well, we have some things in common, Captain. Now, Sarah Jane," and Miss Cassidy turned to her charge, who flinched somewhat under the forthright gaze, "tomorrow morning we shall take a long brisk walk up to the town, and you will tell me all about it. What can you be about, to live in such a fascinating place and have nothing to say about it, I do not know. You will show me where you purchase your things, so that I may run your errands for you. Have you any friends of your age in these parts?"

"No, I am the only English girl of my age."

"Are there no good families among the local folk here, who might visit with you?"

There was a pause.

"The local folk will not come here," said Captain Bendemeer. "I suppose Ah Nai will have told you. Some superstition about the house."

"Indeed! You must tell me more about this superstition. I make no sense of it."

Captain Bendemeer turned away. Sarah Jane fingered her Bible.

Miss Cassidy tapped an impatient fingernail upon the arm of her chair and then asked, "What is a pontianak?"

A cold wind wafted through the room, redolent with the fragrance of frangipani. Captain Bendemeer shivered again. The leaves of the banana trees rustled and whispered.

"A pontianak," said Sarah Jane in a low voice, "is a kind of...I suppose we would call it a vampyr. It is a monster they have around these parts. A demon woman who hunts men and drinks their blood."

"And is there one meant to haunt the house?"

"Yes."

"Have you seen it?"

The banana leaves rustled again, more loudly, and Sarah Jane said, "Miss Cassidy, I beg you not to trouble yourself with these native superstitions. You will probably come across many of them in the time you are here with us. We just...we learn to live with...them."

"I see," said Miss Cassidy, and asked no more.

It was nearly three in the morning when Miss Cassidy woke up. The old iron key she had hung over her window carefully, on a particular bit of string, was gently swinging, striking the wooden shutter in a rhythmic fashion.

There were a few things Miss Cassidy never travelled without. Iron was one of those things. She found it most practical in the shape of a nice big skeleton key. Nobody questioned the possession of an iron key upon someone always attended by a trunk.

She also carried a salt shaker, a piece of blackboard chalk and a ball of string, generally wool. They were handy for practical reasons (such as flavouring soup), apart from their original purpose. Miss Cassidy always liked things to have more than one use to them.

But she didn't need any of them at the moment. Ah Nai had given her a cotton sarong; she now used it as a wrapper, not for warmth but for camouflage. Taking the key down from the hook, she poked the shutter open a small crack, and peered out.

Leaves rustled through the branches of the sprawling rain tree. In the deep moving darkness, Miss Cassidy saw Captain Bendemeer walking up and down his untidy garden, making slow circles along the line of banana trees. The big floppy leaves brushed his shoulders as he passed.

Miss Cassidy said, "Hmph."

There was a glass of water she'd placed at her bedside earlier. Carefully she picked it up, tapped it three times, then lifted it and looked out at the world through the glass and its contents.

And she saw the pontianak.

Miss Cassidy had never seen anything like it—and she had seen quite a lot. It was indeed a woman. She appeared to be unclothed; her body was pale and flawless, moonlit and gleaming. Her hair was very long and very dark, drifting around her as if she were immersed in deep water. She moved without movement; it was as if the shadows were carrying her, and she went gliding between the banana trees like a fish through water. She hovered over Captain Bendemeer's shoulder, whispered to him, hissed, smiled, blinked great dark sleepy eyes.

Then she opened her mouth, filled with an impossible number of incredibly sharp teeth, massively wide, and clamped down over his left eye.

The Captain merely stood there, absolutely still, as the creature seemed to drink from him, greedily. Blood trickled down his cheeks, which she licked up hungrily.

Miss Cassidy had seen enough. Silently she closed her shutter. Silently she put away the glass and the key.

"Well," she said after a moment to herself, "I can do nothing of use now. We shall see about it in the morning."

She went back to bed, and fell soundly asleep.

II

Miss Cassidy &
the Banana Tree

"H MM," said Miss Cassidy the next morning.

The banana tree looked no different from any other in the brilliant light of day. It was perhaps a particularly lush specimen, with unusually bright green leaves; but it was in no way more interesting or sinister than any other in the compound, except that a length of bright pink silk had been tied around it.

Miss Cassidy fingered the silk—it had probably once been some young lady's headscarf, but was now ragged and thread-bare. When the fabric touched Miss Cassidy's fingertips, she winced slightly. This might perhaps be more difficult than she had first imagined.

"Miss Cassidy, do be careful." Sarah Jane's voice listlessly drifted towards her. "Ah Nai doesn't like us touching the banana trees."

"Ah, and do you know why this bit of cloth is here?"

24

"To scare off the monkeys, perhaps. There are a lot of monkeys here, and they are quite fearless."

"I see," murmured Miss Cassidy.

"Can we go back inside now?" asked Sarah Jane, with the first touch of temper Miss Cassidy had seen her exhibit. "We have walked ten rounds, exactly as you wanted, and it is very hot. I want a glass of water."

"Certainly we may go in," said Miss Cassidy briskly, tearing herself away from the tree and its odd decoration, and taking Sarah Jane firmly by the elbow. "I think we are quite done here."

After Sarah Jane had gone off to her room to lie down and recover from her "strenuous" twenty-minute stroll (although to be quite fair, the garden path was not easy to traverse in skirts and petticoats), Miss Cassidy sought out Ah Nai in the kitchens. "Give me something to do," she said cheerfully to the somewhat startled old servant. "Sarah Jane is done with her lessons and her exercise."

Ah Nai, who was fanning a coal fire upon which a clay pot was bubbling, thought a little. "Will you mend?" she asked, mimicking a needle and thread to express herself clearly.

"Yes, if that is what you need."

If there was one thing Miss Cassidy was good at, it was waiting. Of course, she was good at many (many, many) things, but she had perfected patience to an art.

However Miss Cassidy's patience was not of that tranquil sort that allows venerable religious teachers to sit under a tree for outrageous lengths of time. Generally, when Miss Cassidy waited, she was also watching, and listening, and taking note of things and people around her, with an insight particular to a lady of her unique talents. By and by, she would hum a little, and chuckle a little, and drop an interesting observation or humorous word, and by dint of these little incursions, those around her found themselves compelled to engage with her.

Thus it was that, while Miss Cassidy sat comfortably at the kitchen door (for the sake of the breeze), mending one of the Captain's shirts, and Ah Nai brewed her curious concoction, and despite the relative silence in which they did both tasks… in some curious way, they quietly became firm friends.

"So that is a tonic of some sort," said Miss Cassidy with interest, as strong, bitter scents filled the kitchen from Ah Nai's clay pot.

Ah Nai nodded. "For the Captain. For his health."

"Hmm. His health is certainly poor. Tell me, Ah Nai," said Miss Cassidy casually as she busily stitched away, "what ails him? Is it this house? Why do they not simply leave it, and move to a healthier clime?"

The story unfolded at a gentle pace, punctuated by the bubbling of the pot. When Ah Nai had come to the family, the Captain was a happy, healthy, strong man—a sailor of humble background who had risen to become captain of his own vessel. His wife, Maria, was a striking beauty: tall, proud, raven-haired and exotic, born in the West Indies somewhere (Ah Nai could not remember the name of the island, but Maria apparently spoke both Spanish and French fluently, and it seemed likely she was from either Jamaica or Haiti). She was an ambitious woman, asking her husband to leave the seas and take up a position in the British East India Company, in order to better their position in society. When they arrived in Singapore, they already had their first child with them—the infant Sarah Jane.

They were given these splendid quarters which they renamed, simply, Bendemeer House. The couple did well at first; the Captain proved himself a much-valued employee, with his extensive knowledge of the sea (more to the point, he was also familiar with pirate routes and routines, and adept at plotting paths to avoid them). Maria added to their family every other year, and though she was a firm and rather imposing Mama, nevertheless the children were healthy, strong and intelligent, and all seemed to be well.

Then came that one dreadful year. First Mrs Bendemeer fell ill, then her husband, then the children, in quick succession, including Sarah Jane. Ah Nai herself nursed them as best she could, but she herself became ill. She recovered only in time to help Sarah Jane—the only surviving child—arrange the funerals.

Ah Nai paused over the fire to gently beat her chest with her hand, and Miss Cassidy understood that this was the old woman's way of keeping her emotions in check. She let the quiet moment draw out a little before asking gently, "And what disease was this, Ah Nai?"

Ah Nai shook her head. The doctor was a white man; she didn't understand what he had written down. In any case, she knew the symptoms: fever, flux and rash; she had seen many people die like this, especially those living close to the jungle or wetlands. And Bendemeer House was situated right up against the jungle, amid wild banana trees. The Bendemeers had had difficulty finding servants when they first arrived because of that.

"Hmm," said Miss Cassidy. "How long have the trees been there?"

Ah Nai shook her head. Longer than the house, for certain; these wild trees had always been part of the jungle, till the British cleared the land to build the bungalow.

"And did no one, well, cleanse the house?"

Ah Nai knew what she meant, and took it matter-of-factly. "There was a priest," the amah said, somewhat obliquely. "The Captain would not allow...anyone else."

"And the priest was ineffective?"

"He was young," said Ah Nai gently.

"And he faced something ancient? I see."

Ah Nai shrugged, indulgent of the white man's ignorance. "It was all right for a while."

"Until it wasn't." Miss Cassidy put in a few more neat stitches. "And what do you do with the bananas from these fearful trees, Ah Nai?"

Ah Nai looked surprised. "We eat them," she said.

"I have brought you your tea, Captain," said Miss Cassidy cheerfully.

Captain Bendemeer looked up from his papers. For a moment he seemed puzzled, as if he did not recognise her; then, as she entered, his vision cleared. "Ah, thank you, Miss Cassidy. You can leave these tasks to Ah Nai, you know."

"Oh, it is no trouble, I assure you, Captain," she said briskly as she set down the tray. "This daily tonic you drink—how did you come by the recipe?"

Again it seemed to take a moment for the words to filter through to the Captain. "Maria—Mrs Bendemeer, my late wife. A family recipe, I believe. She makes us all drink it—well, she used to," he corrected himself with a wry smile. "I apologise—she has been gone a long while, but I still feel her presence in this house."

"Is that why you stay here? It seems a very large house for a family of two."

"Well, we were a family of nine before...before that year." He shook his head. "I am sorry, Miss Cassidy, but I have much work to do. Just leave the tray there, and I will help myself. I thank you for your assistance."

Miss Cassidy was a woman who knew what the looming ubiety of death felt like. It was not a terrifying thing to her—all mortal creatures must die—and there was no place in the world where she did not feel its presence. Sometimes it was a low, gentle undercurrent, as it was in most places rich with life; other times it was a roar that drowned out all else, on battlefields, in the dark places of the world, where light and warmth and growing things had fled.

She was also not unacquainted with the beings who existed in-between life and death. For the most part, they did not trouble her—she was not their prey, and Miss Cassidy was of the opinion that creatures which did not trouble her, and did no harm to others, were best left alone.

But the farther east she went in the world (east, that is, from where she originated), the more difficult it became to avoid the ones who passed between worlds, especially since Miss Cassidy's path often crossed somewhat through their realm. Generally they ignored one another—the neutral coexistence of those who moved through shadow depended on them all being able to actively ignore one another, no matter how startling the appearance or menacing the aspect. Miss Cassidy was consequently not easily frightened.

Indeed, she was not afraid now, but she was troubled. Bendemeer House was echoingly empty, yet its stark and scrupulously cleaned rooms, with their abandoned children's cribs and trunks filled with toys and camphor, clamoured noisily with the weight of angry memory. Death still clung to every corner; not the sad, gentle death of recently lost loved ones, but something far older, darker and more dangerous.

Ordinarily, Miss Cassidy would have tried to bide her time a little. Information was necessary, but Sarah Jane and her Papa were clearly not the sort to instantly take Miss Cassidy into their confidence, or to pour out their troubles in a flash. They would need many months to warm to her, and Miss Cassidy was quite certain the Captain did not have months to wait.

"I suppose I will have to make time," she murmured to herself.

"What?"

Miss Cassidy blinked. Sarah Jane looked at her, and for a moment both ladies were frozen, caught in the middle of their respective reveries; looking into Sarah Jane's pale blue eyes, Miss Cassidy saw straight into her soul, and was...well, surprised. She was not sure yet if the surprise was pleasant, but it was at least something to consider.

"I will have to make time to write letters," Miss Cassidy said cheerfully, taking Sarah Jane's arm as they continued their promenade (very reluctantly, on Sarah Jane's part) on the manicured lawns of the Botanic Gardens. "I notice you do not write many yourself, Sarah Jane?"

"I have no one to write to," she said, trying in vain to adjust her hat to keep the sun off her pale face. Miss Cassidy's insistence on a vigorous daily walk was very trying to the languid girl, but she had at least given up protesting.

It had been three weeks now, since Miss Cassidy had landed at Collyer Quay. The small household had grown accustomed to her very quickly. Miss Cassidy was like a rushing river—bright, sparkling and inexorable in its passage—so people generally found it easier to paddle their boat to the impetus of her current. This was certainly true of Ah Nai, who had come to enjoy both Miss Cassidy's company as well as her strong arms, and stomach; Miss Cassidy had once been a nurse, among other things, and chamber pots, spittoons and soiled intimates did not faze her. So much did Ah Nai already trust her, Miss Cassidy had now taken over the brewing of Captain Bendemeer's daily tonic, and if it had a slightly different flavour since the pot's watcher had changed, Captain Bendemeer never noticed the difference—in this, or anything else.

Sarah Jane, however, had. "Papa sleeps better these days," she remarked as they marched along, Sarah Jane perspiring under her parasol, Miss Cassidy looking as fresh and cool as if the sun's worst rays were simply sliding off her skin like silk.

"He certainly sleeps more *soundly*," said Miss Cassidy carefully. There were many ways to induce in someone a sleep so deep *nothing* could possibly wake them; some skirted very close to simply having the sleeper never wake again. "I have convinced him to keep the windows closed and the shades drawn. The room may seem a bit stifling, but I believe it is better for him."

"I have heard that the night air in the tropics carries a miasma," said Sarah Jane doubtfully.

"Well, it certainly carries mosquitoes, and they are not pleasant evening guests either."

"In any case, I am glad he seems better. He is the only family I have now."

They walked a little more, and in the shade of a glorious spreading rain tree, Miss Cassidy allowed her charge to sink gratefully into a welcoming bench. "I am so thirsty," sighed Sarah Jane.

"I have the very thing," said Miss Cassidy brightly, and produced from her deep pockets a handful of brilliant pink fruit. "Ah Nai says these are called water apples. They are full of juice."

"I have never had them." Heat and thirst overcame Sarah Jane's usual reluctance to try new things, and she took a fruit, carefully wiped it and bit into it. The look of relief and surprise on her face cheered Miss Cassidy up considerably—it was rare to see Sarah Jane enjoy anything, even something as simple as a cool fruit on a hot day. "Why, they are delicious!"

"You grew up here—did you never have these?"

"Mama was careful with what we ate. She didn't want us being too... oh, I don't know. Too 'native', I suppose."

"Your Mama, bless her soul, must have been a...firm sort of woman."

Sarah Jane bit her lip, and after a moment murmured, "Mama meant everything for the best. She wanted us to grow up to be a credit to Papa's name—to be proud, fine and strong. I am the oldest—was the oldest—and Mama always insisted I must lead the way, make a good marriage, become a fine lady."

"And what did you think about that?"

"It was harder on my younger sisters, I think. But Mama meant it for the best," repeated Sarah Jane quietly. "We were always rather afraid of her; she had such a temper. She had this sewing kit that was always on her lap. It was full of huge, black pins and needles and scissors that she had brought over from the West Indies."

"She must have been very attached to this sewing kit, to have carried it across the sea."

"I suppose so. She used to make little dolls, and perfumed sachets and suchlike, which we put with our things to keep the insects out. I never liked them; I thought they smelled odd. But when we were naughty, she would threaten to stitch our mouths shut, or rub chilli seeds in our eyes, or poke us with her needle—and they were all such enormous needles. Of course she didn't truly mean it, but it still used to frighten us, and we would run to Papa to hide."

"I see," said Miss Cassidy carefully. "And what happened to the little dolls and bags your Mama made for you?"

"They were burned…with all the sheets and things. It was after all—everyone—John and Emily and Charles and… everyone…" Sarah Jane subsided, wringing her hands in her lap. "It was the fever…they said we should burn everything."

Miss Cassidy was quiet, taking Sarah Jane's hand to soothe her restlessness. "What a racket those birds make," she said after a moment, cheerfully.

"I like them," said Sarah Jane wistfully. "We don't get so many birds around Bendemeer House."

"Mm, I have noticed that. Now, shall we go and see the orchids? I am curious about this Miss Agnes Joaquim—they say she has created a new type of flower. Isn't that marvellous?"

Sarah Jane did not seem to think much of this feat, but she stood, and allowed herself to be gently guided away.

III

Miss Cassidy &
the Chinese Wedding

Miss Cassidy adjusted Sarah Jane's hat, then stepped back to view the results with satisfaction. Sarah Jane was actually a rather pretty girl, merely pale in her colouring. Her white-blonde hair and washed-out blue eyes gave her an unfortunate pallor. But the addition of rose-coloured ribbons and a charming hat had worked wonders, and Miss Cassidy and Ah Nai had worked hard to refresh some of Sarah Jane's dresses. Without her keen-eyed Mama, Sarah Jane had been left to run to seed, fashion-wise.

"Lovely," said Miss Cassidy.

"Yes, lovely," echoed Ah Nai, and only then did Sarah Jane smile. Miss Cassidy had learnt, after only being in the house a week, that Sarah Jane adored her amah, and would do anything to please her. Except for that one day in the Botanic Gardens, Sarah Jane did not speak of her own

Mama much, though that lady's photograph took pride of place on the family mantle (under which there was no fireplace). Maria Bendemeer had certainly had a forbidding look about her.

Miss Cassidy had learnt now that Ah Nai's place in the family was beyond that of a nursemaid or servant. An amah considered herself bound for life to the family she served. She raised the children, ran the household and took a vow of celibacy so she would never marry and leave them. Miss Cassidy had seen a number of amahs by now, in their signature white-and-black outfits. The understanding was that the family would eventually take care of their amah in turn, when she was too old to work.

Miss Cassidy couldn't say if any family merited such loyalty, even if their blood ran pure blue in their veins, but it was not for her to comment upon.

Ah Nai had raised all seven children for the Bendemeers, of which the only survivor was Sarah Jane, whom she accordingly loved far too much, and indulged far too freely.

Before Miss Cassidy's advent, Sarah Jane had led a secluded life. Her father was whisked away daily in a rickshaw to the East India offices (where Miss Cassidy suspected he was not entirely applying himself to the company's satisfaction), and Sarah Jane was just left to muddle about till he returned for his tea. It was too hot, she always complained, to go out. She liked to be home. She enjoyed needlework. She was happy to be taught both French and German, and to learn to read in both. Miss Cassidy's insistence on long walks remained trying to the girl, though she did her best these days to comply.

She was, alas, not very bright. Miss Cassidy had not even made it through one lesson of French (which Sarah Jane had allegedly been learning all her life) before she knew that the girl would have no claims to join the bluestockings. She had no option but to marry someone, and soon.

About two months after Miss Cassidy's arrival, Captain Bendemeer placed an invitation in Miss Cassidy's hand. "I would like Sarah Jane to attend this," he said. "Make her ready."

It was, to Miss Cassidy, very interesting. A local business-man's oldest son was getting married—a business acquaintance of the East India Company. It was to be an elaborate affair. There would be seven days of Chinese celebrations, including a wedding luncheon that would be in a "Western" style, for the businessman's many British and Dutch business acquaintances. This was what they had been invited to.

The invitation was worded in formal, Oxford English. There was a large, flourishing Chinese symbol on the front.

"Double happiness," said Sarah Jane, surprising Miss Cassidy. "We get many wedding invitations," she added by way of explanation. "They always have that symbol on. Papa works with lots of Chinese merchants and traders and…and whatever they are. They think it a sign of their status if there are plenty of Westerners at the party. It impresses the others."

"Hmm," said Miss Cassidy. "Well, you are going to this one."

Sarah Jane looked haunted. "Must I? I don't like them. They're terribly loud and…and uncouth. There's fireworks, and these dancing lions with great wobbly eyes, and I can't eat any of the food, and it's ever so hot."

"It says here you will be served cucumber soup, fish, roast mutton, cheese and fruit. I see nothing objectionable here."

"But you don't understand. Here, when they want to cook English dishes, they hire Hainanese chefs."

"Eh?"

"People from Hainan."

"And?" Miss Cassidy drummed her fingers impatiently. She would find it hard to curb her temper with this docile, forlorn girl, she had come to realise.

"They don't cook the same way."

"I should imagine people from Hainan would well be baffled by cucumber soup, but as long as it is edible, does it matter? The purpose of a luncheon is not the luncheon, but the people who attend it. This man, this Mr"—she peered at the card—"Mr Kay Wing Tong is clearly an important man. All the right people will be there."

"Mr Kay is a trader. He is in the Straits Steamship Company, I believe. They are all Chinese."

Miss Cassidy glanced at Ah Nai, who was in the room, apparently invisible, sweeping the floor. Ah Nai caught her eye, smiled faintly, and continued to sweep.

"My dear, there shall be no more argument," said Miss Cassidy briskly. "Your Papa has said you are going, so you are going. Your Papa will be there, and I will chaperone you. If you are so afraid of the heathen Chinese, you may take refuge behind me."

And thus it came to pass. No white at Chinese weddings, said Ah Nai, so they dressed the young lady in pale pink. Miss Cassidy still only had her grey poplin, but she brushed it out, scrubbed the hem as clean as she could, and pinned her single ornament on, a brooch with a deep green stone.

Ah Nai was impressed by the brooch. "It looks like jade," she said, displaying a small flat coin of that precious Chinese stone in her ear, on a piece of red string.

"Ah! It's only malachite, I fear."

"Does it have…" Ah Nai paused, trying to find an English equivalent, and failing.

"It does not bring luck," said Miss Cassidy, correctly guessing her meaning. "But it is—well, I suppose one can say, it brings optimism."

Madam Lim was exasperated.

"We have to find the pig's head," she tried again. "It has to be returned to the bride's family. It's an essential part of the wedding. We cannot proceed without it!"

Mr Kay Wing Tong looked up from his desk. He was a mild-mannered Chinese gentleman who looked somewhat younger than his forty-four years, with his neatly trimmed hair still jet-black. At first glance he had a menacing aspect, for he was very tall and possessed a severe countenance. His cheekbones were high and prominent, and his jaw very strong, so that he often intimidated others around him simply by standing a little closer to them than was necessary. He had always found this to be an effective tactic, since he was not naturally disposed to be either firm or menacing.

Madam Lim, the matchmaker, had known him a long time, and was not impressed by his unusual height or the angle of his jawline or any of these other details of his appearance.

She had known him since he was a gangly, pimply teenager, so awkward that his parents despaired of ever finding him a wife, and with such ambiguous omens in his fortune that they were nearly resigned to his early death before he had cut his first adult tooth. But Mr Kay had survived—had, indeed, thrived, and was now one of the most successful and wealthy traders in the Straits Settlements, with a fleet of steamships to his name.

Madam Lim was inclined to take some of the credit for this, having successfully matched him to a wife whose Eight Character reading was meant to boost his own mediocre fortune in the appropriate way. Consequently, she was never afraid to speak her mind, especially not now she had made a successful match for his own son.

"I have scolded the cook all morning," she repeated, "but they cannot find it. I'm sure your servants have eaten it."

Mr Kay inwardly gave thanks that he had not been in the kitchen to witness the altercation between the cook and Madam Lim. There would probably be some smashed pots and bent utensils to replace, but that was a small price to pay.

"Well, Madam Lim, that is unfortunate," he murmured. "I'll ask the kitchen boy to run to the market now and buy another roast pig. We will remove the head and return that to the bride's family."

"And where will you find a whole roast pig now? You have to order those well in advance!"

Mr Kay waved his hand. It had been his experience all his life that most problems of this kind were solved very quickly when enough money changed hands. "Madam Lim, calm yourself, I beg. The matter will be settled satisfactorily. Now, if you will excuse me…"

Mr Kay could not remember much about his own wedding, which took place nearly twenty years ago. It had been an affair of three days, with a great deal of noise and tumult, a lot of feasting, and much going to and fro between the two houses. He had never had any idea what was happening, allowing himself to be manhandled into this outfit and that, hustled along here and there. Various implements appeared in his hand: a red umbrella, a pair of shoes, a rice ball in a porcelain spoon, a smoking joss stick; he did what he was told to do, recited whatever he was told to say and swallowed whatever was put in his mouth.

Even when it was all over and he was finally alone with his new wife, he was not really alone. The bed looked alien with its garish red sheets, gloriously embroidered with a large dragon and phoenix. There were two enormous candles burning at the head of the bed that had been there two days. There were squashed dates and sweets on the sheet, because a young boy had been asked to roll about in it for luck. Altogether it was very bewildering.

His new wife sat waiting for him, with her ceremonial red dress and veil still on.

He sat down next to her. The wedding feast was still going on—it would continue till morning. The noise rose up around them, the crash of mahjong tiles, the clink of glasses, the smell of roast meats. Drunk men shouting, "More, more!" Women laughing. Children screaming and setting off fireworks.

"Well," he began, and his wife started to giggle.

41

Mr Kay had never been one to be easily offended, otherwise it would have all been over that moment. Instead he chuckled and said, "Yes. It's all a bit much, isn't it?"

She giggled even more. Then she put up her hand and pulled her own veil aside, which was not what was supposed to happen, but it was stiflingly hot. She was not traditionally beautiful—beautiful women could pick husbands with glorious fortunes, and Mr Kay did not have a glorious fortune then—but there was such merriment in her smile, such sparkle in her eyes, that Mr Kay immediately loved her.

Chen Choo, third daughter of a landowner from Malacca, had made Mr Kay a very satisfactory wife. She gave birth seven times, of which four children survived to adulthood, including the youngest twin girls. She managed the household well, with a natural instinct for practicality and economy. She did not get in his way, was unfailingly cheerful and accommodating, and her only vices were a loud laugh and a disdain for education. Women, she felt, had no business reading or writing. Consequently, Chen Choo had gone to her early grave never able to write more than her own name, having died from complications in childbirth with the twins. Mr Kay still missed her. She had been a merry fool, but she had filled the house with a certain energy that had been missing since her departure.

Their oldest son had been Chen Choo's pride and joy; a firstborn son is always precious, especially to his mother, who through him has proved her worth. Now that this precious son was getting married, his wedding had to be splendid, so that Chen Choo's spirit would be pleased.

Mr Kay did not mind the expense. Madam Lim more than earned her salary with her skilful management. What he disliked was all the noise and fuss and bother, but it couldn't be helped. A wedding was a wedding.

His son had insisted on the Western luncheon as well. Mr Kay was not quite so sure of this part, though he went ahead to please his son. As part of the Straits Steamship Company, he had plenty of dealings with both the British and Dutch East India Company, and he knew that these people were...well, touchy, was perhaps the right word. Quick to take offence. Quick to perceive a snub when none was intended. And their rules of etiquette were so complicated! Madam Lim would not touch the Western luncheon with a bargepole; she had no patience for the ang mohs.

He had hired a team of Hainanese wait staff and chefs for the purpose, straight out of one of the hotels that served the British. Mr Kay had been to British houses, had sat down to English tea, had negotiated contracts in their manicured gardens among their Malay and Chinese staff. They were a confusing people. Sometimes, if he was lucky, they would have an Indian lawyer or secretary. With an Indian secretary, he at least knew where he stood.

The Hainanese chef showed him the menu. "Do as you please," Mr Kay said, without looking at it.

The house was looking splendid. Pandan Villa earned its name twice over, from the proliferation of pandan trees surrounding it, and the jade-green colour it was painted. Chen Choo had consulted her fortune teller after their first son was born, who advised her that the colour would balance her warm energies and help her produce more boys. Since Chen Choo had thereafter given birth to another son in quick succession, she had made sure the Villa remained a brilliant green, periodically repainted. The villa was so outstanding that the road leading up to it was now called Pandan Villa Loop.

It was a large villa, made up of three separate wings surrounding a courtyard. Madam Lim had rented enough red cloth, red candles, red lanterns, dragon-phoenix banners and so on and so forth, to profusely decorate the entire courtyard. The dais set up with the ancestral shrine was huge, glittering, impressive.

Mr Kay skirted the edge of the courtyard to remain out of the way of the labourers still unloading chairs and tables from trucks. If they spotted him, they would stop and bow and so on, and he found it most uncomfortable.

The Western luncheon was to take place in a separate enclosure, where the air would be cooler, and it would be marginally—marginally!—less noisy. The Hainanese team had set up the place exactly as if it were a hotel ballroom lunch. Mr Kay was pleased. Perhaps his guests would not be too uncomfortable.

"Papa, Papa!"

He was smiling as he turned. His wife had loved her sons, but Mr Kay loved his twin daughters the most. Giving birth to them had cost Chen Choo her life, so Mr Kay thought them doubly precious.

He burst out laughing almost the moment he turned. Yeling and Yezi—two pretty, perfect, delicate Chinese girls—were dressed in heavy, fluffy, overwhelmingly multilayered Western-style dresses.

The twins, who were only fourteen and full of ideas, looked identically chagrined.

"Isn't it pretty, Papa?"

"Can't we wear these, Papa?"

"Are you hiding cha shao bao in your sleeves?" Mr Kay asked, and roared with laughter.

Yeling and Yezi pouted. Their large gigot sleeves were extremely fashionable. It was not their fault that both girls were so small that the sleeves obscured their faces and swallowed their torsos.

"This is very modern, Papa!"

"The Western women all dress this way!"

"You want us to be modern hostesses, don't you, Papa?"

"You want us to look nice, don't you?"

Mr Kay relented, as he usually did with his daughters. Madam Lim was always saying he was a dreadful father; after letting his daughters rule his home in this unseemly manner, they would be impossible to marry off, et cetera. "If they never marry, they may stay with their old Papa forever," he said fondly, and Madam Lim would toss up her hands in despair.

"Wear whatever you like, my dears," he said, "but go and ask your brother first. It's his wedding, after all."

"They say Oldest Sister-in-Law"—the new bride—"will wear a Western wedding dress and come to meet your guests here. We hear it is very pretty, very modern."

The horror, thought Mr Kay; the poor girl will also look like a leg of mutton. "As long as your brother is happy," he said indulgently. "Now run along, girls. Don't get underfoot when all these men are carrying furniture and chinaware about."

*

Miss Cassidy had never seen anything like it.

It was delightful. The jolly noise, the brilliant colours, the clash of cymbals and gongs and drums. The lion heads were not like any lions Miss Cassidy had ever seen, brightly patched, heavily patterned, with large mouths hanging open, through which she could glimpse the acrobatic dancer expertly manipulating the creature so that it seemed sharply alive.

There were two lions, each operated by two men, surrounded by a very noisy orchestra that beat in time to their dance. They rolled, they jumped, they snapped at each other, they bowed to the audience, to the wedding couple, and to Mr Kay and his business associates, standing in a row and laughing. The couple were brightly dressed in red and yellow silk, and the bride's face was obscured behind an elaborate headdress and red veil.

The Chinese guests were gathered in the courtyard, along with tables for Malay and Indian friends, neighbours and associates, who had completely different menus arranged for them, were dressed completely differently, and yet looked perfectly comfortable where they were. The Western guests—or so they were termed in a lump, though it was not entirely an accurate designation—could see the courtyard from the veranda of the dining hall in which they had been sequestered. They had been invited to view the lion dance for luck, just before the coffee and sweets were brought in.

Miss Cassidy, of course, was not part of the luncheon; she, along with a passel of other chaperones, ladies' maids and valets, had taken her tea in the senior servants' quarters with Mr Kay's Chinese amah, Malay chauffeur and Indian groundskeeper. The English ladies' maids were inclined to be offended, considering themselves a few cuts above local servants, but Miss Cassidy (who by age, bearing, education and experience, entirely out-classed them all) had sailed in with perfect equanimity and helped pour the tea, and these ladies could only sit and stew in silent dudgeon.

When the lion dance started with a crash of cymbals, news came that Mr Kay wanted everybody to see it for good luck, and so they were ushered back onto the veranda along with the guests, much to Miss Cassidy's gratification.

"Oh!" she exhaled. "Why, look how clever he is, standing on top of that pole!"

The chauffeur chuckled. Miss Cassidy's delight was infectious.

But her enjoyment was dampened when she looked over at the guests. Sarah Jane was covering her ears and retreating hastily into the dining hall. Captain Bendemeer was still on the veranda, but he was not watching the lion dance; another gentleman, red-faced and portly, had trapped him in a corner and was vigorously remonstrating in a manner that appeared decidedly threatening. However, the Captain was not reacting; he merely stared, blank as a brick wall, waiting to be released.

Miss Cassidy caught up with Sarah Jane, who had collapsed back into her chair. "My dear! Are you quite all right? Is it the heat?"

"It is the heat, and the noise, and...oh, everything! Everything is so dreadful!"

Someone else had entered the room after her. He was in an English coat and breeches, but he was most decidedly not English. He had luminously olive skin, lush black curls and enormous eyes of quite startling brilliance. He was, in short, very handsome. "Are you all right, Miss Bendemeer?" he enquired anxiously.

Miss Cassidy stood up, astonished. "Why, that is a Malayalam accent!"

"And that is a Scottish one. Aberdeen, I think, but there is a touch of Ireland in it."

He regarded her dryly, and she burst out laughing. "Oh my goodness, forgive my dreadful manners, sir! I am not a guest here—I should not be bellowing rude personal remarks at you!"

"Well, since I am but a lowly law clerk, Madam, I forgive you the terrible breach of etiquette. And you are right—I am from Kerala."

"And I am from Scotland," she replied, eyes twinkling.

"Oh, Mr Nair, I am ever so hot," whispered Sarah Jane faintly.

Miss Cassidy hmmed inwardly as Mr Nair bent solicitously over Sarah Jane. Outwardly she said, "I will go to the kitchen and bring some ice."

Her progress was a difficult one, with guests and serving staff all squeezing and pushing and trying to get by. Miss Cassidy was glad she had left out her petticoats; she was much inclined to make herself a pair of cotton trousers like Ah Nai's.

It grew hotter, noisier and more crowded the farther she went, till she was gasping for fresh air. In desperation, she lunged through the closest door, just for a little relief, and shut the noise out for a moment.

She was in a study of some sort, dominated by an enormous ivory sculpture in the middle of the floor. It was an amazing thing, still in the shape of the elephant's tusk, but cunningly carved with intricate detail as if it were a mountainside covered with trees, flowers, rivers and little miniature houses with patterned roofs. Children with strange hairstyles were running across tiny bamboo bridges, and women in drifting scarves were playing with butterflies in pavilions.

Miss Cassidy reached out to touch the sculpture, and shuddered a little. Such amazing beauty! But such profound suffering!

"I never liked it either," said a voice quite suddenly, startling her. "But it is a family heirloom, so I must respect it. Since I cannot give the tusk back to the elephant, at least the artist who sculpted it will get his due."

And Mr Kay, whom she had seen from across the courtyard earlier, stepped out from behind a screen, smoking a pipe.

"Well! I feel as if I'm in one of those frippery novels by Mrs Radcliffe, wandering about a castle and stumbling upon the king," said Miss Cassidy, to cover her confusion. She was not sure how to greet a Chinese gentleman of standing. Did she curtsey? Bow? Kowtow?

"I am Mr Kay," he said simply, "and you look a little warm, Miss. Sit down a moment, and I will bring you tea."

"Oh, gracious heavens! I mean—I am not one of your guests, Mr Kay. I am paid companion to Miss Sarah Jane Bendemeer—her chaperone."

The name seemed not to ring obvious bells with Mr Kay, but he smiled politely. "The chair you sit in does not mind who you are," he said, and handed her tea in a small celadon cup. "Hold it in both hands," he instructed, recognising her puzzlement.

Miss Cassidy, seeing no polite way to escape her predicament, sipped the tea. It was startlingly sweet, with little red berries in it.

"It is a cooling tea," he said, which was confusing, since the tea was hot. "It will balance out your heatiness. Help clear your freckles."

Miss Cassidy was not sure whether to be offended or amused. "I should hope not," she said at last, "I am quite fond of my freckles."

Mr Kay laughed. Miss Cassidy realised abruptly that he was rather handsome. He had severe features and was monstrously tall, but when he laughed his face changed, his eyes twinkled, and he had a rich deep voice that suited laughter well. It was infectious laughter, and Miss Cassidy laughed too.

"Are you enjoying the party, Miss...?"

"Cassidy—I am Miss Cassidy."

"Cassidy. I knew a Cassidy once. He was Irish."

"My father was Irish, but I was raised in Scotland."

"I like the Irish, more than the English," said Mr Kay, nonchalantly puffing on his pipe. "There is less nonsense about them. I have not yet had dealings with Scotsmen."

"Well! I assure you, we would agree with you about non-sensical Englishmen, at least."

Mr Kay laughed again. Miss Cassidy was starting to feel far too comfortable; Sarah Jane would be wondering where her ice was.

"Mr Kay, I thank you for your truly lovely hospitality, but I must find my way to the kitchens. My mistress is feeling faint, and I was meant to fetch her some ice."

"Ah, is that all? I will send a boy. You will stay here."

"Eh? I mean, I cannot. I must go."

"Well, if you must, you must. I will send a boy anyway. Go back upstairs, Miss Cassidy, and be sure your mistress has not come to mischief."

So saying, Mr Kay simply turned away and disappeared behind the screen again. Miss Cassidy blinked, put down her celadon cup, bobbed a curtsey just in case and hurried out.

IV

Miss Cassidy by the Seaside

"I CAN see you," remarked Miss Cassidy.

The portly Caucasian man looked startled. Splashing about in the water, he roared, "What's this, what's this then?"

"I merely wished to let you know you are quite visible to anyone passing by," she said matter-of-factly. "Dear me, what a lovely view."

The sea off Singapore was not blue and crystal clear—quite the opposite—but it was still a beautiful sight, framed by palm trees and dotted with fisheries on stilts. Not far from where Miss Cassidy stood admiring the view was a low bungalow, built almost up against the tide-line, upon which hung a weather-beaten sign: Singapore Gentlemen's Swimming Club.

"Now see here," blustered the "Singapore Gentleman", hurriedly retreating to the safety of the deep sea, which was all that protected his modesty, "ladies are not permitted at this club."

"Indeed! But I am not at your club—I just happened to stroll by. You have floated a fair distance away from your swim-cabins, you know."

"This is most intrusive!"

"Now then, sir," said Miss Cassidy easily, "this is a public beach you have floated into, and I happen to be waiting for someone, and have been a while. So it is you who are intruding, really, not I."

The man, perhaps thinking it unseemly to continue the conversation in his current state, turned and vigorously splashed away, no doubt grumbling under what little breath he had left after such exertions.

"Now we are alone," said Miss Cassidy, watching the man gradually become an irate bobbing dot on the waves, "you may come out."

There was a strange, windy rustle, and a hollow groan, and then a husky voice asked, "But you are not afraid of me?"

"No, I am not."

"You will be afraid if I show myself."

"Not I. But if you are bashful, you may remain hidden behind the palm tree."

The palm tree in question rustled, and its shadow quivered haughtily. "I am not bashful. I merely wished to spare you the sight of—"

"Now, let us have enough nonsense," said Miss Cassidy briskly. "Show yourself, or not, it matters nothing to me—but I have summoned you, and while my iron is in your tree, you must answer me." She tapped, sharply, the great black nail that protruded from the bark of the otherwise entirely unremarkable tree.

Its shadow seemed to flinch, and there was a general sullen aspect to the droop of its leaves as it demanded, "What do you want from me? You are not from these shores. I can give you nothing."

"Fear not, I do not wish to win money at the horse races. I merely want some information."

"About what?"

"About pontianaks."

The palm tree bristled. "We do not speak of the banana tree ghouls," it said, snarling.

"You will speak of whatever I ask you, as long as my iron holds you here. There is a banana tree bound in pink silk—what is tethered there? Why is she there? What does she want?"

"They all want the same thing. They are scorned women, seeking vengeance upon mankind."

Miss Cassidy sniffed. "Scorned women" made her impatient. It seemed a particularly ineffective way to gain vengeance against men by being eternally obsessed with them. "And how can they be stopped?"

The palm tree chuckled. "You cannot stop them. Not even you. They are ancient, terrible, bloodthirsty—"

"But people still eat their bananas."

"You need to find a mightier spirit," said the palm tree sourly, perhaps feeling Miss Cassidy was not playing the part of humble supplicant with sufficient panache. "A female spirit, stronger and angrier, with greater claim over the victim."

"And how am I to do that?" mused Miss Cassidy. "I cannot raise the dead. I can reach trifling lesser demons like you, but not a true spirit, not one who has crossed over."

"I cannot help you," said the palm tree, now well put-out. "Let me go now, you rude pampuvan. Your time is up."

Miss Cassidy pulled the iron nail out of the palm tree. With a squeak of outrage, the curious presence vanished, and the palm tree was just a palm tree once more, swaying in the breeze. There was the faintest after-image of what might have been a man's shadow, except it appeared to have fins and a tail; and then that too faded into the sand.

"Hmm," said Miss Cassidy.

Maria Bendemeer's photograph was unusual in that she looked directly into the lens and out at the viewer, despite what must have been a blindingly bright flash. She glared out at the world with hard, dark, very beautiful eyes, clear and cold as black diamonds; the lush ruffles and folds of her elaborate dress attempting, and failing, to soften the blade-edges of her stance, her jawline, her square shoulders. Her hair was very dark and seemed to be naturally curly, but it was all mercilessly pulled back and smoothed down into a waxy gloss.

Despite the photograph's prominent position on the mantel, both the Captain and Sarah Jane hardly looked at it, perhaps avoiding that gimlet gaze. Miss Cassidy was confident nobody would notice her quietly taking the photograph down and tucking it away in a voluminous pocket. It should not have weighed much, but Miss Cassidy staggered, as if she had dropped a boulder into her bosom.

"Ah," she murmured.

That evening, Miss Cassidy bewildered Sarah Jane as they stitched their embroidery hoops. (Miss Cassidy disliked embroidery as a rule, but Sarah Jane seemed to find it comforting.)

"You want to see Mama's sewing kit?" repeated Sarah Jane, startled. "Whatever for? You have your own, much better sewing kit, Miss Cassidy—Mama's is very old-fashioned. Her needles are thick, very crude."

"Indeed, that is the very reason I want to see it! I have a bit of old leather I need to mend—shoe leather, you see—and my needles will not do."

Sarah Jane did not look convinced. "There are cobblers in Telok Ayer; you do not need to mend your own shoes."

"I only need to set a few stitches. Besides, I am curious about her sewing kit, now that you have told me about it coming from the West Indies."

Sarah Jane, unable to come up with any other excuse in the light of Miss Cassidy's beaming smile, reluctantly got to her feet and left the room. She returned with a large wooden box, polished nearly black and monogrammed in faded gold with a curlicued "MB".

It was certainly like no sewing kit Miss Cassidy had ever seen. It smelled, as Sarah Jane said, "odd"—like dried flowers both poisonous and beautiful—and looked rather ominous, like a doll's coffin. Inside, neatly sorted into trays and velvet bags, were an assortment of truly intimidating-looking needles, pins, scissors and thimbles, all made of heavy, tarnished iron, so that everything seemed black as blood.

There were some formidable needles indeed, as long as Miss Cassidy's finger, as thick as a small nail, and Miss Cassidy could not imagine the dress Mrs Bendemeer could have tried to put together with such a weapon. There were many odds and ends, bits of scrap fabric, locks of hair bound in thread; and, in fact, there was not a great deal of thread for a sewing kit, except for a spool each of black, red and white thread, all of very strong, high-quality silk.

Miss Cassidy weighed each item in her hand, exclaiming over their weight and size. Sarah Jane, after some abrupt responses, turned right away and muttered something about practising her French. "Take what you want from the kit, Miss Cassidy," she added as she crossed the room, getting as far away from her Mama's sewing kit as possible. "It is of no use to anyone now."

Miss Cassidy's fingers alighted upon item after item—scissors which had cut coloured thread, pins which had bitten lace—and finally closed upon a particular item. "I will take this one, if that is all right."

"If you like," said Sarah Jane listlessly. She glanced up for only a moment to remark, "That was Mama's favourite. She used to threaten us with that one. I don't think she ever even sewed with it."

"It is perfect," said Miss Cassidy cheerfully, and put away the large black needle.

The mother and six dead children of Bendemeer House had been interred in a Christian cemetery in Bukit Larangan. The oldest after Sarah Jane was Emily, who had died four days short of her thirteenth birthday. The youngest of them was Charlie, only three years old at the time of death; he had been buried together with their mother, since his body was too small for a ready-made coffin, and it had been imperative to bury them both quickly in case of contagion.

This made things complicated. It was Maria Bendemeer Miss Cassidy had many questions for, but there was no way to reach her without possibly also raising the spirit of the poor little child. From what Ah Nai had said, young Charlie had suffered quite enough.

Officially, the children and Maria had died of "malarial fever", all within six months of one another, although it seemed more likely there had been a cross-infection of more than one disease, from Sarah Jane's description. Her Mama had very likely died of malaria, but little Charlie appeared to have suffered the symptoms of cholera. Some exhausted doctor, wanting to get away from this cursed family, had signed off all their death certificates identically.

Not that it mattered; they were all dead, buried and asleep. Sarah Jane did not often visit the cemetery, claiming its associations were too painful, but Ah Nai visited the graves when she had a chance, to clean and tidy them and make offerings. This was not often, for Ah Nai was busy and the cemetery was a long way away, so she was glad when Miss Cassidy volunteered to accompany her.

The Captain had forbidden Ah Nai to put up incense and joss sticks, so the faithful servant instead brought votive candles and flowers, "the white man way" as she called it, to make him feel at ease.

58

Miss Cassidy liked the cemetery, where gentle souls lay in repose; more to the point, at Bukit Larangan's elevation, there was always a good chance of a nice fresh breeze. Ah Nai tasked Miss Cassidy to trim the weeds (a job no longer suited to Ah Nai's old knees) while Ah Nai rinsed each headstone with water, and murmured softly to each lost child. She treated the white votive candles precisely as if they were joss sticks, holding them in both hands and bowing to each headstone before placing them carefully amid the flowers.

Miss Cassidy found the arrangement of the graves rather interesting. Emily was interred at a distance from the others—a full three feet away from the rest of the cluster. "By her own request," explained Ah Nai. "She asked Miss Sarah Jane to be sure to place her by herself, away from the others."

"That is a strange request."

"Miss Emily was a little bit different," said Ah Nai indulgently. "Her father and mother had trouble with her. But she loved Miss Sarah Jane very much."

"And you, surely, Ah Nai."

Ah Nai smiled. "She was a good girl," she said, "it was only her temper. She would have outgrown it."

Miss Cassidy gazed thoughtfully at the epitaph on Emily Bendemeer's gravestone—*Dearly beloved sister, daughter and friend*—and then at the Bible psalm underneath—*the LORD is a refuge for the oppressed, a stronghold in times of trouble.* An interesting choice, thought Miss Cassidy.

When night fell, for once, Miss Cassidy was not within the walls of Bendemeer House. She did what she could for the

Captain for the night, then once he was asleep, she ventured out to see what she could do for him for the rest of his life.

Bukit Larangan at night was not the same friendly, peaceful hill as it was in the daytime. The swaying trees became ominous silhouettes; the heavy air grew thick and strange. Nobody came here after nightfall, but Miss Cassidy was unconcerned. Cemeteries, in her experience, rarely held anything dangerous; troubled souls were not tied to their physical remains, but to the person or place that troubled them, and this was almost never a cemetery full of other dead people.

Miss Cassidy was very good at remaining unseen had she wished it, and if anyone was to pass her on the lonely roads at midnight, they would instantly forget it and go on their way. She knew where to go as well in the dark as in the light, and the shifting shadows and strange shapes did not faze her, even though some of them might have been trying their best to.

She knelt by Emily Bendemeer's grave and sighed. "I am so very sorry," she murmured gently, patting the cool grey stone, moist with the night air.

She took Maria's photograph out of her pocket, and exhaled as she placed it on the ground, at her own feet. Then she took out Maria Bendemeer's great black needle and plunged it into the earth before the gravestone.

The night was rent with a terrible cry. It might have been a bird or a cat or some unfortunate prey animal set upon by an owl's sharp talons.

Miss Cassidy stood as still as stone. She felt her skirts rustle and heard a curious sobbing sigh, then cold, small fingers gripped her hand, fingers as thin as bare bone.

Miss Cassidy spoke, but her voice was not like Miss Cassidy's at all; instead, it contained the stern inflections of a West Indies accent. "What have you done, you foolish girl?"

"Mama," came the high, sobbing whisper, "I didn't mean it. I couldn't stop it."

"What did you do?"

There was no answer, just unhappy sobbing, and the small cold hand gripped Miss Cassidy's fingers fiercely.

"Answer me, child."

The sobbing grew louder.

"Who is she?"

"I took the nail out," whispered the unhappy ghost at last.

"Out of the tree with the pink binding?"

"I took the nail out. It was under the pink cloth. After that I could not find the nail. I could not put it back in. I only wanted you to stop, Mama," whispered the cold little voice, and the small, strong, skeletal hands dragged hard at Miss Cassidy, but she stood her ground. "I didn't mean to hurt Papa. I only wanted you to stop. Why did you not love me, Mama?"

"What is her name?"

"I saw her in the garden. We were friends. She said she would show me her baby if I took out the nail. We were friends!"

"What is her name, Emily? This is important."

"I didn't mean to hurt Papa. Mama, Mama, forgive me." The scrabbling hands now grew frantic, grasping, seizing, dragging her down. "Mama. Mama. Forgive me. Mama. Take me with you. Mama."

"I cannot take you with me."

Another high, keening, terrible scream; Miss Cassidy felt the weight of something cold and heavy, the weight of rage and sorrow and regret; it pulled at her, pulled hard, and if she had not been Miss Cassidy, her soul would have been lost.

"Emily, what is her name? Tell me now," said Miss Cassidy urgently. The pawing hands were so frantic, it was hard not to turn; but if she looked upon Emily (or whatever was left of the poor child's troubled spirit), the girl would vanish, and this frightful spell could not be cast more than once without danger.

"Mamaaaaa!!!"

Miss Cassidy became desperate. "Emily, if you do not tell me the girl's name, I will take this needle and—"

"No, no! Her name is Asheekin! Asheekin!"

Miss Cassidy pulled the needle out of the ground.

The night was still and calm. Over Emily Bendemeer's grave, and the graves of all the lost children, leaves rained softly down.

"It was never your fault," said Miss Cassidy gently. "You should not have blamed yourself, so much that you wanted to lie apart from your family. I will help you, poor child. I will free your Papa, and you may rest at last. I promise."

V

Miss Cassidy & the Twins

"M iss Cassidy, I have here an unusual request which concerns you," said Captain Bendemeer. Miss Cassidy looked up from her beadwork. Ah Nai was teaching her how to make decorative Chinese knots out of red satin cord. It was very therapeutic work for a hot, slow day.

Captain Bendemeer's health had not improved since Miss Cassidy's arrival, but Sarah Jane's had. Forced walks around the Botanic Gardens, obligatory visits to other suitable families, and a course of vigorous geography lessons had both put some colour in her cheeks and added some structure to her life. She was still inclined towards pallid and fretful, but there was no denying that Miss Cassidy was doing her good.

The Captain appeared to be pleased about this, but seemed disinclined to join them. Miss Cassidy looked up at him expectantly, wondering if perhaps she had ordered too much silk for Sarah Jane's new walking dress, but he placed a folded letter in her hand.

"It is from Mr Kay Wing Tong."

It took a while for Miss Cassidy to process the syllables in her mind. "Oh!" she said at last, none the wiser.

"He is looking for an English tutor for his two daughters. They learn it in school, but not well enough to please him. He has asked if he may request your services, on any afternoon Sarah Jane does not need you. You will be paid for your time, naturally."

For the first time in her life, Miss Cassidy did not know what to say. "Well," she began. "I. Well. Of course, if you think it suitable—"

"Certainly I do. Mr Kay and the Straits Steamship Company are indispensable partners with the Company." He meant the East India Company. "Anything that pleases him will help us."

"Very well then," said Miss Cassidy doubtfully. "When should I present myself to Mr Kay?"

"Now, if you please."

"I beg your pardon, Captain?"

"He has requested to see you the moment you are available. I see you are available now. I know it seems odd, but I have long since been familiar with Mr Kay's quirks. He is an impatient man. So please just go. The servants will let you in, and if he is busy, you need only wait till he may see you. Bring the letter with you and present it at the door."

Captain Bendemeer left the room without any further comment. Miss Cassidy looked down at the letter in her hand. It was phrased in formal English, as if it were a business document. There was a Chinese chop on it, with a neat character in a circle.

"It says 'ji'," said Ah Nai. "In Cantonese, 'kei'. The family name. I will get Ah Kio to call you a rickshaw."

Miss Cassidy curiously regarded the twins. The twins stared back. She had glimpsed them during the wedding, first in Western-style gowns far too mature for them, and later in green silk brocade blouses that were much more charming, though they hadn't seemed to think so.

Even for identical twins, they were almost disturbingly alike. Each had their father's strong jaw and high, broad cheekbones, but their full cheeks, pert noses and small, bright restless eyes were probably their mother's. They were small for their age, chubby enough to have dimpled knuckles, and both had their shoulder-length black hair parted in the middle and bound in two pigtails, ending with yellow satin bows.

They were clearly uncertain what to make of their new instructress, restlessly shifting in their seats and twisting over to whisper to each other. They had both politely asked her, "Hallo, how are you," in slow, butchered English syllables, and then looked confused when she replied, "Very well, thank you. And yourselves?" So conversation had flagged as they all sat waiting for Mr Kay in his study, in the shadow of the huge, carved ivory tusk.

Miss Cassidy tried the effect of a friendly smile. They appeared startled; then they grinned back, broadly, and giggled again.

One of them reached out, across the low rosewood table that separated their chairs, and touched Miss Cassidy's hair. She smiled. Her hair was not just a pleasant auburn or delightful strawberry, but that fiery orange-red that Europeans associated with savage barbarian roots. Miss Cassidy had never been troubled by her unfashionable hair colour, only by its untameable texture, but she could see why it would be fascinating to the twins.

Suddenly both girls snapped back to military posture, crossed their ankles under their chairs, placed their hands in their laps and stared demurely straight ahead. The door opened, and Mr Kay entered.

He beamed at them. "Yeling, Yezi."

"Good morning, Papa," they responded politely.

Miss Cassidy, who had risen, curtseyed in a vague, uncertain manner. Mr Kay looked different when not dressed formally. Like his girls, during the wedding he had briefly worn a Western dinner jacket out of respect for his special guests, but spent most of the day in an expensive-looking grey Shantung silk coat, his height and presence making him look perfectly at home in both. Now he was in a comparatively ordinary black silk jacket, rolled up to his elbows because the weather was hot, his fingers stained with ink. There was a small silver reading glass dangling from a fine chain poking out of his breast pocket.

"Miss Cassidy," he said.

"Boss Kay," responded Miss Cassidy, trying to say it the way Ah Nai had taught her. "Kei Loban."

The girls giggled, and Mr Kay chuckled. "I appreciate the effort, Miss Cassidy, but you may address me as Mr Kay, as all the Westerners do. You do not have the ear for either Cantonese or Mandarin, and it is hard to learn at your advanced age. Which brings me to this matter," he continued before Miss Cassidy could ponder upon her "advanced age" (which, on paper anyway, was thirty-eight). "These daughters of mine. I have sent them to an English-speaking school, CHIJ."

Miss Cassidy blinked. "CHIJ...The Convent of the Holy Infant Jesus? The one run by French nuns?"

"By French missionaries," he corrected. "Some of whom are, indeed, Catholic nuns. It is unimportant what they are, except that they cannot seem to whip any decent level of English into my daughters. So I wish them to have an instructress at home. As Captain Bendemeer has no doubt explained, you will be suitably compensated."

"I am flattered you have thought of me, Mr Kay. Though indeed, your level of English is highly competent, and so was your son's when he addressed us at the wedding. Surely—"

"I thank you, Miss Cassidy, for the compliment. When my wife was still alive, we had a tutor for my boys, an English priest. He taught us all, even my wife, who was a rather stupid woman."

Miss Cassidy blinked, but Mr Kay had spoken with fondness, not insult. It was offered as a fact rather than a flaw. "He, er, did a good job then," she murmured.

"He did, but he has been dead eight years, sadly. Malarial fever. He died in this house," added Mr Kay.

"I see," said Miss Cassidy, not knowing quite what to say since Mr Kay was now lighting his pipe, and there was an odd sort of pause in the conversation.

"And of course," he continued, "everyone keeps telling me the girls do not need English. They must sew and cook and learn to manage a household, and I agree that they must. But they will also learn English. It is of no use to be fluent in a single Chinese dialect when they live in a land that speaks twenty languages, and which is governed by Englishmen. How will they know the laws of the land, its practices? You never know where life might take you, what crosses you may have to bear." He smiled fondly at his uncomprehending daughters. "I wish them to be prepared for any eventuality."

"Well," said Miss Cassidy, "I am not sure I can prepare them for any eventuality, but I can certainly teach them English."

"Yes, Miss Cassidy. Teach them English, and also the ways of the English."

"The ways of the English? Though I am not English?"

"I have found that one learns best of English ways," said Mr Kay, puffing his pipe, "from those who have been obliged to adapt to them. I have adapted to them, but I am in business with Englishmen, and Dutchmen, and sometimes Portuguese men. I know nothing of female Westerners." He did not add, *They do not interest me,* but the expressive way he smoked his pipe conveyed the same meaning.

"So you wish your girls to learn the ways of Englishwomen?"

"Not to adopt them. Merely to understand them."

"I see. And you have explained as much to the girls?"

"I have explained that you are to be their instructress, twice a week, two hours each time, and they are to obey you as they would their own mother." He turned to the girls and said in

Cantonese, "Be good, and listen to Miss Cassidy." He said "Miss Cassidy" in precise English, and the girls murmured, "Yes, Papa," also in English.

"Very good. Now, commence the lesson."

He turned his back, in that nonchalant way Miss Cassidy was starting to find exasperating, and retreated behind the painted screen that separated his desk from the waiting area of the study.

"Excuse me?" she called, bewildered. "Commence the lesson...here? Now?"

"That is correct. Commence." There was a scrape as he pulled up his chair, a rustle of papers and then the clickety-click of abacus beads.

The two girls looked up expectantly at Miss Cassidy.

"Well!" she exclaimed, thinking hard. "I suppose I should begin with your lessons. Will you bring me your school textbooks?"

The girls frowned, concentrating on her words. "School...?"

"Yes. English books? From school."

From behind the screen, Mr Kay barked something sharply, and the girls' faces cleared. They shot up from their chairs and ran out of the room, a tumble of limbs and flying ribbons. Miss Cassidy could hear Mr Kay chuckling from behind the screen.

The first lesson progressed better than Miss Cassidy expected, considering the circumstances. Yeling and Yezi were brighter than Sarah Jane, at least, and were eager to learn. Miss Cassidy could see why they were not getting much out of the convent school's textbooks. It was no use saying

"A is for Apple" to children who didn't eat apples, or using Bible verses for sentence construction out of context. The girls were able to phonetically gabble off the Lord's Prayer and the Hail Mary word-perfect, without the least clue what they were saying.

The enormous, dreadful elephant tusk came into use, as Miss Cassidy pointed out little scenes carved into it and described them in English. "The girl is crossing the bridge." "The boy is playing with the dog." "The man is wearing a hat," and so on. Miss Cassidy also found it personally instructive. Between the girls' excited exclamations and Mr Kay's occasional monosyllabic translations from behind the screen, she was improving her Cantonese vocabulary as well.

By the end of two hours, the girls were able to echo in unison, "Goodbye, Miss Cassidy, you have been very kind. We will see you again next week." In addition, because they were very restless and Miss Cassidy needed to keep their attention, they also knew how to create various shadow puppets on the wall, sing the refrain to "The Bonnie Banks o' Loch Lomond", and were amazed and deliciously horrified by Henry VIII and his six wives.

Mr Kay rematerialised from behind the screen. Throughout the lesson, his clerks and household staff had come in and out, some of them nonplussed by Miss Cassidy's presence. But both business and English lessons had progressed unimpeded nonetheless.

Now Mr Kay dismissed his girls, and unceremoniously handed Miss Cassidy an envelope of banknotes. "Thank you, Miss Cassidy, you have taught them well," he said, his eyes twinkling. "If Father Brunty had been as entertaining, even my wife might have learnt something."

"Your daughters are delightful, Mr Kay."

"They are spoilt rotten," he said proudly, and waved his hand.

Miss Cassidy found herself staring at his palm. Mr Kay noticed her staring. "Ah," he said, "do Irishwomen practice palmistry?" And, unselfconsciously, he offered her a full view of his outspread hand.

"Scotswomen. And no, we do not, as a rule."

"Still, you notice something here?"

"I do."

"All the fortune tellers tell me it is a most foreboding hand. But it writes good script, counts off the abacus correctly and guides my chopsticks without incident into my mouth, so thus far I am satisfied with it."

Miss Cassidy laughed politely. Inwardly, she said, "Hmm."

VI

Miss Cassidy &
the Hungry Ghost

PANDAN Villa's gates were never short of rickshaws, but Miss Cassidy shook her head and kept walking.

She did not particularly like being dragged along in a rickshaw, and it was an unusually cool day, excellent for trying out her newly completed cotton walking skirt, in a durable shade of brown.

She was beginning to like Singapore very much, three months after having arrived to the heat and smells. It was an untidy world, but not disorganised; there was place for everything, from the Indian dhobi launderers to the Chinese medicine shops to emporiums with imported British goods. She could now go out on her own for errands; Ah Nai had shown her where to purchase fabric, groceries and ladies' items. The vendors of the Telok Ayer markets had grown accustomed to seeing her; some hailed her by name, "Miz Cazdee!"

She'd found it hard to learn much Chinese, mostly because the Chinese people around her were from all over China, and not everyone spoke either Mandarin or Cantonese. And she found the little bit of Malayalam she'd learnt in India was useless with the largely Tamil-speaking Indian populace. But Malay was easy to pick up in bits and bobs, and most people could speak it in the same bits and bobs, so Miss Cassidy got by on that. She liked Malay as a language. There was an elegance to its simplicity, like a song with all the right notes.

She stopped at a snack stall for a paper cone of flavoured peanuts. The stall was mounted on the sidecar of a bicycle, a variety of crunchy snacks rattling in large tins. The boy running the stall looked about thirteen but was probably older; he wore nothing but a grubby blue sarong and a broad grin.

"Ahmad, is your sister better?"

Ahmad grinned even more broadly as he handed her the newspaper-cone of nuts. "Better, since you gave her the medicine," he said in a mix of pidgin English and Malay. "We went to the bomoh to clear her spirit also."

"What is a bomoh?"

The answer to this question was beyond Ahmad's limited English, but by dint of much complex mimicry and physical exaggeration, Miss Cassidy understood that a bomoh was a form of shaman. "Why, that is marvellous," she exclaimed. "Where can I find the bomoh?"

"On the hill. But he won't see you, Miz Cazdee. He does not see mat salleh."

"But I have a particular reason. I have a...a mok-mok problem."

73

Ahmad shrugged. "The bomoh is not for orang putih. You ask the Chinese amah. Maybe Chinese temple can help."

"But I do not think this is a Chinese ghost," said Miss Cassidy doubtfully.

"Ah! My nenek would say, Chinese ghost, Malay ghost, Indian ghost, all same-same—if you want them to go away, you must find out what they want."

"Your nenek sounds like a wise woman."

"She is a scary woman." Ahmad's grin, if possible, grew even wider. "She hit my father with a broom yesterday, piak piak piak! That's why I am running the stall today. Pak cannot stand up." Ahmad roared with laughter.

"Why did she hit your father with a broom?"

"Mak complained to Nenek that Pak has another woman. He doesn't come home at night. So Nenek waited for Pak the whole night at the door, with her broom. And when he came home, whack whack whack!" Ahmad roared again.

Miss Cassidy paid for her peanuts and sauntered along, raising her parasol. It was the Chinese Hungry Ghost Festival, and all around her people were burning hell notes in repurposed tins and canisters, and setting up altars with food and drink, for the enjoyment of the family ghosts. Miss Cassidy chose her steps carefully without appearing to do so deliberately. There were ghosts, and then there were ghosts, as Ahmad's nenek might say.

The Hungry Ghost Festival was a sore point in the Bendemeer household. Ah Nai and Ah Kio lived with the family, Ah Nai in the house itself and Ah Kio in a little self-built shack at the back of the property—a dire place, but he apparently preferred it to living in the house and being relentlessly bossed around by Ah Nai. There was a small Chinese altar by his shack, and there both he and Ah Nai made their offerings to the dead, and burned hell notes and joss sticks, as quietly as possible, and only when the wind did not carry the smoke indoors.

The two Chinese servants were strictly forbidden to practise any sort of ancestor worship within the house itself. Both Captain Bendemeer and Sarah Jane found the ruckus and paraphernalia of the festival deeply repellent. They tolerated every other holiday, largely because the others were easy to avoid—Chinese New Year, Ramadan, Deepavali, Vesak Day, even Thaipusam—but it was impossible to avoid the Hungry Ghost Festival, with the drifting ashes, noisy getai concerts and hundreds of altars laden with food swarming with ants, which could be set up at any corner or sidewalk. Sarah Jane could not be compelled to go out while the festival was in force, and the smoke in the air apparently gave her a perpetual headache that stopped her from doing any lessons, sewing, music or, indeed, from moving at all from the confines of her bed. This was why Ah Nai and Miss Cassidy had both found themselves with time on their hands to bind decorative Chinese knots.

A sense of foreboding started gradually building up in Miss Cassidy as she approached Bendemeer House. The banana trees were rustling noisily in the wind; a storm was coming, one of those furious whipping monsoon storms that would force the reluctant Ah Kio out of his shack and into the shelter of the kitchen. Grey clouds were steadily blotting out the sun.

Miss Cassidy was unsurprised when she walked into the house to find: Sarah Jane, weeping and clinging onto Ah Nai; Ah Nai, standing very still and trembling; Ah Kio, hiding in a corner, clutching his things, unable to cross the room; and Captain Bendemeer, in a rage. Bits of yellow paper littered the ground and were clutched in his fist.

"Ah Nai, I've told you this hundreds of times! I want none of this... heathen rubbish in our home!"

"They are for you and Miss Sarah Jane," persisted Ah Nai, pale but stubborn. "This house is no good. There are dirty things all over it." There was no proper English translation for the Chinese phrase "dirty things". It did not refer to hygiene.

"How do I know they are not some sort of witchcraft, some horrible magic?"

"They are from the temple," said Ah Nai, insulted. "From the nuns."

"Those temples! With the great gold idols and mad priests going into convulsions!"

"Those are Taoist priests. I am Buddhist."

"I don't care!" roared Captain Bendemeer. "You will remove these—these—things from the house, do you hear me?"

"I cannot," said Ah Nai, totally pale. "Forgive me, but I must not."

"Then I am forced to dismiss you."

"Papa, no, please!" cried Sarah Jane.

Miss Cassidy judged it a good time to intervene. "Captain Bendemeer, what is wrong?"

He turned to her. She had never seen him blaze with such anger; indeed, he had never blazed with any type of emotion. "Miss Cassidy, look at this." And he took her hand and filled it with little yellow triangles of paper.

Miss Cassidy suppressed a gasp, as if she had received a jolt of electricity.

"I found them all over the house. There was one under my bed, and one under Sarah Jane's. They were in our drawers, our linen, in my study, in her sewing basket. Everywhere!"

"Ah Nai means well," cried Sarah Jane. "She says they are talismans—charms to protect us."

"We are a Christian house! I will not permit this...this blasphemy!"

Miss Cassidy unfolded one of the little triangles. It was a perfect square, with red Chinese lettering. "Captain," she said at last, "you read your Bible, do you not? And say your prayers, and trust in God?"

"Of course I do," he said uneasily, and Miss Cassidy thought, Unlikely, but never mind.

"I know Sarah Jane does," she continued. "If your faith in God is perfect, you know that nothing can harm you. What difference does it make if there is a bit of paper under your bed?" She held out the unfolded charm. "It is only paper. There is nothing terrible about it."

"I dislike witchcraft, Miss Cassidy."

"Well, what era are we in, Captain, that you should give credence to the idea that witches even exist?"

"I do not want these things around me," he said stubbornly, skirting the argument. "That is the end of the matter. I trust you, Miss Cassidy, as a British woman. You will go through the house with Ah Nai, and remove all the rest of these, and burn them. Is that clear?"

"Of course, Captain."

He stalked out of the room. Sarah Jane was sobbing violently, almost hysterical.

"My dear, lie down a moment," said Miss Cassidy, putting some cheer into her command. "You have had a shock."

"Oh, oh, oh! Ah Nai, why did you do it again? Why? You know Papa, you know Papa—"

"Lie down," commanded Miss Cassidy imperatively, and practically shoved Sarah Jane into a reclining position upon the sofa. The girl continued to sob and gasp; Miss Cassidy placed one hand over the girl's damp eyes, and another over her heart.

Sarah Jane fell asleep.

Ah Nai was tearfully gathering up the talismans from the floor. "Miss Cassidy," she began, but Miss Cassidy interrupted her in a whisper.

"Sew the paper into their clothes," she said. "Put one in the Captain's shoe-heel, where he will not notice; Ah Kio can do that. Into his coat lapel, also. I will sew them into the lining of Sarah Jane's skirts and inside the ribbon of her hats. We will find places for them."

"But he wants you to burn them!"

"Give me some hell notes, and I will burn those instead— he won't know the difference. Now take the talismans away, quickly. I must pretend to search the house."

*

78

Miss Cassidy went to bed that night, but did not sleep. At midnight the scent of frangipani flowers rose redolent in the air, and the iron key began to swing gently at her window—tap, tap, tap.

She pushed the shutter open a crack. Sure enough, there was Captain Bendemeer, making his slow, methodical way under the banana trees.

By the time Miss Cassidy made her way to the garden, the Captain had reached the end of the path and was turning back. He gazed straight at Miss Cassidy, unseeing. She reached out to take his hand...

...and something passed through her, like a pale trickle of light.

Miss Cassidy froze. Captain Bendemeer kept walking, pacing, moving past her.

"Who is it?" she asked sharply. "You are not the pontianak."

And abruptly there was a woman standing before her, smiling. She was Chinese, in a blue cotton outfit and a kind of red headscarf. She had broad country features and small sparkling eyes, and was eating a steamed bun. She did not speak, but made a gesture: go back, go back, all is well.

"Who are you? Have you chased her away?"

The woman smiled, and munched on her steamed bun.

Miss Cassidy thought a moment. "You are a ghost who is being fed from the altar of this house today. Are you an ancestor of Ah Kio's or Ah Nai's?"

The woman raised two fingers, gestured again.

"Both? Ah! You are their mother! They are siblings!"

The woman nodded happily, still chewing with vigorous satisfaction.

"You will take care of this house while you are here?"

Again she nodded.

"Oh, thank heavens. I am so glad. I only need a little more time, and you have granted me that, bless you."

The old lady beamed.

Captain Bendemeer had returned to the house. The woman's ghost vanished when he shut the door.

Before she headed back indoors, Miss Cassidy hurried to the banana tree bound in pink silk. It gave off a sullen, thwarted air, which she ignored, and she knelt to carefully place Maria Bendemeer's photograph amid the weeds tangled around its roots.

A sudden cold wind made her shiver. "Really," she muttered to herself, "I must write some letters."

VII

Miss Cassidy &
the Two Temples

"WHY, Mr Nair, how nice to see you!"
Mr Nair smiled as he made his way down
the pews. The church was mostly empty now,
except for a few older ladies in the back pews, which were
reserved for non-white worshippers. It was quite a beautiful
church if small, and some wealthy member of the congrega-
tion had donated several brilliant stained-glass windows. A
winsome wooden Jesus, pinned to a large cross behind the
altar, appeared to doze peacefully from his nails.

Miss Cassidy was waiting for Sarah Jane. The girl went
to church three times a week; it was the only trip she was
actively willing to make. Surprisingly, she was Catholic; she
had converted to Catholicism after her mother died. Her father
remained nominally Anglican, but did not go to church at all,
Protestant or otherwise.

Miss Cassidy, busying her hands with plaiting Chinese
knots, privately suspected that Sarah Jane had converted

to Catholicism purely for the rite of confession. She confessed her sins to the priest every week, dutifully; she carried scented red rosary beads in her pocket; she had an altar to the Virgin in her bedchamber, where she said her bedtime prayers. In one way or another, she was constantly confessing and doing penance for a multitude of sins only she seemed to perceive.

The Bendemeers had assumed Miss Cassidy was also Catholic, and she was content to let them think so. She was very familiar with the rites of Catholicism, and had no objection to attending a Catholic church if the preaching was reasonably entertaining. It at least was a good reason to get Sarah Jane out of the house. Miss Cassidy knew all the hymns and responses, and accepted the communion wafer with the respectful deference she accorded to all long-standing religious rituals.

"Always a pleasure, Miss Cassidy," said Mr Nair.

Miss Cassidy, who knew perfectly well he had not come over for the pleasure of her exclusive company, mildly explained, "I am waiting for Sarah Jane—she is in the confessional booth. Are you waiting your turn, Mr Nair?"

"I do not generally practise confession, I fear. Father Andrews is a good man, but God has not granted him the ability to comprehend the trials of an Indian Catholic law clerk in Singapore."

"I don't meet many myself, and I have lived in India. Have you been away long?"

"Four years. A long four years."

"Do you dislike Singapore?"

"Not at all! But the position I am in is…uncomfortable."
He said nothing more, but Miss Cassidy nodded briskly.

"You work for the East India Company, do you not? With
Captain Bendemeer—Sarah Jane's Papa."

A faintly embarrassed look came over Mr Nair's face. "I
do indeed, Miss Cassidy."

"What do you think of him?"

Mr Nair appeared taken aback, as well he might be. "I
beg your pardon?"

"I am merely curious," said Miss Cassidy lightly, "to know
if he is well-settled here. It concerns me a great deal, of course,
since I have sailed here at great discomfort, and I find Sarah
Jane is not particularly well-disposed to remain in Singapore."

"Is she not?"

"No, she is not. She finds the heat oppressive and the,
er, the native folk, confusing. I fancy she would prefer to be
home in England or, at least, in some land with wide green
fields and far fewer people."

"I see," murmured Mr Nair, perhaps thinking of his own
home.

"She will, of course, follow her Papa wherever he goes. So
you see, it is important to me to know if Captain Bendemeer
is happy here."

Mr Nair coughed. "He is…well, I am hardly the right
person to ask…"

Miss Cassidy waited, looping a small amber bead through
pink satin cord.

"We all work under the same man," said Mr Nair at last.
"Mr James Henry Kingsbright."

"And what sort of man is Mr Kingsbright?"

"Well," began Mr Nair, appearing to ponder his fingernails. "He is… the second son of a baron, I believe."

"Hmm," said Miss Cassidy, remembering the stout, red-faced, middle-aged gentleman bellowing at Captain Bendemeer at the wedding in Pandan Villa.

Mr Nair's carefully worded description told the tale without needing further explanation. James Henry Kingsbright should have been safe in England, enjoying his status as a wealthy landowner's son. Instead, here he was in the East Indies engaged in trade, about as far from his father's seat as was possible. Unlike most of the British here, he was not a middle-class man trying to make his fortune. He was most likely a disgraced aristocrat who had, probably, already lost one.

"Mr Nair!" Sarah Jane had finally emerged from the confessional, dabbing with some confusion at her cheeks with a lace handkerchief. She smiled, however, as he bowed gallantly over her hand.

"Miss Bendemeer, a pleasure as always. I have come to ask if you would like an escort home?"

"Oh, you are most kind! But Miss Cassidy is with us, and we cannot all fit in a rickshaw."

"Perhaps I might persuade you to walk, Miss Bendemeer? It is not far, and I know a path that is shaded."

Sarah Jane usually took a great deal of persuading to walk with Miss Cassidy in the streets, but she consented very easily to Mr Nair's proposal, and off they all went.

For etiquette's sake, as Mr Nair was not a British man, Miss Cassidy remained by Sarah Jane's side, holding up her parasol, while Mr Nair escorted them at a polite arm's length. Even then Miss Cassidy could feel the weight of many eyes upon them. Beside her she could sense Sarah Jane's tension, and as they left the church grounds, she half-thought Sarah Jane would change her mind and ask to summon a rickshaw.

Miss Cassidy was pleasantly surprised, therefore, when Sarah Jane said, in a burst of courage that must have taken a great deal of effort for her, "Mr Nair, I must beg you for your arm—I am not accustomed to these uneven paths."

Mr Nair's handsome face lit up, but he said nothing, and offered Sarah Jane his elbow. Sarah Jane placed her gloved hand upon his forearm, and then asked for her parasol.

"Are you certain, Sarah Jane?" asked Miss Cassidy. "Your father would not like you to be...unattended by me."

"I will answer for it, Miss Cassidy."

Miss Cassidy, as her paid chaperone (paid by, after all, Captain Bendemeer), could not say, *Bravo!* But she meekly relinquished the parasol and fell back three paces from the happily defiant couple—as she would have done from the start if Mr Nair were British, or at least a white man.

She was quite aware as they walked that most of the passing rickshaws were carrying British churchgoers, staring at them; that a few, indeed, were carrying Indian churchgoers, also staring. It was hard to say which one of them was receiving the most ire: the English girl disgracing her race, the Indian man disgracing his, or the paid companion failing utterly at her duty.

Ah Nai was waiting for them at the gates of Bendemeer House. She, too, stared with all her eyes, although she clearly knew Mr Nair, and smiled at him pleasantly enough. They exchanged polite greetings in pidgin Malay.

"Mr Nair, thank you for your kindness," said Sarah Jane. Her cheeks were flushed pink, her eyes bright, but Miss Cassidy could see her nerves beginning to fail.

"Will you be at the Friday mass?" he asked.

"Yes," she murmured in a low voice. "I shall. Miss Cassidy," she said abruptly, before Mr Nair could speak, "I am sorry to ask you this when we have only just returned, but I have just remembered the shoes I sent to be mended. Will you collect them for me? Here is the money," and she pressed something into Miss Cassidy's hand.

"Of course, my dear," said Miss Cassidy, quickly pouring the contents of her palm into her pocketbook. "You had best lie down. You are not used to walking such a long distance."

"I shall. I... Thank you again, Mr Nair."

The cobbler was in Chinatown, which was on Mr Nair's way, he said, so he offered his escort a second time. Miss Cassidy laughed. "You have definitely been well-schooled in English manners, Mr Nair."

"I am. I quite like English manners, to be honest, Miss Cassidy. There is something very well-organised about them, to my mind. There is a mode of conduct prescribed for every possible situation."

"Even the situation we have just come from?" Miss Cassidy's eyes twinkled.

Mr Nair laughed. "Well, we all behaved with perfect propriety. I cannot help that my skin is not of the prescribed colour."

"You laugh now, but there will be consequences."

"Life has consequences, Miss Cassidy."

Miss Cassidy could by now navigate Chinatown on her own with great skill, despite the narrow winding streets and bullock carts. She knew which places to avoid, where the stink of opium drifted through tattered curtains; she knew to cross the street when she recognised the markings of secret society warnings on the walls, though she could not read them; she even recognised certain members of the secret societies, to whom she bowed politely.

"You amaze me, Miss Cassidy," said Mr Nair as she collected Sarah Jane's dancing shoes from a wiry Chinese cobbler in a noisy square.

"Do I? Do you mean the gang bosses? It was Ah Nai who taught me to recognise them, Mr Nair, specifically to keep me safe. Even Mr Kay accords them respect. He has met them in his house, and given them food and wine."

"Mr Kay is expected to do so, as a Chinese man. They must all pay the gangs protection money. It is sheer extortion."

Miss Cassidy smiled. "Your lawyer's mind dislikes the untidiness of it? But you must be just to the gangs as well, Mr Nair. The best of them behave with honour. They genuinely guard Mr Kay's interests, have defended his coolies and warehouses, and have even helped put out a fire or two. For him, at least, they are more effective than the police. They were at his son's wedding, you know."

"I am a law clerk, not a lawyer. But you appear to know a great deal about Mr Kay's affairs, Miss Cassidy."

Miss Cassidy felt a blush rising, and resolutely damped it down. "I teach his daughters English."

"I see. And meanwhile, Mr Kay discusses the details of his business with you?"

"Well, we are...that is, his daughters and I are...in the same room while he transacts his business."

"And is this common practice among wealthy Chinese parents?"

"Mr Kay is fond of his daughters and likes to monitor their progress," said Miss Cassidy with some asperity.

"Mr Kay is a widower, is he not?"

"Mr Nair!" Miss Cassidy wanted to be outraged, but it was hard to do so with such a handsome young face grinning mischievously at her. "Whatever you are implying, it isn't so."

"I never imply anything, Miss Cassidy. I always state facts. My lawyer's mind, you know."

Miss Cassidy fell silent and dignified, which clearly amused Mr Nair greatly. "Come now, let us be friends, Miss Cassidy. My first name is Haresh. What is yours?"

"Leda," she said coolly.

"Leda? As in—Leda and the swan?"

"Good heavens, Mr Nair—you are certainly a wide-ranging scholar."

"What else is a bachelor to do with his days, but read? Come, Miss Cassidy. If you will be kind to me, you can meet my cousin."

"Your cousin? I did not know you had family here."

"We are barely family, but technically yes, we are cousins. I am going to see her at the Hindu temple. She has asked me to read a letter for her. She is not yet twenty, but has three children already. She was sent from India to her husband in an arranged marriage. Come, Miss Cassidy! You know you are interested—you can't help yourself."

"How dreadful to be so easily understood by a near-stranger," murmured Miss Cassidy.

"Are we friends, Leda?"

Miss Cassidy sighed. "Yes, we shall be friends, Haresh. Shake hands."

They shook hands. A faint expression of surprise passed over Mr Nair's face as Miss Cassidy pressed into his palm what Sarah Jane had earlier put into hers. It was a small gold locket with an ivory frontpiece, upon which Sarah Jane herself had painted a spray of yellow roses.

It was a gift that could not be officially acknowledged, so Mr Nair could only say, fervently, "Thank you for your friendship, Miss Cassidy."

"Much obliged, Mr Nair. Now tell me about your cousin, do."

The Hindu temple was one Miss Cassidy had passed by many times. It was on the same street as a Chinese temple; the two pantheons appeared to coexist quite happily. The Hindu and Taoist worshippers, explained Mr Nair, had decided—as the Romans of the Empire once had—that if particular gods or deities were similar enough, it was actually the same deity under a different name. The Taoist and Hindu monkey gods, for instance, were interchangeably appealed to by both sets of devotees.

"Polytheistic religions are curiously all-inclusive," said Mr Nair. "I've always found it terribly confusing myself."

"Do you? I think it all very jolly. A single god all by himself must surely get bored."

"A curious opinion from a Catholic."

"Is it? Ah, is this your cousin?" added Miss Cassidy hastily, as a young woman wrapped in a bright purple sari hurried towards them on bare feet. She was carrying a baby, whose dangling feet jingled with silver bells. She was in some distress, handing Mr Nair a telegram in English.

Mr Nair read it, and looked exasperated. "It is about her brother, a sailor. He has disgraced himself and is in jail in Madras. Excuse me, Miss Cassidy, I must advise her. You are quite welcome to walk about the temple, if you wish. Many British visitors do."

It was certainly a fascinating temple. The roof was many levels high, and intricately decorated with Hindu deities painted in brilliant colours. The walls were embellished with scenes from the life of Lord Krishna. Devotees made offerings of fruit, flowers, milk and incense; some were praying, some were gossiping, some were shouting at children—not at all unlike the church before service began. White and orange flower petals were scattered everywhere underfoot.

Left to wander mostly at will, Miss Cassidy found herself presently in a little garden, with a small stone fountain. Sitting by the fountain, opening the folds of lotus flowers with her fingers, was a woman of extraordinary beauty, in a brilliant peacock-blue sari. She looked up in surprise when Miss Cassidy entered. Then she smiled.

Miss Cassidy paused on the threshold, dumbstruck. Then she curtseyed, as deeply as she could.

"Oh, please don't," said the lady, laughing. "It's very odd, when folk like you go about bowing and curtseying. It makes me wonder if someone is about to leap out at me from behind a rock."

"Alas, there are not enough of my folk left to risk foolish pranks on goddesses," said Miss Cassidy, smiling.

"Yes, it's a pity. Life used to be much more interesting when you lot were about. Come and sit with me a minute. What is your name?"

"Leda Cassidy, milady."

"Well, Lady of the Sidhe, what are you doing here, so far from your ancestral land?"

"Trying to decide what to do with my life, I suppose, milady. I have lived in your land as well, where the Ganges flows."

"Indeed! You astonish me. Although, I suppose, I should not be so surprised. Everyone is everywhere these days." Miss Cassidy had seated herself on the ground by the patterned feet of the beautiful goddess, and felt her hat being removed and her hair being unknotted and smoothed out by strong, busy, life-giving hands. "Ah, such colour! It reminds me of Boadicea. Such a stunning woman."

"Yes, she was. I rather admired her."

"Heavens! Don't. You won't get far in this new world if you model yourself on Boadicea."

"Milady," said Miss Cassidy after a moment, "I have been biding my time, hoping to meet one of your wisdom. May I beg advice of you?"

"You may, if you promise me you will buy three jasmine garlands from old Moti at the temple gate. She has had no business today, poor thing, and her husband will beat her."

"I shall," said Miss Cassidy, peeking into her pocketbook. "I have enough."

Miss Cassidy explained about the pontianak and Captain Bendemeer. The great goddess, having completed a complex winding braid on Miss Cassidy's hair, pondered. "Mm. The monsters of this land are rather dreadful. And the desert god would be puzzled to deal with them. Have you not written to Inanna?"

"Anna's reply has not yet reached me."

"And the people cannot sell the house, and let the monster alone? Well. The talismans are excellent, but they do not last forever. What about the man on the hill?"

"I am told he would not help me. Besides, seeing how frightfully the Captain reacted to a few talismans, I doubt he would permit a bomoh in his house."

"A pity. The man on the hill is exactly what is needed. I will put a dream in his ear. Go and see him, and perhaps you may find a way."

It was a while before Mr Nair had finished his business with his distressed cousin, and he was a little alarmed when he realised the time. However, he found Miss Cassidy looking quite content, laying jasmine flower garlands at the feet of the statue of a many-armed goddess.

"Miss Cassidy, you constantly surprise me."

"Indeed, why? This is a lovely temple. I merely wanted to make a small contribution."

"You know that is Kali, the goddess of death?"

"Is she?" Miss Cassidy murmured mildly. "Goodness. Has your cousin left now, Mr Nair? What a pity. Perhaps there will be another chance for me to speak to her. I'm afraid it is getting rather late; may I trouble you to find me a rickshaw? Thank you so very much."

VIII

Miss Cassidy Makes Mischief

"THE gods are angry," said Ah Nai worriedly.

It was an unusually cool evening, and even in Ah Nai's humble little room, the wind could be heard moaning and thrashing about the trees.

All three of them—Ah Kio, Ah Nai and Miss Cassidy—gazed at the wooden crescent blocks, presenting their unpleasant round sides face up, where they lay on Ah Nai's clean floor. Ah Kio murmured, "Aiyoh, aiyoh," softly under his breath and shook his head, and repeated the performance until Ah Nai impatiently yanked on his ear, whereupon he subsided.

"Try again," said Miss Cassidy, resting her chin against her knees. They were in front of Ah Nai's small altar, where reposed a tranquil cross-legged Buddha and a small jade Kuan Yin with a hand raised in graceful benediction. There was no joss-stick holder, as Ah Nai was not permitted to burn incense or joss sticks within the house.

94

Ah Nai gathered up the jiaobei stones and tried once more. Murmuring softly under her breath, she asked the gods again: Would the house be clean?

She dropped the stones. "No," she said, resigned.

"Hmm," said Miss Cassidy.

She thought a moment. Then, from her own pocket, she took out an odd assortment of miniature things: a lychee pip, dried and polished; a wee, blue stone; the tiny bone of some small animal, probably a bird; a coin. With little ceremony she dropped them, directly on top of the jiaobei.

"What do your gods say?" asked Ah Nai, absent-mindedly smacking Ah Kio's curious pointing finger away.

"My gods?" murmured Miss Cassidy distractedly. "Well... the outcome is uncertain. Will you put the flowers into Sarah Jane's bath tonight, Ah Nai?"

"I will go to the temple," she said.

It had been a fine day. The monsoon rains had prevented Sarah Jane's usual trip to the church in the morning, but after the clouds cleared, the air was cool and fresh. After two hours of mediocre French and unnecessary embroidery, Sarah Jane astonished Miss Cassidy by exclaiming, "I want to go out. I am sick of sewing. I can't bear it a moment longer." She glared at her needle in distaste. "Miss Cassidy, I pray, let us leave the house."

"Why, certainly, my dear. Where do you wish to go?"

"Oh, I don't know. I'm just sick of being cooped up in here. I feel restless, Miss Cassidy. I feel like I must busy myself with this and that today, and keep my mind occupied."

Miss Cassidy understood. "Well, let us walk to the Ladies' Lawn Tennis Club. We can look in at Robinsons, perhaps, and then stop for tea."

Sarah Jane was usually a listless walker at best, but to Miss Cassidy's surprise, this time she was out the door the moment her boots were laced, and set a clipping pace. It was all very mysterious, but the mystery began to clear eventually, as Miss Cassidy found herself on a completely different street, nowhere near the Ladies' Lawn Tennis Club. It was the extremely busy thoroughfare upon which the British East India Company offices were located.

"I thought I might look in on Papa, and see if he would like to... to..." Sarah Jane stumbled awkwardly.

"To stop for tea with us? Certainly," said Miss Cassidy easily. "Let us go in and see if we can find him. Quickly," she added, as a rickety bicycle went careening past, bearing a precarious load of lunch tiffins. "I fear we will cause an accident."

The Chinese clerk at the door looked startled, as well he might, when the two ladies walked in. "Er," began Sarah Jane. "Oh, dear. Ngor hai..." she began in atrocious Cantonese. "Ngor hai...lei ji mm ji do..."

"Can I be of assistance, ladies?" asked the clerk woodenly.

"Oh! I am...the daughter of Captain Bendemeer. I was wondering..."

"Have you any idea if Captain Bendemeer is available at the moment?" Miss Cassidy took over.

"Captain Bendemeer, I believe, is with Mr Kingsbright. They are in a meeting with the Straits Steamship Company."

Miss Cassidy wondered crossly why she could feel a blush rising. "I see," she said brightly. "I suppose we should not disturb them."

"Is there," tried Sarah Jane helplessly, "Is there…oh dear."

"Is there a Mr Haresh Nair in the office, by any chance?"

The clerk began to answer, frowning, and just then the side door opened, and out walked Mr Kay.

Miss Cassidy's first instinct was to shrink out of the way into the shadows, a reaction clearly shared by Sarah Jane, who seized her elbow and dragged her aside. From the very edge of the doorway, by the great iron grille, the two ladies skulked in the shadows as the room suddenly filled with men.

Mr Kay was part of a contingent of other dignified, visibly very wealthy Chinese tradesmen. In their wake trailed Mr James Henry Kingsbright, portly and red-faced; Captain Bendemeer, looking pale and exhausted; and, bringing up the rear with an armload of ledgers, Haresh Nair.

Nobody looked particularly happy, but the meeting was clearly over. The Chinese businessmen, muttering a little amongst themselves, trooped out of the room to waiting rickshaws; all except Mr Kay, who was almost out the door before he spotted Miss Cassidy.

A curious light came over his face: astonishment, pleasure and confusion. He began to speak, but was interrupted by Mr Kingsbright, who abruptly shouted, "Don't speak to me, Bendemeer! Do you know what your incompetence is costing us? I'll be damned if I keep you on here, drawing a salary you do nothing to earn."

"Sir," began Mr Nair urgently, for he had spotted Sarah Jane in the corner. Miss Cassidy could feel the grip on her elbow becoming painful in its intensity.

"Shut up!" shouted Mr Kingsbright in a fury. "You impudent dog!"

And, without warning, he seized the nearest thing to hand—an inkwell—and hurled it at Mr Nair's head.

Captain Bendemeer, to his credit, had enough presence of mind to seize Mr Nair and drag him out of harm's way. The inkwell, which might have struck the law clerk's forehead, instead hit him in the shoulder, scattering ink all over his coat. The ledgers fell loudly to the floor.

Nobody saw Mr Kay move, in the horror of the moment, but he was suddenly standing directly in front of Mr Kingsbright, looming threateningly over him with all his great height.

"I suggest you calm down," he said evenly. "There are ladies present."

Mr Kingsbright, red-faced, was glaring from Mr Kay to Mr Nair to Captain Bendemeer, apparently on the verge of apoplexy. "Ladies!" he exploded, and cast a vicious look at Miss Cassidy. He could not glare at Sarah Jane, because Miss Cassidy had physically blocked the girl. "Who let ladies in? Why are they here? You fool!" he now shouted at the Chinese clerk.

"It is hardly his fault we walked in through your wide-open front door," said Miss Cassidy sharply.

"Is he hurt?" cried Sarah Jane.

"Your Papa is not hurt," said Miss Cassidy quickly.

"Nor am I," said Mr Nair in a low voice, "but I wish to tender my immediate resignation. Captain Bendemeer, I thank you. You, at least, have always been a gentleman."

"A gentleman! Hah! Yes! A useless little—"

"*Mr Kingsbright*," said Mr Kay at the top range of his booming voice, drowning out the rest of the abuse.

There was a tense silence. Then Mr Kingsbright growled, "Go on then, you pathetic savage. Starve in the streets with the rest of your kind. See how your fine clothes and fine speeches serve you then."

"They will serve very well with me," said Mr Kay evenly. "Mr Nair, if you are willing, come to see me at Pandan Villa tomorrow morning. I have a place for you. No, do not thank me yet," he added, "let us escort the ladies from this place first."

Outside, Miss Cassidy fully expected Sarah Jane to dissolve into hysterics, but the girl surprised her again by instead falling into a rage, the like of which Miss Cassidy had never seen. "That dreadful, dreadful man! How dare he speak to Papa that way? And how could he…could he…" She stared at Mr Nair, covered in ink and tense with rage and humiliation. Then, abruptly, she seized his hand and declared passionately, "Mr Nair, you are a fine gentleman. I am…I am proud to know you. It is dreadful…dreadful…"

She burst into tears, and it seemed the most natural thing in the world for Mr Nair to take her in his arms and comfort her.

Miss Cassidy was aware that Mr Kay was finding this quite entertaining. She pointedly avoided meeting his eyes.

"Sarah Jane," she began after a moment, intending to remind her they were in the middle of a very busy street.

"Sarah Jane!"

Miss Cassidy's warning was too late. Captain Bendemeer stood aghast at the doorway, watching his daughter being embraced by a poor, jobless Indian law clerk. Miss Cassidy found it in her heart to be sorry for the Captain—he was certainly having a trying day.

Mr Nair immediately released Sarah Jane, but he stood nevertheless clear-eyed and unashamed, gazing back at Captain Bendemeer. Sarah Jane, for her part, appeared to undergo several emotions all within the space of a heartbeat. The final one she decided on was made of the finest stuff she had in her, and she kept her hand in Mr Nair's, and looked up at her Papa with admirable calm.

Nobody spoke, but as it became evident Sarah Jane was not going to release Mr Nair's hand, Captain Bendemeer demanded in a low but commanding voice, "Miss Cassidy, I ask you to take my daughter home immediately. I cannot think why she has even been permitted to come here."

"Sir, I am an honourable man," began Mr Nair, but Captain Bendemeer turned upon him with alacrity.

"Rumours have reached me," he said through gritted teeth, "which I disregarded. My daughter is a well-brought up, decent, God-fearing girl, I said. And she has a chaperone besides." The daggers shot at Miss Cassidy were marvellous in their intensity. "If she was seen in the company of a gentleman, whatever his complexion, surely it was innocent."

"It was, Papa. There is no... understanding between us," said Sarah Jane quietly.

"Since I have not been consulted, there had better not be," he snapped. "But now that you have paraded yourself on a very public thoroughfare, with all the world and their bloody buffalo staring at you, I cannot think how you intend to comport yourself next."

"Captain," interjected Mr Kay, "please calm yourself. I will undertake to send Mr Nair and Miss Bendemeer their separate ways. You had best return to Mr Kingsbright."

"Indeed I must. *His Majesty* still has a great deal to say to me." The vicious sarcasm was unexpected and rather bracing, or so Miss Cassidy thought. "Mr Kay, I thank you for your kindness to these two foolish women. I hope it does not put you out too much."

"Hardly at all." Mr Kay, deciding the street opera had best be ended, was already gesturing to his waiting rickshaws. "Whatever else you need to say, let it be said this evening. Good day, Captain."

Mr Nair was unceremoniously packed into a rickshaw and sent off, despite his clumsy protests that he could not afford it (Mr Kay simply pushed money into his hands and told him impatiently to get himself gone). Sarah Jane and Miss Cassidy took another, and Mr Kay took a third by himself, a pipe in one hand and an ebony fan in the other. Miss Cassidy could have sworn she could hear him chuckling over the raucous noise of the streets, though it was hardly possible.

They reached Bendemeer House first, and when Miss Cassidy went to Mr Kay to thank him, he smiled broadly and said, "Do not forget, today you are teaching my daughters."

"Yes, I remember, Mr Kay, but if Sarah Jane needs me—"

"She will not need you. She has her amah and she will be in bed with a headache till her Papa comes home. This sort of scene always induces headaches in her type. My daughters' lesson will proceed apace, and you will come tell me about this interesting matter. After all, if I am to hire Mr Nair, I must know everything about him."

"Mr Kay," exclaimed Miss Cassidy, "I declare you mean to gossip with me like an old woman."

Mr Kay neither agreed nor disagreed with the accusation. He merely smiled even more broadly—a little mischievously, Miss Cassidy thought—and commanded his rickshaw to move on.

Mr Kay's prediction was astute; Sarah Jane sobbed on Ah Nai's shoulder for a moment, then retired to bed for the rest of the day. What was Haresh Nair doing? Probably, thought Miss Cassidy practically, trying to wash the ink spots out of his one good coat.

Miss Cassidy was glad of the long walk to Pandan Villa to clear her mind and calm her nerves. Captain Bendemeer was not wrong—she had failed in her duties, for the primary duty of a young girl's companion is to preserve her innocence. A young English lady of station was not permitted to fall in love without her Papa's sanction, certainly not with someone as "wildly unsuitable" as Haresh Nair. Strictly speaking, Miss Cassidy should have stopped their acquaintance; certainly she should have done nothing to encourage it. But she had, and she was not sorry, not a jot. Still, it would be unfortunate to be removed from her position now, and possibly sent home without a reference.

About an hour later, as Yeling and Yezi pondered over their English exercises, Mr Kay sauntered over in his usual insouciant manner, filling the air above their heads with tobacco smoke. He glanced at the exercises and chuckled. "Henry VIII was fat, and had six wives. Henry VIII will be fat, and will have six wives. Henry VIII is fat, and..." He paused. "Has six wives? Surely not. He did not have all six at the same time."

"Mr Kay, you are distracting us," said Miss Cassidy, who was putting away a Chinese chess set. The twins loved Chinese chess, and part of their spoken English lesson was to teach Miss Cassidy to play it.

"I must teach you some Chinese history to put in your grammar exercises. Wu Zetian is fascinating. Or the philosophies of Kongzi."

"Is that Confucius? Since you are educating your daughters, I hardly think Confucius is a suitable philosopher."

"One can still learn from a great man's philosophies, without necessarily agreeing with them all. Or, indeed, a great woman." He puffed on his pipe. "I have asked Mr Nair to see me tomorrow, at ten o'clock. It is fortuitous that I do, in fact, need a clerk well-versed in the British East India Company's business, especially while inept men like Kingsbright are trying to run it for their own personal profit."

"He is a horrible man."

"He is a man made horrible by circumstance." Mr Kay pulled up one of the heavy rosewood chairs and sat down with grace and ease by Miss Cassidy's side, his long limbs outspread and encompassing the room. "He is the second son of a baron. He disgraced himself in England with some dancing girl, but it was not the dancing girl alone who doomed him"—the pipe gestured enthusiastically in emphasis—"it was that this girl was already the possession of another, greater man. There was a fight, some say, and the girl was found dead."

"Mr Kay, this is a terribly sordid story to be telling in front of your daughters."

The pipe waved dismissively. "Found dead," he repeated, delighted with Miss Cassidy's scandalised expression. "Mr Kingsbright was implicated. His father pulled a string or two, and a mighty friend of a friend arranged for him to be sent to the West Indies as an undersecretary for the Company. He performed poorly, and was sent on to Ceylon, then to Bencoolen, then here. He is a fool and an incompetent, who makes life miserable for his subordinates, and exasperating for the Company's partners and associates. The meeting we had, which you saw, was to deliver him an ultimatum. If he does not accede to certain of our requirements, we will demand to have him replaced. And there is nowhere else for him to go. He must either be demoted, or sent home in absolute humiliation."

"An unpleasant story," said Miss Cassidy primly, "but none of my business, Mr Kay."

"Ah, but it is mine. I prefer my associates to be honest men."

"As do we all, I am sure, but at the moment I am more concerned for myself."

"Ah!" Mr Kay leaned back in his chair with an expression at once ludicrous and engaging. "You refer to our star-crossed lovers! Tell me, what do you make of their chances?"

"Very poor."

"And yet you do not discourage them."

"They may choose their own path as much as anyone else, Mr Kay. It is the prerogative of the young to break their hearts at least once or twice in their lives. It would be a dull sort of world if all young ladies let their Papas choose their husbands."

"Is that a jibe at our customs?" asked Mr Kay with interest. "Do you disapprove of arranged marriages?"

"Not at all. I merely state the simple fact that children who rebel against their parents add a great deal of spice to society."

"And is this good or bad?"

"It is interesting. And it is…character-building, I suppose."

"Miss Cassidy," said Mr Kay, puffing on his pipe, "I begin to suspect you of a love of mischief. There are spirits in Ireland, they say, who lead travellers astray simply for the joy of it. Are you of that ilk?"

"Hmm. Have I led you astray, Mr Kay?"

"That depends."

"Depends? On what, pray?"

"On what I am meant to be straying from."

Miss Cassidy turned resolutely away from him, and asked the twins crossly what was taking them so long.

*

Miss Cassidy returned to Bendemeer House with some trep-idation. Just before sunset, as expected, Captain Bendemeer summoned her to his study. Sarah Jane was already there, pale but calm, clutching her morocco-leatherbound Bible in her lap. Captain Bendemeer, looking exhausted, stood at his desk, gripping a tumbler of whisky he was not drinking from. Miss Cassidy entered, stood quite still, and waited.

"Miss Cassidy, Sarah Jane absolves you of all blame," he said coldly. "She says you have done nothing to encourage this...unpleasant situation."

"Miss Bendemeer is very kind," said Miss Cassidy gently. "But I must accept my part in this. I have not been a stern enough monitress."

"No," said Sarah Jane, gripping her Bible. "You have been good and kind, and tried to advise me sensibly. If you had been as stern as...as I have once experienced...I would by now have done something far more foolish, probably. Eloped, or run away, or worse."

"I do not think Mr Nair would have done any of those things," said Miss Cassidy.

"Nor do I," said Captain Bendemeer. "I will admit he has always been a practical fellow, and honest. I believe he is sincere in his intentions. But Sarah Jane, it was unlady-like of you to encourage his affection—yes, and unkind, when you know full well that nothing can come of it. He is a clerk whose wages barely feed himself, apart from him being Indian!"

"There is nothing wrong with his race," said Sarah Jane passionately.

"Do you think I mind his race? We are nobody; no one would care. But you would have to live within his world, his culture. Perhaps his country, if he is sent home eventually."

"His family is Catholic."

"And they are still Indian. What do you know of their ways, their rules, their lives, Sarah Jane? Do you imagine, as an English girl, that you will have some form of special status in an Indian family? You have never lived without luxury—you have your own rooms, your amah, your companion. You cannot do plain cooking or sewing or manage a household. You do not speak a word of Hindi."

"Malayalam," murmured Miss Cassidy.

"Excuse me, yes, he is from Kerala. Do you even know the difference, Sarah Jane? Between Hindi and Malayalam? Or Tamil and Hindi? Or, indeed, anything about India?"

Sarah Jane stared at her Papa. "I am sure he will teach me," she said in a faltering tone.

"Will he? Will that be enough?" Captain Bendemeer sighed.

"Captain," ventured Miss Cassidy, "if I know Mr Nair, I think he will come to you as soon as he can tomorrow. You have said it yourself, he is an honourable man."

"Indeed. All I cling to now is Mr Nair's sense of honour." Captain Bendemeer laughed mirthlessly. "Very well. Go then, both of you. I have nothing more to say."

IX

Miss Cassidy & the Bomoh

"Miz Cazdee, Pak Labah says come."

Miss Cassidy stared at Ahmad, somewhat distracted, as he peered through the gates of Bendemeer House. The Bendemeers and Haresh Nair were, at that very moment, gathered together in the Captain's study with the doors closed. Miss Cassidy had waited an hour, then decided to leave the house, and was pacing restlessly in the garden, under the banana trees. In the brilliant sunlight there was nothing sinister about the trees, or the bobbing frangipani flowers. Indeed, the banana trees produced delicious creamy yellow fruit when the season was right, very different from the small, sweet bananas Miss Cassidy had eaten in India.

Ahmad, the kacang putih seller, was peering in through the gates of Bendemeer House, scratching his belly. Miss Cassidy offered him a banana, which he took without thanking her, and consumed in three great bites.

"Who is Pak Labah?" she asked.

"Bukit Labah," he said, "Spider Hill. Pak Labah. He had a dream. You must see him."

"Oh! The man on the hill! But I can't go now."

Ahmad shrugged. "He says to come through the fire."

"Eh?"

Ahmad, having tucked the banana skin into a fold of his sarong, had nothing else to say, and ran off in a tumble of limbs.

"Naughty boy," said Ah Nai behind her, as the old amah came trotting up the path. "He is not supposed to shout through the gate."

"Oh, well, it was only for a moment. Are you going to the temple, Ah Nai? Are the Captain and Sarah Jane still...?"

Ah Nai sighed, and nodded. "You come with me?" she suggested. "The Captain says we should go out. He does not want us to hear."

"But what if they need something?"

"Ah Kio is there." With a single expressive gesture, Ah Nai indicated that it did not matter what Ah Kio overheard, since he would not understand anything.

Thian Hock Keng temple was one of the most impressive, and busiest, temples in the settlement. It was dedicated to the Hokkien sea goddess Mazu, but Ah Nai visited it for the smaller Kuan Yin shrine in the back. The temple had many wealthy sponsors, and consequently was a marvel of elaborate construction, part of which had been completed by Indian workers. It even had a wrought-iron gate that had been shipped in from Glasgow.

Miss Cassidy thought the temple beautiful, but unlike the little Hindu temple Mr Nair had brought her to, Thian Hock

Keng was famous and therefore full of casual visitors. At its gates and around its walls called the vendors, selling flowers and joss sticks and incense and talismans, and itinerant fortune tellers had set up shop at little tables, trying to persuade visitors to sit for them. Miss Cassidy only ever came to Thian Hock Keng in Ah Nai's company, for the amah ferociously shooed away anyone she thought was being too bothersome, in a voluble flood of whatever dialect happened to be called for.

Ah Nai took Miss Cassidy by the elbow and led her to a great shrine, so crowded with deities it was hard to make anything out amid the incense smoke. A group of kneeling nuns chanted sonorously, ringing a little silver bell to keep time. Ah Nai patted one of the cushions before the shrine, indicating that Miss Cassidy should kneel, then put in her hands a bamboo container full of little sticks. "You have good hands," she explained, and took Miss Cassidy's hands in hers. Together they shook the bamboo canister vigorously, Ah Nai murmuring softly under her breath, until one of the sticks fell out.

"Come," she said, picking up the stick, leading Miss Cassidy to a wooden booth where dozens of fortune-stick containers were arranged neatly on shelves. The nun there accepted the fortune stick, and looked up the corresponding fortune from a large cabinet with multiple drawers neatly numbered.

There ensued a great confab between Ah Nai and the nun. Miss Cassidy waited patiently, gazing at Kuan Yin's tranquil face. Finally Ah Nai sighed, accepted the fortune, and said, "A great separation is coming. We must prepare ourselves."

"Hmm. An unavoidable separation?"

"Yes, unavoidable."

Miss Cassidy left the temple gloomily. Ah Nai stayed to seek advice from the nuns, and offer more joss sticks, but Miss Cassidy wanted to walk the streets and think. Telok Ayer was, as usual, very busy at this time of day. She bought a paper cone of roasted chestnuts from a street vendor, and walked and ate at the same time. It was a rather unladylike thing to do, but Miss Cassidy always thought best when she was eating—

—and then, quite suddenly, she was no longer in Telok Ayer.

She looked around, exasperated, casting away the last of her chestnut shells. Around her was a yard, which held a small makeshift chicken coop and a hut made of leaves and attap. A small fire was burning very close to her, and Miss Cassidy gathered up her skirts hastily.

She nearly stepped on a small, wizened old man who sat cross-legged by the fire. He wore only a sarong, and held a half-coconut bowl with some small items rattling about inside. A few coins, a pebble and a banana skin.

"Good gracious," said Miss Cassidy blankly, "have you... summoned me?"

The old man regarded her out of shrewd, beady black eyes, and spat betel juice out of the corner of his mouth.

"Nobody has had the power to summon me for hundreds of years. Certainly not as I am now," she said with asperity. "Whatever do you want? Oh," she exclaimed at last, "are you Pak Labah?"

"Pak Labah," agreed the old man in a hoarse, gruff voice. He stood up and regarded her calmly, his hands behind his back. "Eh," he added non-committally, unimpressed.

"Do you know about the pontianak at Bendemeer House?"

"Pontianak," said Pak Labah, nodding, moving towards his hut. "Nanti, nanti."

Miss Cassidy obediently waited. She could not move far anyway; the bomoh had cast a very small summoning circle.

Presently he returned, holding a length of red string. He took Miss Cassidy's hand and looped the string round and round her wrist, finally binding it in a loose knot. Then he pointed at her pocket.

Miss Cassidy took out the ball of wool she always kept with her, and handed it over. "Be careful with it," she said sternly. "If you break it, you will be lost in the place you follow it to."

The bomoh grunted as he accepted the ball of wool. Then he went to the fire and stamped it out.

Miss Cassidy was once again in Telok Ayer.

It was later than she expected, and she hurried back to Bendemeer House, being careful to tuck the red string well under her sleeve.

She arrived just in time to see Mr Nair leaving. "Miss Cassidy," he said with a rather ghastly smile. "Always a pleasure to see you."

"What has happened?" she demanded without preamble. "Have you come to an understanding with the Captain?"

"Of a kind, Miss Cassidy," said Mr Nair, running his fingers through his already dishevelled hair. "Sarah Jane and I are...not engaged to be married."

"Ah."

"Not yet. The Captain—quite sensibly, I suppose—wishes me to establish myself in a manner he feels would sustain Sarah Jane in the lifestyle she is accustomed to."

"Gracious. What does that mean?"

"It means, Miss Cassidy, that unless I have an income that is equivalent to Captain Bendemeer's own, I cannot marry Sarah Jane. Beyond that, if we marry, we will live within the Straits Settlements. We will not return either to England or India."

"And what do you think?"

"Think?" Mr Nair produced a gloomy laugh. "I think he has set me an impossible task. Yet I cannot fault him. He was...more of a gentleman than most might have been in his circumstances. In short, Miss Cassidy," he said at last, beginning to trudge slowly away, "Sarah Jane remains free. And so, I suppose, do I."

"Ah," murmured Miss Cassidy as she watched him leave, "young love."

Sarah Jane was waiting for her in the hallway. Her usually pale face showed two burning red spots on her cheeks, and though she had clearly been crying, her eyes were bright.

"Miss Cassidy, help me," she cried, seizing Miss Cassidy's hands. "Help me convince them both."

"Of what, my dear?"

"Of my willingness to be poor."

Miss Cassidy kept her face mild and serious, seeing how passionately earnest Sarah Jane was. It was nice to see her so worked up. "Do you mean, with Mr Nair?"

"Yes! Papa has convinced him that poverty is too great a hardship for me. That he must be able to provide me a house, and dresses, and servants, and...and...pineapples, and I don't know what else. It isn't true, Miss Cassidy! I don't need all these things; I have never been concerned with them."

It was true; Sarah Jane had certainly never been much concerned with her surroundings or her personal appearance. She spent most of her time reading the Bible in the same chair, and never looked twice at the fashion plates from which Miss Cassidy and Ah Nai did up her dresses. "My dear, I think your father's greater concern is your lack of practical skills," said Miss Cassidy gently. "Poor women must economise, manage a household, do our own sewing and cooking. You may not have a maid for the rough work—for chamber pots and laundering and so forth."

"I could learn. I am willing to learn, from you, from Ah Nai. Why should they dismiss my ability to learn these things before I have tried my hand at them?"

Miss Cassidy accepted the undeniable logic of this, but continued, "And Mr Nair's salary would need to feed you both."

"I could work. I could...I could teach English. You could show me how."

"Nobody could afford to hire you."

"They needn't pay me in money. Ah Kio and Ah Nai often trade the bananas from our garden for other things. I could do that, trade lessons for necessities."

"Well," said Miss Cassidy at last, "I confess, Sarah Jane, you have thought it through far more than I expected."

"Will you speak to Papa for me? I know I can convince Haresh, but Papa—it is hard for Papa. I am his only surviving child, and he wants… he has better hopes, I suppose, for me."

"Of course he does, but I will do my best, Sarah Jane."

"Thank you! Oh, thank you!"

Miss Cassidy was not sure she merited such heartfelt gratitude, but there was no time for further discussion; Ah Kio was hovering at her elbow. Captain Bendemeer was asking to see her.

She was alarmed by how dreadful he looked. He stood by the window of his study where the warm evening light cast deep shadows over his cheeks and eyes. He appeared paler than ever, more drained of colour, and though it was as hot a day as always, no perspiration was on his brow.

"Miss Cassidy, I may as well tell you at once that I have decided Sarah Jane and I must leave Singapore."

Miss Cassidy took a deep breath before speaking. "Captain Bendemeer, I am sorry to hear it."

"I have been in the colonies for nearly fifteen years. Sometimes as I think of it, I am amazed I have stayed this long. The fetid air, the noise, the chaos. Once I had a wife and a home full of children, and servants," he murmured dreamily. "She was a magnificent woman, my Maria. My family would not recognise her worth because she was quadroon."

Miss Cassidy thought of the picture of the forbidding woman in the drawing room. Dark, beautiful, stern. Certainly Captain Bendemeer would have thrived under the management of a strong-minded, ambitious wife with nothing to lose, but Sarah Jane was an entirely different matter. "Does Sarah Jane know her Mama's history?" asked Miss Cassidy.

Captain Bendemeer looked faintly surprised. "Of course. It is unimportant. I have said before, Miss Cassidy: we are nobody. We have no blue blood to taint. If not for Maria, I would still be sailing with the fleet, or drowned and dead by now. Whatever respectability or gentility I now have is due to my late wife. I am nothing—a sailor, son of a blacksmith and a dairywoman. That I have raised my daughter up this high is a miracle, nothing less. I have nothing but respect for Haresh Nair; we have much in common. But you see, Miss Cassidy, what it would mean if Sarah Jane were now to return to the mode of life both Maria and I have emerged from. It would mean I have come this far for nothing."

"Captain, forgive me but…you know that you could simply dower Sarah Jane with an income. That will keep them from poverty."

"I could. I have. And I hoped that her income would find her a husband of equal standing. The only way to found a great family is to keep combining lesser fortunes till they become a great fortune. That was Maria's ambition for her children."

"And that is why you have asked Mr Nair to improve his income?"

"Of course."

"Will you not grant Sarah Jane the engagement, at least?"

"No. She is only sixteen. She has matured greatly since you arrived," he nodded at Miss Cassidy politely, "but she still has no inkling of the hardships that would face her, as the wife in a mixed-race marriage. Both in England and in India, her life would be unbearable. It is why Maria and I came here. Sarah Jane was still a very small child, then. It was for her sake we left England, and for the sake of all our children. Imagine their lives in school, with their drop of non-British blood? No," muttered the Captain, "no. It was not to be borne."

Miss Cassidy was silent. Privately she wondered if the Captain was a little delirious. It was not like him to be this verbose, to say this much to a paid dependent who had no proper right to pry into his family's history.

"We will leave Singapore," said the Captain at last. "I will be glad to be rid of that swine Kingsbright. I will be glad to leave this house. It is full of ghosts for me; every night they seem to walk across my shadow. Every night...every night..." He paused, as if confused.

"What about the servants and myself, Captain?" asked Miss Cassidy briskly, and he blinked at her as if wondering why she was there.

"Ah Nai may come with us if she wants. She might not. I do not know yet where we are going. I only know we must leave...must leave... this place..."

Miss Cassidy was ready for it, and just managed to catch the Captain as he collapsed. He was thin and light, and she was strong and solidly built, so it was no great hardship to carry him to his chair and make him comfortable. She loosened his collar and checked his pulse; he was breathing, but not conscious. Indeed, he appeared almost to be dreaming.

Miss Cassidy quickly unlooped Pak Labah's red string from her wrist. She tied one end to the Captain's fourth finger, just under his wedding ring, and the other to her own corresponding finger.

Then she took a packet of salt from her pocket (the other item, apart from string, that she always carried with her) and scattered the salt liberally all over the floor.

Finally, she pinned to her blouse the most important item: Maria Bendemeer's enormous black iron needle.

This done, she sat, and waited.

The daylight was all gone when she saw it: a footprint, appearing in the salt, right in front of the Captain. Then another, leading away. Then another.

Captain Bendemeer's eyes opened, blank, unseeing. He stood up.

He began to walk, appearing to carefully place his feet in the footprints already marked for him. Miss Cassidy waited till he had paced out the length of the red string. Then she stood up and followed him.

They passed both Sarah Jane and Ah Nai in the hallway. Sarah Jane had been waiting to speak to her father; she now slept soundly in the window seat. Ah Nai slept where she stood, still holding a feather duster. Ah Kio was in the garden, dozing in the shade of the banana trees, his mouth still half-full of mashed banana.

Miss Cassidy could just hear the sound of her iron key at her own window—tap, tap, tap.

The garden was a fog of frangipani flowers, the white and yellow petals drifting in spiralling circles although there was no breeze. Miss Cassidy kept a steady eye on the Captain's back as he moved deliberately beneath the banana leaves, step by careful step.

Then abruptly, he vanished.

Miss Cassidy swore in a language that was guttural, ancient and magical, seized the red thread around her finger and tugged.

Something tugged back.

"I am ready for you now," said Miss Cassidy quietly. "Let this begin."

She seized hold of the thread and pulled it taut, then ran down its length till she could run no more—till she reached a place of darkness so dense she could not see, could only smell the cloying scent of frangipani closing in around her, and hear the breath of some sibilant creature by her ear. The red thread remained taut in her fingers, but she could not see what it was now tethered to, nor could she see the Captain.

"I knew you wouldn't let him go," Miss Cassidy said sharply to the being she could not see. "I knew you would choose to finish him now, rather than let him out of your clutches. It is delicious, isn't it? The lifeblood of a loyal man, the soul of true courage. You have almost drained him dry, but your kind are never satisfied."

The shadows flickered. They uncovered, gradually, Captain Bendemeer's still, prone form on the ground, so pale and white Miss Cassidy feared he was already dead. She started to bend over him.

The red thread around her finger became painfully tight, and then tugged sharply at her. It was an irresistible force;

stumbling, pulling at her skirts, Miss Cassidy was dragged forwards at breathless speed.

And then a monstrous face was very close to hers.

Its eyes were huge, black, slanted, without whites; its great red mouth was full of teeth as sharp as needles; long, dark hair drifted about the terrible face, and the smell of decay struck Miss Cassidy like an assault. In blackened, clawlike fingers, the pontianak held Pak Labah's red thread twined and knotted.

It hissed at Miss Cassidy, "You do not belong here. This land is mine."

"That is true. You have more power than me. But I am stubborn. I am renowned for it. And now we have everything we need to bind you."

The pontianak cackled. "You! You cannot bind me. I am beyond the power of your twinkly moor lights. This one is mine."

"Not quite, my dear. There is someone here with a higher claim."

The pontianak laughed, a screech of rusty nails.

Then it attacked, so fast Miss Cassidy had no time to react.

Its claws were sharp as knives, and Miss Cassidy's human flesh, clad only in cotton and muslin, was instantly pierced through. All ten of the creature's fingers were driven deep into her chest and belly, and the long blades emerged again from the other side. Her white blouse was immediately covered in gore and blood.

"Hmm," said Miss Cassidy. A corset might have been handy.

Then, suddenly, she wasn't there.

120

The pontianak growled, screeched and hissed. It returned to Captain Bendemeer's still form, and crouched over it territorially.

"Sluagh," Miss Cassidy's voice echoed with strange notes, "get away from him."

The pontianak bared all its hundreds of terrible teeth. "It cannot be," it snarled. "Your kind cannot hold me."

"You are quite right," said Miss Cassidy primly, "but it is not into my power you have now fallen."

And all of a sudden—quite new to the pontianak's experience—someone pulled its hair. *Hard.*

It whipped around and snapped and clawed, but the tug only grew firmer and tighter. A face gazed down at the pontianak, stern and forbidding—but it was not Miss Cassidy's face.

"Release my husband," snarled Maria Bendemeer in a husky voice as cold as iron. "Or I will have to punish you."

Cold, dark and dreadful was the former mistress of Bendemeer House. In one hand she gripped the red thread that bound all creatures in her circle, a circle Miss Cassidy had cast for her; in the other, in a fist like stone, the pontianak's hair. The pontianak clawed at her, screaming, fighting, but Maria was larger, stronger and more brutal.

"My claim is greater," said Maria, beautiful, terrible, perilous as night. "Over both your victim and your thrall, my foolish daughter who freed you. I kept you at bay from the moment I came to this house. This place is *mine*."

"No!" roared the pontianak, struggling in Maria's brutal grip upon its face and neck. "No, her kind cannot summon you—this cannot be!"

"*She?* Summon *me?*" Maria's mocking laughter was like fire in a thunderstorm. "Pitiful monster, I summoned her. There are so few of her kind left—it took so long—but the spirits told me, it must be her and no one else. Only she could put together the pieces that would bring me back. It took her far too long, but it is now done. The fay is under *my* summoning, and you are bound by *my* circle now."

The tall and terrible woman pushed down on the monster's face with all her might and forced open its jaw, disregarding the teeth still snatching at her fingers. She kept a firm grip on its hair, and knelt on each of the long-clawed hands.

"Asheekin," began Maria, and the pontianak shrieked at the invocation of its name. Into its scream echoed Maria Bendemeer's icy voice. "Asheekin, I bind you, with the power of blood and iron. Miss Cassidy, hold this naughty child down."

Miss Cassidy—who did not look very much like Miss Cassidy at that moment, but there were no human eyes to notice this—did as she was bid, for her kind had to when a summoning was in effect.

And with a grin of sadistic pleasure, Maria started to press fistfuls of bright red chilli padi into the creature's mouth and eyes.

Miss Cassidy winced. "This is not part of the ritual," she ventured.

"It is part of mine. Hold her still."

"I must obey you, but still I object," said Miss Cassidy stoutly. "Surely you did not do this to your own children?"

Maria Bendemeer's mouth twisted with scorn, but she responded shortly. "No, of course not. But this is not my child."

Chilli padi seeds burned like acid; a single seed in one's eye could be excruciating. With Miss Cassidy's grip rendering the pontianak substantial, forcing it to remain in the physical realm, Maria Bendemeer's favourite threat for naughty children would be a torment beyond measure.

The pontianak was struggling violently, but Maria had clearly planned this punishment for a long time, and continued to force chillies down the creature's throat and push paste into its eyes. It screamed and shrieked and began to sob.

But Maria Bendemeer was pitiless. "When you take what does not belong to you," she said sharply, "you must be punished." And she raised her great black needle.

Miss Cassidy had seen some frightful sights in her time, but Maria Bendemeer threading her black needle with the bomoh's red thread, her grey face cold as stone, was one of the most terrifying. She turned away primly as the pontianak began to scream again. It seemed to her that Maria took her time over the task.

When the pontianak's lips and eyes had been sewn firmly shut—both filled with chilli seeds—Maria bit off the thread from her needle, and nodded with satisfaction at the suffering creature trembling in Miss Cassidy's grasp. "It is done," she said. "She is bound."

"Then end it, milady," said Miss Cassidy urgently.

Maria Bendemeer gripped the weeping creature's head, bent it forward and drove her needle deep into its neck.

The pontianak began shrinking, changing; beneath Miss Cassidy's hands the monster became a woman, quite a young woman, who was probably rather a beautiful woman, but her face was now swollen and red and covered in blisters and her eyes were bloodied and watering. The shrieks were now childlike human sobs. Smaller and smaller she became, till Miss Cassidy was gripping a weeping teenaged girl, no older than poor Emily Bendemeer—once, long ago, a wronged child named Asheekin, her spirit now bound again by Maria Bendemeer's great iron needle.

"Thank you, Mrs Bendemeer. She will harm no one else."

"Make sure of it." Mrs Bendemeer gazed down at her unconscious husband. "I told him so," she added. "He believes in nothing. He thinks it makes him safe. But if you do not honour your dead, what are you? Do you live in a void, linked to nothing that has gone before? The dead are important, where I am from, as they are here. I told him so."

And, without another word, with no tender message for those she had left behind, Maria Bendemeer was gone.

The night was calm again. The scent of frangipani was fading.

There was no one in the garden now except Miss Cassidy (who once again looked like Miss Cassidy) and the Captain. Miss Cassidy bent over him. He opened his eyes and clutched his head. "Miss Cassidy...why, what is this? When did we come outside?"

"You have been dreaming, Captain. You have been ill, but you will be better now. Here is Ah Kio, come to help you to bed."

Miss Cassidy left the old servant to help his master. The first thing she did was to retrieve Maria's photograph from where she had previously left it, beneath the banana tree bound in pink silk. It now weighed no more, to Miss Cassidy, than its silver frame, as she popped it safely back into her pocket, to be returned to the dim shelf where she had found it.

She removed the pink silk scarf from the tree. It was no longer needed.

She then hurried over the grass, towards the gate. She did not want to undergo the indignity of being summoned through a cooking fire again.

Ahmad was waiting, eating a bar of chocolate, with a rusty bicycle that should have been far too big for him. He matter-of-factly accepted the pink scarf, into which Miss Cassidy dropped the large black iron needle and the remainder of Pak Labah's red thread. She then folded the cloth in a particular manner. "Be quick," she said, "and don't lose it."

"I know, I know," said Ahmad with a huge grin, accepting the princely sum of twenty cents from Miss Cassidy. He took his precious package, mounted his bicycle, and pedalled away.

Pak Labah would add the Bendemeer House pontianak to his collection, where it would be safe...at least, for now.

X

Miss Cassidy Finds a New Job

BENDEMEER House was finally empty. Ah Nai and Ah Kio stood before the gates, with their belongings neatly bundled into gunny sacks at their feet, watching as Miss Cassidy came down the steps. She smiled at them. "You have a long way to go, my dears. I hope you find the English climate comfortable; it will be colder than you are used to."

Ah Nai waved her hand dismissively. "They go, I go," she said simply.

"Will you and Ah Kio ever return to China?"

"Ah Kio was born in Singapore," said Ah Nai. "For me, it does not matter where I go."

Sarah Jane and Captain Bendemeer had left Bendemeer House two weeks ago, the very day after the Captain's dreadful nightmare of his wife standing at the gates of hell with a black needle and red thread. That afternoon, he resigned his position at the British East India Company and purchased first-class tickets on the earliest available ship, which would leave that night. He had paid Miss Cassidy, Ah Nai and Ah Kio that evening, and gave all three the option to come with them—particularly Ah Nai, who had raised Sarah Jane from a baby. Ah Nai had agreed without considering, as long as Ah Kio could come with her.

Miss Cassidy had decided to stay.

"You are certain, Miss Cassidy?" asked the Captain. "I will give you a good reference, of course, but it will be hard for you to find another place here."

"I will manage," said Miss Cassidy briskly. "I always do."

Sarah Jane had been inconsolable. The Captain had grudgingly given her and Mr Nair permission to write letters to one another, but he still refused to sanction an official engagement.

"I will make my fortune, Captain Bendemeer," promised Mr Nair stoutly. "I will not rest till I have a home worthy of your daughter."

"I sincerely hope you will, Mr Nair, for Sarah Jane is very fond of you."

"Till then, I hope we part as friends."

"We do, Haresh." The two men had shaken hands.

Although there was to be no formal engagement, Mr Nair had pressed upon Sarah Jane a gift of five silver bangles, which tinkled like bells when she wore them. "One day I will give you gold ones," he added fervently, in a piercing whisper. Sarah Jane could only weep silently, and hold his hand as long as she dared.

Captain Bendemeer had already begun to look better, healthier and stronger almost from the moment he awoke in the garden. By the time he and Sarah Jane actually boarded the ship, he looked ten years younger than when Miss Cassidy first saw him.

Despite her sorrow, Sarah Jane bore up well in front of her Papa, and as she kissed Miss Cassidy, murmured, "I hope this is not goodbye forever, Miss Cassidy. You will take care of Haresh as well as you did of me and Papa, I know."

"I certainly will, Sarah Jane. He will be plump and rosy by the time you see him again."

Sarah Jane managed to laugh through her tears—a significant change from the pale creature Miss Cassidy had first met—and embraced Miss Cassidy heartily.

Ah Nai and Ah Kio were to follow the Bendemeers on a later ship, after packing up the rest of the house. They would catch up in Hong Kong, and continue on from there together.

Miss Cassidy was sad to see them go. She and Ah Nai had become very good friends. "You will write to me?" she asked. "I value your wisdom, Ah Nai. Write to me in Chinese and I will go to the temple and find a translator."

"I shall, Miss Cassidy. And...thank you for what you have done."

"I am glad to have been of service."

Miss Cassidy stood on the dock and watched the ship till it was a mere spot on the horizon, disregarding the chaos and noise of the quay. In her pocket was a ball of red silk cord that Ah Nai had given her, to replace that which she had traded to Pak Labah.

She stood watching till it seemed silly to stay any longer, then turned, dabbing at her eyes with a cotton handkerchief... and walked rather violently into Mr Kay.

"Oof! You are a solidly built woman, Miss Cassidy."

"For heaven's sake!" exclaimed Miss Cassidy crossly. "Where on earth did you come from, Mr Kay? I declare you were not there five minutes ago."

"Five minutes? You have been standing here a good one hour. I have been looking down at you from my warehouse window. All my coolies were saying there is a mad red-hair on the dock, standing like a statue, and I supposed it must be you."

"I have just said goodbye to my friends, Mr Kay. And furthermore, I am now without work or home. I am rather preoccupied."

"Indeed. I have seen your advertisement in the newspaper. Respectable middle-aged lady seeks place as governess or lady's companion to European or British family. Proficient in French, German, English, arithmetic, geography, dance and drawing. Experience in nursing. Interested parties please—"

"Good gracious," growled Miss Cassidy irritably, "have you memorised the entire advertisement for the sole purpose of teasing me, Mr Kay? I declare it is no laughing matter. I have rooms now in the same boarding house as Mr Nair, and while it is perfectly respectable, it is meant for working men. I am the only woman apart from the landlady herself, and were it not for the colour of Captain Bendemeer's money, I fancy she would suspect me of being a particularly specialised specimen of a certain kind of professional woman. Oh, I am sure it amuses you," she added tetchily as Mr Kay chuckled, "but you forgive me if I cannot find the humour in the situation quite yet."

"Well! You are quite right, and I should stop laughing at you, for I have a proposition."

Miss Cassidy took a breath, and began, "Mr Kay, I cannot—"

He held up his ill-omened hand to stop her. "Do not argue," he commanded, "not till I have spoken. I propose to hire you as tutoress for my daughters, and my daughters-in-law—I have two now, you know—as well as for my forthcoming grandchild, whatever its gender, for it will not matter when it is still a child. The quarters we once gave to the good priest who taught my sons are still empty, and quite respectable; set apart from the main house, but not with the servants. I know this is not a customary situation among your people," he added, raising his formidable voice so that it drowned out her protest, "but I have my arguments prepared.

"Firstly," he ticked off one finger, "you are nobody important, Miss Cassidy, and any potential scandal is irrelevant to you. Secondly," he continued, disregarding her expression of outrage, "I am a respectable widower of great wealth and influence, in good graces with the triads and secret societies besides; no one will dare speak ill of anything I do. And finally, it is practical. The women of my household must know English, and they are not all teenagers with malleable minds—you will have to deal with mature women, who have barely learnt to read in Chinese, much less any other language. Two-hour lessons twice a week will do them no good.

No, the tutoress must live with us, and must converse with them; must, indeed, force them to converse with her. Come, Miss Cassidy," he concluded at last, "are my arguments not persuasive?"

"Mr Kay—"

He raised his dreadful hand again. "If you are going to say that it is an unsuitable arrangement, I have already given you the reasons why it will not be—or rather, the reasons we do not have to care, if it is. Have you any other argument?" He looked down at her, waiting.

Miss Cassidy was at a loss for words. Nobody else had such an effect on her, from demons and shamans to goddesses and ghosts; only this mere mortal man had such an astounding ability to continually stagger her.

He was still looking at her. He was looming, quite deliberately, she thought in exasperation. It was such an effective way to blockade a person's thoughts, this heavy presence standing in one's shadow.

"Very well," she said at last. "I...cannot find any reason to refuse."

"Excellent." He stepped back, and Miss Cassidy realised abruptly she was flushed pink. This annoyed her greatly, and she stepped away from him as well.

"When may I present myself at Pandan Villa?" she asked, hastily rearranging her hat to shade her face.

"Present yourself?" He chuckled again. "Am I the Queen? You will go immediately, Miss Cassidy, to these rooms you have rented amongst the bachelors' caves, gather up your things, and 'present yourself' at my gate in forty-five minutes."

"Forty—"

"The rickshaw is waiting for you now," he interrupted her. "Go. Good evening, Miss Cassidy."

He turned on his heel and left, just like that.

Miss Cassidy glared at his retreating back for a moment. She considered all the many swear words she knew, in many colourful languages. She could find none suitable.

"May you choke on your pipe," she exclaimed at last.

This appearing to satisfy her soul, Miss Cassidy lifted her skirts and headed to the waiting rickshaw.

THE CURSE OF PANDAN VILLA

XI

Miss Cassidy's New Pupils

"AH! You are afraid? But it must be quick or the chicken will not die."

In the sun-drenched, steamy kitchen of Pandan Villa, Mr Kay's oldest daughter-in-law, Mui Ee—whose wedding reception Miss Cassidy had attended in the courtyard almost two years ago—gripped the squawking chicken by the neck in her strong, meaty fist and, with expert efficiency, slammed the bird's body heavily onto the table. The sound of its neck snapping was sharp and alarming; the chicken's wings twitched spasmodically, but it was already dead.

"It is how my mother taught me," she said, handing the bird back to Miss Cassidy. "The chicken dies quickly. If you do not do it right, the poor chicken, you know—it runs around."

"Without a head? Yes."

Miss Cassidy settled down to begin plucking the chicken. Mui Ee and her younger sister-in-law, Wong Mi, were busy with the chopping of many vegetables, and the old amah of the household was stirring the rice. Mui Ee, as wife of the oldest son, was in charge of the kitchen, and was not shy about bossing everyone around, including their red-haired English teacher.

The household of a wealthy Chinese merchant was not at all what Miss Cassidy had originally expected. Although there was no shortage of servants, including a full-time cook, the daughters-in-law were fully expected to take on important household tasks such as the cooking and sewing. Mui Ee, in particular, was expected to oversee the kitchen, the household expenses, the servants and the children. She usually cooked the late meal along with almost all the womenfolk in the household, because it was the most important meal; and she did the sewing both for her own husband and children, and for Mr Kay himself.

She was more than up to the task; indeed, Madam Lim the matchmaker had specifically chosen her for her management skills. The oldest daughter of a landowner, she had raised her own nine siblings, nursed her late mother and trained a household of maids by the time she was eighteen. She married into Mr Kay's family at twenty years old, and was a cheerful, diligent, energetic addition to it. Mr Kay stayed out of his daughters-in-law's way, but Miss Cassidy was very fond of Mui Ee. They had much in common and got on splendidly well.

Wong Mi, on the other hand, was very quiet and rather slow, inclined to be afraid of everything. She was much prettier than practical Mui Ee, little and lithe, rather fragile. She was not the matchmaker's choice; no responsible matchmaker would have picked Wong Mi for a large, practical household that demanded constant physical labour. But Mr Kay's second son Leong had fallen in love with her, and decided he must have her. Ever indulgent, Mr Kay allowed him to marry for love, even disregarding the fortune teller's warning that their Eight Character readings did not match well, and went so far as to let them have a quiet Western-style wedding at City Hall, with no fanfare whatsoever.

It was fortunate for Wong Mi that Mr Kay's wife was not still alive. It was the prerogative of a mother-in-law to fully train and test her daughters-in-law. From what Miss Cassidy could gather, Chen Choo would probably have liked Mui Ee very much, and disliked poor Wong Mi, who was such a stark contrast. But there was no mother-in-law to worry about, and Wong Mi plugged away as best she could under Mui Ee's impatient, but not unkind guidance.

Mr Kay's oldest son, Boon Ming, was a serious, solemn, rather stern young man, who looked strikingly like his father. He was an avid pupil of the business and was his father's bookkeeper, being a precise accountant and paymaster. Like his father, whom he clearly emulated, he wore Chinese coats and used an abacus; unlike his father, he was solidly traditional, and disapproved of his young sisters' indulged and petted lives.

He himself was now the father of both a son and a daughter; the daughter was only a toddler, and spent her days tethered to her Mama or to a nearby bit of furniture. She was a happy, contented baby who rarely cried unless she was hungry. She was also currently the innocent cause of some tension in the family: the issue was whether or not to bind her feet. Mui Ee, whose feet had not been bound (always designated as the "useful" daughter), was inclined to bind them, as was old Madam Lim. Her father and grandfather, however, were totally against it.

Miss Cassidy stayed firmly neutral, listening with interest to both sides of the argument. Mui Ee was exasperated with the menfolk. "What use is a daughter in an influential family, if not to make alliances with other good families?" she asked as she fried meat and vegetables in a spitting hot wok. "What is her value to be, if she is a girl with a good dowry but big feet? Is she to be a farmer's wife? No, no, Miss Cassidy. My daughter will not labour as I have. She will have her feet bound, and I will wash her skin with milk and give her good food. She shall be pretty, and plump, and valuable, and marry well and live an easy life. As her mother, I must be sure of this."

"Why does your husband disagree?"

"Ah! That man." Mui Ee always referred to Boon Ming, impatiently, as That Man. For Mui Ee, this was as close to a public expression of tenderness as she could ever get. "He says tradition is all very well, but foot binding seems a waste of time. And the Old Man"—referring to the senior Mr Kay—"says it will be painful. What do they know? Two of my sisters had their feet bound. I did it myself, with our amah. Of course it hurt them, but it increased their value, you see? It was easy to find them husbands of good fortune. They live well now, doing nothing but playing music, sewing, eating delicate foods and having babies. They do not even have to feed the babies, since they have wet nurses. Their husbands treasure them, you see, because we bound their feet and kept them pretty."

Privately Miss Cassidy thought it sounded like a dire life, but she made no comment. "Do you wish you had your feet bound, Mui Ee?"

"Me?!" Mui Ee laughed without bitterness. "Ah, when I was born, our family had no such luxury. We had no great wealth then. We had land, and my father worked the land with his men, and my mother cared for the house and my grandparents. I helped them both—in the house, in the fields. I needed my feet for practical purposes. I did not think I would marry, though I saw all my sisters off. I was grateful when Madam Lim said she had found me a good husband. Even then, I am older than That Man by a year, but he said it did not matter to him. Otherwise in my family home now, there are too many women. My sisters-in-law, you know. The house is really Oldest Sister-in-Law's by right. I should not be battling with her over it."

Mui Ee had learnt English quickly, primarily because she loved to talk, tell stories and gossip, and she found Miss Cassidy an excellent listener. While her grammar was not always perfect, she was quite understandable, and Miss Cassidy thought her progress remarkable. It was amazing what a driving force mere gossip could be.

Madam Lim also liked Miss Cassidy tremendously. The matchmaker was often in and out of the household, taking outrageous advantage of her status as a close family friend to eat at their table and drink their wine, but nobody seemed to mind much. Mui Ee often asked her to mind the children or watch the servants. But what Madam Lim liked most was to sit with Miss Cassidy in the shade, eating sweets and fanning herself, while Miss Cassidy did her sewing or arranged her lessons, or was tutoring the twins.

"I worry about that Wong Mi," Madam Lim often confessed in a conspiratorial whisper. "Her fortune and Kay Loban's fortune, both together in the same house—it is bad. It is a curse."

"Mr Kay seems to be doing well, for a man under a curse."

"Ah, but it is like that. You must have a great deal to lose, before the curse can take full effect. Nobody would curse a beggar, do you see? It would be a waste of energy."

Miss Cassidy could not argue with this.

Miss Cassidy's classroom was no longer confined to the anteroom of Mr Kay's study. Often it was in the courtyard, the same courtyard in which they had all witnessed Mui Ee's wedding being held, where the two daughters-in-law could get on with some sewing while Yeling and Yezi could run about with their little niece and nephew, and everybody could learn their English phrases in whatever individual way suited them best. Madam Lim often joined them. She was now trying to persuade Mr Kay that his daughters needed marrying off. They were now fifteen; they would finish school in another year, and what was he going to do with them, if not marry them off to good families? They could not stay underfoot all their lives.

Anna's letter had finally reached Miss Cassidy.

My dear Leda,

First, let me say how much we all miss you here! Cas and Pol both say it has been difficult without their dear little mother to take care of them. I agree with them whole-heartedly. I cannot imagine why you have chosen to stay in that terrible place of fevers and swamps when you could be back here by now, with us, and having a lovely time. It has been such a jolly summer, you know. So many new children born.

Now, as to the advice you have asked of me. The magic on that side of the world is different from ours, as you well know; we are not privy to its secrets. Do not speak to gods, for they will ignore you; but if you meet a goddess, ask her blessing.

Fresh eggs are the best fix for most things. You already know about needles. Find the places in the palms of the hands, the armpit, and the back of the neck. Colours vary—it might be white, red or even green. Mothers and babies, for the most part. It is inevitable, I suppose. None of our kind of folk there, but you might find distant kin in the water.

The letter continued for a few more pages, detailing all of Anna's adventures. Miss Cassidy read it a few times, then burned part of it, including the page about the fresh eggs. Keeping such things about oneself could often be dangerous.

Miss Cassidy did not eat with the family—it was far too formal, though Mr Kay often asked her to join them. She sat with the old amah, Yoke Jie, and the Malay chauffeur and groundskeeper, whom they all addressed simply as Mat. Mat was in charge of Mr Kay's motorcar, which was very seldom used, because Singapore's streets were narrow and crowded and a rickshaw always worked out better. Mat seemed to prefer it that way; he could keep the automobile pristine and perfect, a showpiece in the house. Mr Kay always joked that the vehicle was really Mat's; he was just allowed to ride it sometimes.

Mat cooked his own food, since he was Muslim; sometimes his wife or one of his children brought him a huge lunch wrapped in a banana leaf, which he ate with his fingers. Miss Cassidy, who loved spices, sometimes came in for a share when the family had extra. It was always delicious.

Miss Cassidy had discovered that food was the great leveller in a Chinese household. Her willingness to participate in the daily food preparation (which was incredibly time-consuming), her adventurous ability to consume all manner of curious dishes from chicken's feet to fish head curry, and her unflagging interest in culinary matters earned her the goodwill of most of the womenfolk in the household, including the cook (who had frequent sullen clashes with Mui Ee), the old amah, and Madam Lim. It even earned Mr Kay's admiration—the sight of Miss Cassidy slurping up pig's intestines with evident enjoyment, he said, was one he wished to have photographed for posterity. Whereupon the womenfolk chased him out of the kitchen.

Mr Kay was, indeed, a problem Miss Cassidy was uncertain of addressing. There was nothing glamorous about Miss Cassidy; she had been very careful to construct an appearance of absolute British respectability, which in most cases was sure to dampen any man's ardour. But Mr Kay was clearly not "any man".

It was his habit of an evening, now, to stroll amicably towards Miss Cassidy's quarters. The room she had been allotted was very much as he had described it: a free-standing little structure built within the servants' compound, but set apart from the dormitories, at the far end of the vegetable garden. It had clearly belonged to a priest, being very spartan—a narrow wooden bed, bare walls and floor, and a wooden cross mounted above the bed. A large bible was still set up on a pedestal beside the bed, very dusty. Since it was a beautiful Bible, Miss Cassidy dusted it but left it where it was. She had initially removed the cross, approving much more of the iron hook it hung on; then she put it back, realising that an empty hook was far more glaringly obvious on its own.

It was a considerable distance out of his way (from the main courtyard and garden) for Mr Kay to wander to Miss Cassidy's little yard, but he managed it all the same, unfailingly, every other night. She would smell his pipe before she saw him; she had come to like the scent of his tobacco, and was rather annoyed with herself about it. But Mr Kay clearly enjoyed his conversations with her, which were entirely unremarkable and not even remotely improper.

"What am I to do about my daughters?" This was his opening remark now, as Miss Cassidy sat sorting silks in her little yard after dinner. Mr Kay never greeted her or gave any other indication why he had come to look for her; he merely sailed straight into the topic uppermost in his mind, and waited for her to enter into discussion.

"Do you mean, with regard to marrying them off?" Miss Cassidy did not look up, continuing to sort coloured cords for the next morning's lesson.

"Yes. Perhaps. I'm not sure."

"Not sure? What do you mean?"

Mr Kay puffed on his pipe introspectively. "I mean, Miss Cassidy, I wonder if I should not simply let them continue their education."

Miss Cassidy now looked up, astonished. "But...how, Mr Kay? You cannot send them to England as you did your boys. They might go to finishing school, perhaps, but those are meant for European ladies, and they are largely to prepare one for marriage into a European family of status."

"Indeed! Miss Cassidy, you are an intelligent woman. Help me find an excuse to keep those girls at home and out of trouble, but without bringing down the wrath of our good Madam Lim."

Miss Cassidy shook her head. "Short of chopping off an arm or leg, and thus making them unmarriageable, I cannot imagine what would deter Madam Lim. You must admit, she is not wrong. You now have two daughters-in-law, and cannot have so many women about the house."

"Indeed," said Mr Kay with feeling.

"Besides which, Mui Ee and Wong Mi work hard for their keep. Yeling and Yezi spend their days learning English and geography and dance and music, and can neither thread a needle nor kill a chicken. At least, not to Mui Ee's liking."

"Perhaps they will not need to thread needles and kill chickens?"

"If I understand it correctly—if you did not want them to sew or cook, you should have had their feet bound."

"And made little playthings of them?" Mr Kay puffed his pipe. "Ah, Miss Cassidy, have you seen the wives with bound feet? The lotus wives, we sometimes call them; bound feet are called lotus feet. They cannot walk without a maid to support them, and spend their days confined in beautiful prisons, waiting for their husbands to visit them to add variety to their monotonous lives. Often they are the second or third or fourth wife, with no official status. It is no life, if you ask me."

"I quite agree with you, Mr Kay, but if you want your daughters to live useful lives, they must be given useful skills."

Mr Kay fell silent, introspectively smoking his pipe. He always stood a polite distance from her, physically far enough separated that nobody had yet commented on his penchant for her company. "Sometimes I wish my daughters might ask to be nuns," he said after a moment.

Miss Cassidy was startled into laughter. "I suspect you are not the first father to say so, Mr Kay. But I have never noticed any zeal for religion in yourself personally, or indeed your whole household."

"Mm. You know, religion—as you understand it—is not native to the Chinese. In times past, we grew up with stories of gods and spirits. Very colourful, they are—we have gods in the heavens, goddesses in the sea, dragons beneath the earth and fairies on the moon. We have a monkey god full of mischief, a beggar god full of vice, and a child god full of vindictiveness. But none of those gods demand loyalty or worship. If you wanted to petition a god for something specific, then you might go to a shrine and light some joss sticks; if you were getting married or having a child, you might go again to seek a blessing. But we were never like the Christians or Muslims; we had no gods who demand obeisance so many times a day, at such-and-such frequency. We left our gods alone when we had nothing to say, and they left us alone if we had nothing to ask."

Miss Cassidy nearly said, "I remember," but caught herself in time and merely said, "Hmm."

"Those were simpler times. Then the Buddhists arrived, and there came to be monks and sutras and chanting. And people started to change the way they thought about gods and worship. Now, other types of gods have been brought to us, and this idea of nuns and priests. And what fascinates me, Miss Cassidy," he continued companionably, "is how useful a nun is allowed to make her life, simply because she declares herself dedicated to this or that god. In that god's name, she may remain unmarried, may go out into the world, may teach and toil and learn and fulfil a personal purpose to her life, that she herself may choose."

"I believe you are thinking of the nuns who teach your daughters in CHIJ, Mr Kay. They came with the Jesuits; their purpose is to spread the word of God—their god, as you call it—through whatever means they can."

"Yes, and so they educate girls who might otherwise be illiterate and unread, as my wife was. There are nuns in the hospital, as well, who have learnt to care for the sick and dying; there are different nuns in the Buddhist temples who tell fortunes and give good counsel. It seems to me my daughters' options in life are tremendously limited—unless they become nuns."

"Well, Mr Kay—they will at least not suffer from lack of money."

"But that is a mixed blessing. If they were poor, they might be apprenticed—as Madam Lim was, to a fortune teller. They might go out to work for a family, and be amahs; they might even choose to teach, as you have. But because they have money, and they are young, they must be married. Unmarried young women are a trial, Miss Cassidy. An older woman such as yourself, past a marriageable age, may move on to other modes of life, but a young woman must still look to her male relatives for guidance."

Miss Cassidy, unable to bring to mind a polite response to this, remained silent.

"Will you help me choose their husbands?" asked Mr Kay presently.

"I beg your pardon?" Miss Cassidy stared up at him blankly.

"They have grown fond of you, Miss Cassidy. And their Mama is no longer living. Since we have agreed now that their options are limited to bride or nun"—Miss Cassidy refrained from commenting that she had not made any such concession—"I think there is no help for it. They must be brides. But how? To whom? Madam Lim has brought me a list of names, which wearies me. But someone must go through the list with her, and decide on suitable candidates. I should like you to do so."

"Mr Kay! You cannot seriously mean this."

"But of course I do. I count upon your wisdom."

"My wisdom?" repeated Miss Cassidy with some asperity. "You appear to imagine, Mr Kay, that I am some ancient fount of great knowledge. I am not—"

But Mr Kay had sauntered off, as was his habit, leaving Miss Cassidy in a tangle of coloured cords and exasperation.

XII

Miss Cassidy Plays Matchmaker

"PALE blue, I think. It is a good colour."

The twins sulked, hanging back and getting in the way of everyone trying to flow past them in the marketplace, as Mui Ee held a swatch of blue patterned silk over Yeling's shoulder. Miss Cassidy found it difficult not to laugh at their tragic faces. She knew her presence was the only thing keeping the twins from positively running out of the market and all the way home; and Mui Ee had made several short, sharp gestures indicating she would like to pull their ears, but was prevented from doing so because the English teacher was there.

Usually, the twins loved coming to the fabric market. Their amah and Miss Cassidy always came with them to choose silks and ribbons for their next dress or blouse or coat. There were dozens of stalls, each with stacks and stacks of fabric in tall rolls, sorted by material and colour. The stall-owners, knowing the twins were good for more than one big purchase, were always eager to spread out multiple swathes of silk and satin and brocade, fine cotton and muslin, and expensive pieces of lace and net and embroidery. The twins could spend hours in the marketplace just choosing buttons. Yoke Jie, who indulged their every whim, would then spend many happy days and nights destroying her old eyes by putting together whatever elaborate outfit the girls had seen in some fashion plate or other. Mui Ee had always disdained to help in such frivolity, but Miss Cassidy did not mind, and so the girls were well-spoilt these days.

For that reason, when it came to the matter of an outfit in which to meet a potential groom, Miss Cassidy asked Mui Ee to come, not Yoke Jie. Mui Ee's taste was practical and age-appropriate, and she would sanction no such ridiculous ideas as Westernised gigot sleeves or lace trim or low necklines.

"Your father is very kind to allow you to meet the men first," Mui Ee said with some sharpness when the girls balked. "He is almost letting you choose your own husbands, what more do you want? The least you can do is look nice, for your father's sake. Do not make him lose face by being naughty."

"I do not want to marry," whispered Yezi to Miss Cassidy, clutching her left hand as they moved through the market.

"Nor do I," said Yeling, clutching her right hand.

"Must we?"

"Can we not stay at home with Papa?"

"Perhaps we can work in his office? We are good in maths."

"Yes, we are. Will you not speak to him, Miss Cassidy? He trusts you."

"My loves, you know your Papa will not do anything you dislike. But your Dai-sou is right," Miss Cassidy added, primly using the proper honorific for one's oldest brother's wife, as the girls were required to do. "Your father deserves respect, so dress nicely, behave nicely, and if you do not like the boy, tell your father so. Nicely. He will not make you do anything you don't want."

"Hmph," said Mui Ee, who not-so-privately felt the girls ought to do a few things they didn't want now and then, but they were not her daughters, she often loudly proclaimed in exasperation.

The twins, who were really very good-natured and really did like their Dai-sou, submitted to the inevitable, and even managed to take some interest in their new clothes. It was decided that, for once, they would wear different colours. Yeling, the older by a couple of minutes, would wear pale blue, and Yezi would wear pale pink. Mui Ee ignored all the excited clamour for loud patterns and exotic prints, and they left with yards of pretty silk with a subtle cherry-blossom pattern, some matching ribbons and cord buttons, and black velvet for new shoes. "I will cut their hair," Mui Ee decided, "and Miss Cassidy, we must be sure to wash their faces well, with the expensive soap."

"May we wear rouge?"

"And a little powder?"

"No," said Mui Ee firmly, and muttered in Cantonese something about old whores in young bodies.

Madam Lim, with a certain indignation, had shared the list of potential suitors with Miss Cassidy, as Mr Kay had instructed. "It is not that I do not trust you, Miss Cassidy," she said as she fanned herself violently and consumed preserved sugared mangoes at an alarming rate, "but it is a scandalous thing to ask a foreigner to do. Choose his daughters' husbands! Why, how could you know what to choose? You would not know our customs, how we match their fortunes, and so forth. That moon-faced priest, who used to teach us English, I could never speak two words to him. He disdained my profession, I could tell, though he was always so polite. He was offended when I asked him why he was unmarried, a sound healthy man like that of decent family. A waste of good stock. If he were Chinese, his parents would have provided him a good wife when he was young, I told him, and there would be none of this rushing about the world, wasting time teaching strangers' children. He told me his God had greater plans for him. There he was, a poor man living in another man's garden, no children of his own, no money, no land, and all his health burned away with fever, and he tells me his God had great plans for him!" Madam Lim scoffed, her spleen vented, and finally waved to the nearest maidservant. "Take it away, I will be fat," she cried, handing over the empty dish.

"Madam Lim, I quite agree with you—I do think Mr Kay ought to be sitting here himself," said Miss Cassidy, who was absolutely sure Mr Kay had delegated the task to her because he wanted to avoid this very conversation with the indefatigable matchmaker. "But since he insists I must do it, I depend upon your guidance. Tell me, who in your list of suitors do you like best for the girls?"

Madam Lim set aside her tea, sweets and fan, and got to work. She was worth every penny of her expensive fee, for she was in and out of the best houses all day, making herself fat and comfortable for good reason. She heard all the gossip about the sons and daughters of each house, and beyond their Eight Character fortunes she also knew their individual quirks and personalities, the types of people in each family, the kind of life the daughters-in-law would lead. She knew which families had the wealth to maintain the girls' present lifestyle, and the same easy-going ways that would not overly emphasise their shortcomings.

It had clearly been difficult for her. Neither of the twins could be an oldest daughter-in-law, because they did not have the appropriate skills. They could not be a junior daughter-in-law in a house with a strict matriarch, for they would be miserable, accustomed as they were to being indulged and petted. Their feet were not bound, and so they could not be some rich older man's second or third wife. They could not be sent away from Singapore because their father would not allow it. And finally, because they shared their father's poor fortune, there were families who simply didn't want them.

"And since their father has insisted the girls must meet their suitors, I cannot pick a man who is ugly, or fat, or has pockmarks, or any of these things," she concluded in disgust. "They would simply refuse. At their age, they are still foolish; they want a handsome husband. Ah, I wish all brides could be like Mui Ee—she was easy. 'Find me a husband who is patient and will not beat me,' she said, 'and the rest can be dealt with.'"

Miss Cassidy had to admit, Mui Ee's criteria summed things up rather sensibly. It was striking how many men failed to fulfil those basic requirements, in Miss Cassidy's experience.

Madam Lim had narrowed down the list to five options. Of the five, Miss Cassidy considered what she knew about both Mr Kay and the twins, and removed two suitors: one from a family she knew Mr Kay rather disliked, and one she knew the twins disliked because he had been in school with the daughters. That left only three men.

Two of these—a rather clever arrangement of Madam Lim's—were actually a pair of brothers, two years apart. They ran a Chinese medicine shop together, a successful business. They particularly wanted wives who would get along, for they both lived in the rooms above the shop, and their wives would always be in close quarters. It would be especially useful to the brothers to have wives who were literate, could keep the books and help in the business.

"Why, how perfect, Madam Lim," exclaimed Miss Cassidy, "you found a use for their learning." Madam Lim beamed broadly, pleased with herself.

The only drawback was that they also required wives who could run a household: cook, shop, clean, sew and care for their own children. The twins would have to be well-trained, but Miss Cassidy felt they would be more amenable to such a lifestyle if they were able to face it together. "I hope the brothers will not mind a few burned meals now and then."

"The brothers are cooking for themselves now. And they are good-natured men, not the sort to shout at women. Besides, the girls will bring their dowries, which will help with the business—and I think it more than likely Yoke Jie will choose to go with them, if the husbands are agreeable. Yoke Jie belongs to Mr Kay's household, so they would get an amah for free. For such benefits, they will put up with a few burned meats and crooked buttons at first."

The third man was Eurasian. He was a cloth trader and had dealings with both the Straits Steamship Company and the East India Company. A mixed-race man was a daring choice, but it was because he was hard to match, said Madam Lim, that he was likely to be amenable to having a rather immature wife he would need to train. He was alone in Singapore—his mother had died—and he wished to settle down and raise a family. He was also an honest man, a hard worker, and Madam Lim knew Mr Kay well enough to understand these things carried more weight with him than the man's birth.

"Charles De Souza," read Miss Cassidy. "I think Mr Nair knows him."

Madam Lim began to fan herself again. She disapproved of the upstart Haresh Nair, referring to him as "that arrogant Indian boy". This was probably because Mr Nair and Mr Kay got along very well, and it irked her feudal Chinese sensibilities to see the lowly dark-skinned law clerk drinking rice wine and laughing with one of the wealthiest Chinese businessmen in the Straits Settlements, as if they were equals and brothers.

"Read your stones, Miss Cassidy," urged Madam Lim now, "see what they say."

Miss Cassidy took her "stones" out of her pocket. Fortune-telling was such a common feature of Chinese life that nobody saw anything remotely odd about Miss Cassidy's ability to "see" things in her seemingly inconsequential collection of pebbles, empty thread spools, beads and small bones. Like Ah Nai, they all merely assumed it was some British version of jiaobei stones. It was rather liberating, when in other parts of the world she might have been drowned as a witch for looking too long into her teacup.

Miss Cassidy scattered her stones on the table, over Madam Lim's neatly notated list. She observed which beads fell over which name. Madam Lim craned her neck eagerly, anxious. "Well? Are the fortunes good?"

"Hmm," said Miss Cassidy. "Overall, Madam Lim, they are good. I think you did very well in choosing. But the twins themselves will not agree."

"Ah, that is to be expected." Madam Lim fanned herself more slowly, satisfied with the reading. "There is nothing for it now but to wait and see."

The meetings were accordingly scheduled. Mr Kay could not wriggle out of these, so he armed himself well, putting Miss Cassidy at his right hand, his oldest son Boon on his left, Mui Ee beside Boon and finally Yoke Jie seated by a side door. In the room beyond this door, the twins sat waiting and peeping, and trying not to make too much noise.

Miss Cassidy, once again making some use of her grey poplin dress and malachite brooch, had decided she would not speak, in the hope that if she remained silent, Mr Kay would be forced to take the lead. Accordingly she brought her sewing, to busy herself with, as did Mui Ee. Sewing was a very good way for the womenfolk to look demure and busy while listening to every word, and appearing to defer to the menfolk.

Charles De Souza was undoubtedly handsome, in the exotic Eurasian manner, with dark brown hair and hazel eyes, and an imposing Portuguese nose. Having been raised Chinese, however, he wore a Chinese suit and conversed fluently in Mandarin, Cantonese, Malay and English. He spoke very little Portuguese, having not had much chance to practise it. He had brought a gift, as he was meant to do: a few yards of beautiful green silk, and some cakes and sweetmeats.

After tea was poured and the necessary pleasantries exchanged, there was a silence. It was for the head of the family to now start politely interrogating his daughter's suitor. Miss Cassidy glanced at Mr Kay—indeed, they were all glancing at Mr Kay—but he sat gazing down into his teacup, with a curiously blank expression. It was Boon, responding to a nudge from Mui Ee, who finally asked, "So, Mr De Souza, tell us what sort of home you offer to my sister."

Mr De Souza, well-prepared, began to explain. He had a small house, not far from Pandan Villa, and employed two servants, a gardener and a maid. His wife would not have to do the rough work, but she would have to cook and sew. Their children would always have the unfortunate heritage of mixed blood, but they would be well-educated and well-provided for. Boys would be part of the business, and girls would be suitably dowered. He did not want a mousy, quiet, obedient wife; he sought someone lively and good-humoured, who would be good company after a long day.

By and by, Yoke Jie stood up and whispered to Miss Cassidy, and Miss Cassidy whispered to Mr Kay, and the twins, eaten up with curiosity, were allowed to enter and meet their suitor. Yeling in blue and Yezi in pink, each bowed politely; each tried and failed to keep their eyes suitably downcast; Charles De Souza greeted each one amicably and easily, with no self-consciousness.

Then it was over; Charles De Souza left, more pleasantries were exchanged, and everyone resumed their places for the arrival of the Tong brothers.

"I liked him," said Mui Ee, raising her eyes from her sewing. "Have you been to his house, Mr Kay? Is it as he describes?"

Mr Kay nodded, still turning his small cup of cold tea round and round in his palm. "He is an honest, hard-working man," he murmured. "He treats his servants and subordinates well. I am sure he will make a fine husband."

The Tong brothers came together, also bearing gifts, this time of ginseng and bird's nest soup and other expensive herbs and tonics. They spoke in Cantonese, so Miss Cassidy was rather lost in the conversation, but she liked the look of them. The older brother, Wang, was quieter and thinner, with a pleasant, kindly smile; the younger brother, Yang, was rather plump, cheerful and amusing. Both were qualified Chinese medical practitioners, though Wang was more of the physician and Yang the businessman. They would welcome wives with learning, Wang explained earnestly, for their business was now thriving, and besides keeping accounts, a woman at the counter would be useful for ladies who came in seeking advice. If the Kay daughters did not mind the work, of course.

"They will not mind," said Mr Kay, smiling faintly. "They adore the chance to chatter to strangers. It is rather difficult to get them to stop."

The brothers both stood when Yeling and Yezi trooped shyly into the room, and formally bowed and greeted them. Yang beamed broadly, and Miss Cassidy could not help but notice that Yeling met his eye and giggled, then clapped her hand over her mouth in embarrassment. But Yezi stayed well behind her sister and peeped nervously over Yeling's shoulder, not quite looking at either brother.

"Hmm," said Miss Cassidy, and Mr Kay—by now accustomed to Miss Cassidy's little mannerisms—gave her a sharp sideways glance.

There was no time for lengthy discussion after the brothers left, each member of the household hurrying off to their delayed tasks. The twins had no lessons, since Miss Cassidy was sure they would not be able to concentrate; instead they were changed out of their nice new clothes and taken on a vigorous walk, where Miss Cassidy could not help but notice that Yeling was bright and chatty and full of questions about the three men they had just met, and Yezi was uncharacteristically quiet.

"Yezi, imagine us being doctors in the medicine shop," Yeling giggled. "Wouldn't it be delightful? Grand ladies coming in to get powders and potions from us, and we would look at them and go, 'Ah! I know what is wrong! You have eaten too many lotus paste buns, that is why your face has gone yellow.'" Yeling squealed with laughter. Yezi smiled obligingly, but did not seem to have heard the joke.

Miss Cassidy sent Yeling and Yoke Jie off to buy roasted chestnuts, and asked Yezi gently, "Did you like any of the men, my dear?"

Yezi shook her head slightly, twiddled her thumbs, then said softly, "I think Mr De Souza is the nicest. But Miss Cassidy! I don't want to marry any of them. Can we just be as we always have been? Why should we have to marry?"

"If you don't want to marry any of them, your Papa will not make you, Yezi. Don't worry."

"But Yeling is so excited now. She has been since we listened to the brothers talking. She keeps saying it will be so much fun, we will still live together in the same house, and we will raise our children side by side, and learn how to run a shop, and we will be grand laoban-niangs and order servants about—oh, all sorts of things!"

"Do you not like either of the Tong brothers?"

"I like them. They are nice. But I don't want to marry anybody."

That evening, Miss Cassidy was ready when the scent of tobacco smoke wafted to her doorway. "Sit down, Mr Kay. I have tea ready for you."

"Do you? How hospitable of you, Miss Cassidy."

"Yes, indeed—and I will shut the little gate to my yard, do you hear, and place my seat just so in front of it, so that you cannot get up and walk away before our talk is done. Now," she added primly while Mr Kay chuckled, trapped in his seat behind the heavy table, "let us discuss these suitors."

"What do you think of them, Miss Cassidy?"

"What do *you* think of them, Mr Kay? And do not think you may avoid the question by smoking your pipe. You will answer if I have to wait till you are out of tobacco."

"Will you? I have quite a lot of tobacco with me, I warn you."

Miss Cassidy said nothing. She simply waited.

Unlike Bendemeer House, Pandan Villa was not far from a major thoroughfare, and it was never quiet. As Mr Kay continued to nurse his pipe introspectively, the noise rose around them: shouting voices, bellowing horses and bullocks, laughing children, the rustle of pandan leaves, the shriek of thousands of crickets. A mosquito buzzed past Miss Cassidy's nose, and Mr Kay slapped it down against the tabletop. "You know," he remarked, "this is very companionable."

Miss Cassidy refused to rise to the bait and remained silent. Mr Kay sighed. "Very well," he said. "The suitors were all excellent. Humble, successful, hard-working men who will probably treat their wives well."

"But...?" prompted Miss Cassidy.

"But." Mr Kay gazed at her, serious for once. "Miss Cassidy, you already know I am a man of ill fortune. Do you know what form this is meant to take?"

"I...know a little. I saw it in your hand."

"What do you see in my hand?" And he opened up his palm again to her. It was a good, strong, rough-edged hand, but it revealed a curiously empty-looking palm, with unusually deeply scored lines.

161

"Mr Kay, I am of a different culture than yours—"

"What do you see, Miss Cassidy?"

She sighed. "Death, Mr Kay. I see death in the palm of your hand."

"Indeed. And not my own death, which would not be so terrible—all men must die—but the deaths of others. Is that not so? My fate is to bring death upon others, particularly those under my roof."

"Do you put much credence into palmistry, Mr Kay?"

"No. I do not." He tapped his pipe gently. "But others do. And there is no denying that my parents died relatively young, that one of my children died in infancy, and that my wife died in childbirth."

"That is hardly unique to you, Mr Kay. Captain Bendemeer lost almost all his children in one short year, you know. You have four healthy, living children and two thriving grandchildren—I think the odds are still in your favour."

"Mm! But it is not death that frightens me." He paused. "I think, Miss Cassidy, I must tell you a secret."

Miss Cassidy waited. Mr Kay smiled. "Look at you," he said, "entirely unsurprised. I think you have become immune to me."

"To your idiosyncrasies, never, Mr Kay. But I have felt sure, for a while, that there is something else I ought to know."

"Well, here it is. My family can see ghosts."

XIII

Miss Cassidy &
the Third Eye

ISS Cassidy quietly observed the tea leaves in her cup. The sun was setting, and the fire in the sky reflected glints of flame in her hair. But she did not move.

Mr Kay leaned back, studied her expression and waited for a reaction. Receiving none, he continued, "I never knew what they were, when I was a child. They are just…people, you know. They look like ordinary people, a little lost and a little sad sometimes. It was when I grew older that I realised not everyone could see them, that they were not…real, I suppose, to others."

"Mm. Have you seen any which frightened you?"

"You seem entirely unmoved by the idea, Miss Cassidy."

"It is perfectly common in…where I am from, Mr Kay. Some call it the third eye. Often you have it as a child, then it closes and you no longer see them. Some, like yourself, have it all their lives."

"Have you got the third eye, then, Miss Cassidy?"

"I do not."

"You cannot see ghosts?"

"Not ghosts," said Miss Cassidy carefully, "no. Not unless they specifically want me to see them."

"And has this happened to you? Ghosts wanting to see you, specifically?"

"Mr Kay, do your children all possess the third eye?"

"My sons do not. My daughters do. It is unusual, my grandmother said, for boys to possess the ability in adulthood."

"Do the twins know about this?"

"I do not know if they have noticed. They lead sheltered lives, as you well know, Miss Cassidy. But I have seen them looking at things that I know only I can see; I have seen them call out to their mother and play with her, when they were little, long after Chen Choo was gone. Their amah tells me that they sometimes ask, who is that staring at them? But there will be no one there."

"Well, by now I imagine they will have noticed something odd, though they may not quite understand it. But in truth, Mr Kay, I do not see how this ability could bring ill fortune to you or your family. The ghosts are there, regardless of whether you see them. They are, by and large, quite harmless creatures."

"You are quite right, Miss Cassidy. But...here, perhaps you may puzzle it out for yourself. I am a man who brings death upon others, and I can see ghosts. Do you see how this might become...problematic?"

Miss Cassidy thought about it quietly, still swirling her teacup. "Do you mean to say," she said slowly, "that...the ghosts of those who have passed untimely…might blame you for their misfortune?"

"Exactly! You have—what do the Englishmen say?—you have hit the nail on the head!" Mr Kay beamed at her like a proud teacher. "Let us continue. What then becomes of a ghost who has found someone to blame for its untimely death?"

"They would hang about you—haunt you, as it were—till they are appeased."

"Precisely. And you see, what can I do about it? Nothing, for I am not the direct cause of their death; how am I to appease them?"

"But Mr Kay…how many of these ghosts are there?"

"Not so many at Pandan Villa. Far more at our wharves. Coolies, sailors, their wives and children sometimes. I employ many, many people, Miss Cassidy, and shipping can be a dangerous business. Wrecks, and pirates, and simple accidents. Drunken brawls in brothels and opium dens. Disease, and fevers they cannot explain. It is well-known that Mr Kay Wing Tong is a man who brings ill fortune—it is easy to lay the blame upon me."

Miss Cassidy tapped a fingernail upon her teacup in a slightly impatient manner. "Mr Kay, you cannot mean to say that people are so credulous as to blame you for scurvy and shipwrecks."

"They do if my name is on the docket."

"If what you say is true, Mui Ee and Wong Mi are very brave women. So, indeed, are Yoke Jie, Mat and Madam Lim—and so am I, for not instantly bolting out the door, now you have told me."

"The people you have named are all fine, practical, no-nonsense folk," he said, while Miss Cassidy frowned faintly, "but sailors and coolies are highly superstitious."

"And how do you explain all this to them?"

"Explain? I don't. It would only make things worse. I pay well and am a fair loban. I cannot alter the beliefs they choose to hold of me, nor the gossip that they hear."

"Does this...this howling mob of angry ghosts—do they harm you in any way?"

Mr Kay chuckled. "No. They drift about, rather lost; the more theatrical ones may hide under my desk, or try to startle me from around a corner, or stand on the ceiling and hold up an accusing finger. But as time passes, they fade away."

"And do these creatures affect Yeling and Yezi at all?"

"I never bring them to the wharves. The few they see in Pandan Villa have been harmless to them. But Miss Cassidy, you see why I am worried," he added. "When they leave this house, what will they see out in the world? What should I tell their husbands, if anything, about this matter? What if they marry the Tong brothers; what if they must deal with the sick and dying? Can you imagine how frightful it could be?"

"Mr Kay, with respect, I think you are underestimating your daughters," said Miss Cassidy, now reaching over to take his teacup. She peered at its leaves, nodded once with satisfaction and put it back down. "They are a great deal more resilient than you think, from being well-raised and well-loved. I advise you to talk to them, tell them of this matter, and thereby prepare them. Whatever it is that awaits them beyond this house, they must face it sooner or later."

Mr Kay smiled at her, tapping the bowl of his pipe. Miss Cassidy avoided his gaze, studiously fixing her eye upon two butterflies that happened to be dancing giddily past.

"That is a mating dance," he said, gesturing at the butterflies.

"I know," said Miss Cassidy crossly. "Now, Mr Kay, to proper business. Which of the suitors do you like best for the girls?"

But Mr Kay was rescued from the question by a loud commotion. A woman's muffled screams, people shouting, a crying child; and, as they both stood up in alarm, old Mat came running towards them, face pale.

"Come quickly! Second lady is ill!"

"What has happened to Wong Mi?" exclaimed Miss Cassidy, but Mat refused to answer, instead speaking to Mr Kay.

"Sir, we let the women deal with this first."

"Be damned to that," he began, but Miss Cassidy was already running, her skirts gathered in both arms. A problem to be dealt with "by the women" could only mean one thing: a miscarriage.

By the time she reached Wong Mi, some semblance of order had been established. All the men had been sent away, and Mui Ee was bending over her sister-in-law. Yoke Jie had been sent away with Mui Ee's two children, who had been present when Wong Mi fell and were very frightened.

Mui Ee had laid Wong Mi on the ground in the courtyard where she had fallen, and covered her in some old blankets. There was blood on the ground, and Wong Mi was pale and breathless with pain. "She cannot be moved yet," said Mui Ee to Miss Cassidy as the teacher reached her. "She is in too much pain. You may look, if you are not squeamish," she added, lifting a corner of the blanket.

Miss Cassidy was not squeamish. She looked. Mui Ee had removed Wong Mi's cotton trousers and undergarments, now all soaked with blood. The half-formed foetus was not yet drawn from the mother's body.

"Did she know she was with child?" asked Miss Cassidy.

"She says she was not sure," said Mui Ee with a moue of impatience. "She told no one, not even her husband. On her feet all day, in the kitchen with me, then the washing, and her husband requiring her duties for—you know—ah, she is a silly child!" cried Mui Ee in exasperation. "Don't you know, you silly child, that it is not only you who will suffer now? I carry some blame, and your husband, and poor old Yoke Jie, and even my children for playing with you. Why did you not speak? You, with your skinny fleshless body, you know childbearing will go hard with you, why did you not tell us, so that we might all have been careful with you?"

"Hush, now, Mui Ee," said Miss Cassidy urgently, "you can scold her later. Let us help her now."

Wong Mi muttered something, but it was too faint to be heard.

Miss Cassidy heard an exclamation. Yeling and Yezi were at the courtyard entrance; one held a tureen of hot water, the other towels. But both were now looking away, staring at one particular corner, at the door that led to the private quarters of Wong Mi and her husband.

"Girls, quickly," shouted Mui Ee, and the twins hurried to her.

"Yoke Jie says she is boiling more water and clean rags," said Yezi.

"And your children are with Dai-gor," said Yeling. Dai-gor was their oldest brother, Boon.

"Shall we bring some chicken broth for Ee-sou?"

"Or shall we make tea?"

"Or will you let us help Ee-sou?"

"We are not afraid."

"You are good girls," said Mui Ee. "Are your hands clean?"

"Yes, Dai-sou," they echoed.

"You can handle a little blood?"

"Yes, Dai-sou."

"Good. Now, Miss Cassidy, lift Wong Mi up on your shoulder. Try to keep her calm. Yeling, you must soak the towels in hot water, and give them to me when I say. Yezi, you must run for more water and towels until this is over. Ask Yoke Jie to put some chicken broth to heat for afterwards. Come now Wong Mi," she said briskly, "let us get the dead thing out of you."

It seemed to take forever, but it was only perhaps half an hour later that Wong Mi was cleaned up and put to bed, exhausted and sobbing. Mui Ee, tired, annoyed and gloomy, went off with Yoke Jie to deal with the remnants of the foetus.

Miss Cassidy walked with the twins back to their rooms. They had comported themselves well; the bloody mess did not faze them, and they had been quick on their feet and light with their hands. "You would make excellent nurses," said Miss Cassidy.

"I should like to be a nurse," said Yezi. "I think it is very interesting to help other people."

"If we marry the Tong brothers, we will be like nurses," said Yeling.

"Girls," said Miss Cassidy after a moment, "did you see something in the courtyard?" She imbued the word "something" with a similar nuance to the equivalent phrase in Chinese, when referring to something supernatural.

The twins looked at her in surprise. "Did you see it too, Miss Cassidy?"

"Wasn't it odd?"

"It seemed to be watching Ee-sou."

"I didn't like it."

"What did it look like?" asked Miss Cassidy.

The twins looked at each other. "Small," they said at last. "Like a small baby. And a funny green colour."

"And did it run off into Ee-sou's room?"

"Yes," they both murmured. Yeling shivered. "It was ugly," she added. "Usually when we see a Thing, it's just like seeing another person. It isn't scary. But this one is a little bit scary."

"I think this one is different," said Yezi. "It is more than just a sad ghost. But I don't think it belongs to us—to our house, I mean. I have never seen it around Papa."

"Hmm," said Miss Cassidy. Certainly Mr Kay had underestimated his daughters.

*

Wong Mi's miscarriage cast a pall of gloom over the household. As Mui Ee had predicted, Mr Kay was very much annoyed with Wong Mi, and somewhat displeased that none of the other women had noticed her pregnancy—especially Yoke Jie, who attended to the intimate needs of all the younger women in the household (except Mui Ee, who pish-poshed any need for an attendant). Poor Yoke Jie reproached herself so much that Mui Ee sent her out of the kitchen, saying her tears would oversalt the food, and Miss Cassidy was dispatched to mediate.

"Miss Cassidy, the reason we still have an amah now that all my children are grown, is precisely to see to the needs of my daughters-in-law and my grandchildren," said Mr Kay, for once implacable and—so Miss Cassidy thought—unreasonable. "Yoke Jie knows perfectly well that her most important role is to notice the signs of pregnancy in my daughters-in-law—especially someone like Wong Mi, who is too young and inexperienced to understand these things herself. I do not think it is unreasonable for a lady of Yoke Jie's age and experience to have suspected something, especially now that Mui Ee has taken over the running of the household, and Yoke Jie has far less to occupy her mind."

"But Mr Kay, you know Yoke Jie is old. She had not noticed that," Miss Cassidy cleared her throat primly, "that two uneventful months had passed for Wong Mi."

"Well, either she must start marking her calendar, or she must teach Wong Mi how to do it, for I will not tolerate a repeat of this incident."

"She will do both. Now Mr Kay, tell me you forgive Yoke Jie, for she is much distressed."

171

"Forgive her the loss of a grandchild? No." Mr Kay puffed furiously on his pipe. "But she has been a faithful old woman, and has raised all my children, and is helping to raise my grandchildren, and we all love her dearly. That does not change." He exhaled heavily. "Now tell the old lady all is well, as long as she keeps a close eye on that silly girl, Wong Mi."

Miss Cassidy did not tell Mr Kay about the little green creature the twins had seen in the courtyard. It was clear he had not seen any such thing, otherwise he would have mentioned it to Miss Cassidy. So the twins were right—this Thing, whatever it was, was not related to him.

Miss Cassidy pondered. The size of the villa was inconvenient, and there were far too many people living there, including two very young children. Many servants as well, who would sweep up any salt she scattered and clear any crumbs or dishes of food left unattended. Since the twins had never seen it before, clearly the creature did not wander the grounds; it was firmly attached either to Wong Mi, to her husband or to something in their living quarters. Miss Cassidy knew better than to broach any supernatural beastie on its own territory, unarmed and with no knowledge of what it was.

Wong Mi refused to see anyone. She had to see Mr Kay, of course—an interview that upset her—and she saw Mui Ee once, to thank her. Other than that, she remained in her room, the shutters closed, only Yoke Jie going in and out to tend to her.

Miss Cassidy tried the most effective Chinese bribe: food. Armed with fatty pork rice dumplings, a particular favourite of Wong Mi's, she tried to gain access. "I made them myself," she said as piteously as she could manage to Yoke Jie. "I just want her to taste them, and see if I did well."

But Yoke Jie shook her head firmly. She was not in a frame of mind to disobey anyone's orders now, and Wong Mi and her husband had ordered that there be no visitors. "I am grateful to you, Miss Cassidy, but no. Second Young Master's Wife wishes to remain very quiet for now."

Miss Cassidy thought of writing a note, but it was no use. Wong Mi could not read much English, and Miss Cassidy could not write anything in Chinese besides her own name; transposed into phonetic Mandarin by the giggling twins, it was Li Da, meaning "Of Great Might". She therefore sighed, and said, "Well, I will put the dumplings in their dry kitchen for now; if she does not want them, you may eat them for your dinner, Yoke Jie."

This was, at least, an excellent reason to go traipsing around the couple's quarters. Both the Kay sons lived within the compound, but in a set of rooms separated from the main house by courtyards and covered walkways. Each separate house had its own name. Boon and Mui Ee lived in Prosperity Wing; Wong Mi and her husband Leong lived in Longevity Wing.

Longevity Wing was slightly smaller than Prosperity Wing, in deference to the older brother, but it was still of a generous size. They had two floors, comprising the bedrooms, an unused servant's room, Leong's study and the two kitchens.

Miss Cassidy had learnt about wet and dry kitchens from the cook when she first arrived. The "wet" kitchen was, quite literally, the kitchen that handled all liquids: cooking oil, sauces, meats and vegetables and their juices, rice and soup and steaming baskets and stews. There was one very large, well-equipped wet kitchen in the main house which was currently the only one in use, for the family was still small enough to all gather at the same table to eat. It was the same kitchen Mui Ee had taken over upon her marriage. The old cook had been pensioned off a month ago.

The "dry" kitchen was not for cooking, merely for preparation. It usually held jars of biscuits, sweets and tea, and wine for the men. Snacks and small meals were prepared there, for guests or simply for teatime.

Miss Cassidy had been to Prosperity Wing a number of times by now. Yoke Jie lived there, in their servants' quarters, the better to mind Mui Ee's children. The dry kitchen was off the main living room, and was always stocked with candied fruit, cocoa, tea, all sorts of biscuits and whatever fresh fruit was in season. It was Mui Ee who had first split open a durian for her, an experience Miss Cassidy would not soon forget.

Mui Ee was a superlative house manager, and both the main house and her own quarters were clean, tidy, well-stocked and comfortable. Wong Mi, on the other hand, was clearly struggling. Although everything was clean, nothing looked quite comfortable. Wong Mi did not have Mui Ee's eye for homemaking. The furniture seemed stark and cold, there were no flowers or decorations anywhere, and the attempts Wong Mi had made to put a vase here and there were clumsy and ill-matched.

As for their kitchens, which should have been the heart of any Chinese home, neither seemed to be in much use. The dry kitchen contained a few half-empty tins, and the wet kitchen had nothing on the stovetop but an iron kettle for boiling bathwater. It seemed a great waste to Miss Cassidy. Few households had the luxury of two kitchens. A home with an unused kitchen was like a body with a missing soul, a shell stumbling about trying to find its purpose.

She searched the place carefully and thoroughly. What she was looking for would need to be well-hidden, if it was to escape the notice of the servants.

She found it at last, in a dark cupboard under the unused sink of the dry kitchen, hidden behind boxes of soap and tins of insecticide and other abrasive things a casual visitor would be unlikely to touch. It was a shallow ceramic dish, the kind used for English teacups, with a crack down the centre where the dish had been carefully glued back together. The dish was full of milk—reconstituted powdered milk—in which a couple of insects had already drowned and died, but the milk had not gone bad. Somebody was refilling this dish regularly.

She put the rice dumplings, still in their banana leaf wrapping, on the countertop of the dry kitchen. Then, from her pocket, she took out a handful of small glass marbles, pretty and shining, and placed them in a neat row on the floor. Around them, quickly, she scattered a little salt.

Then she took a deep breath and closed her eyes.

There was no one in the room, but if there had been someone watching, they would have been rather alarmed. Miss Cassidy was a woman of healthy, substantial girth, half a head taller than the average lady and sometimes twice as broad. It should not have been possible for her to vanish in a small room, certainly not in daylight with all the windows open. Yet vanish she did, and perhaps there was a shadow that should really not have been there, or a flicker of light in the air that appeared to have no source.

Miss Cassidy did not have the third eye; she could not "see" ghosts. But not everything otherworldly was a ghost, and sometimes, if they were careless, they forgot to hide.

She had to wait a while before she heard it. A soft snuffling, scratching, a kind of gurgle. Then the faint scritch-scritch of small feet on a gritty floor.

Miss Cassidy remained as still as she could. The faint noises came and went, came and went, a cautious creature, uncertain of its approach. Then, finally, there was the unmistakable click of glass marbles striking one another.

And the door opened. "Miss Cassidy, are you here?" Yoke Jie peered into the room.

The creature was gone. Miss Cassidy opened her eyes, and had just enough time to bend and scoop up her marbles—now arranged in a wobbly circle instead of a straight line—and then hurriedly dust up the small rodent-like footprints in the salt. "Oh, dear, I'm so sorry, Yoke Jie," she exclaimed, and Yoke Jie jumped.

"Aiyoh! I didn't see you there! What are you doing? Mui Ee wants you in the kitchen."

"Yes, of course. I spilled a little sugar, I'm afraid, Yoke Jie. I was trying to clean it up."

"Oh, is that all? I will do it. You had better go, Miss Cassidy, before Mui Ee gets angry."

Miss Cassidy made her apologies, gathered up her skirts, and hurried out of Longevity Wing as quickly as she could.

XIV

Miss Cassidy &
the Sultan's Daughter

"How does one address a sultan's daughter?" wondered Miss Cassidy.

Haresh Nair, shading his face from the brilliant sunshine of Mr Kay's courtyard, smiled. "We call her Your Royal Highness, and bow, as we would to the British Royal Family. She does not expect everyone to follow the rules of a sultan's court."

Miss Cassidy and the twins gazed with some awe at the magnificent tea set of hammered gold that was winking blindingly in the bright afternoon sunshine. The little celadon teacups next to it seemed to shrink away in terror.

"And why does Her Royal Highness want to visit Mr Kay?" asked Miss Cassidy, as Yeling gingerly picked up one of the gold cups and weighed it in her hand. "It is heavy," she whispered to Yezi, and handed it over.

"She says he did her a great kindness, but does not say what it was. The gift is to thank him, and the visit, I suspect, is out of curiosity. Her father is here on state business, and she is quite a young lady. I doubt she has ever been out of her father's state. I imagine she is no different from our lovely twins here—she is bored and wants to make friends."

"Has she no friends?" asked Yeling, surprised.

"Does she not go to school?" asked Yezi.

"What about her brothers and sisters?"

"Or cousins and nieces and nephews?"

Mr Nair smiled. "She does not go to school, no. A young Muslim girl of status cannot go out unchaperoned, so school would be difficult for her. Now she is old enough to leave the house, she must be covered up in public, and cannot speak to anyone her parents have not approved of, which I imagine makes it hard to find casual friends."

"But there are many Muslim girls in our school."

"They are not all covered up."

"Muslim girls allowed to go to a Catholic girls' school will have fathers like your own; modern and progressive, and not especially orthodox in their religion. A sultan cannot be modern and progressive without considering the opinions of the people of his state."

"How dreadful to have to live by others' opinions," murmured Miss Cassidy. "I am starting to pity the poor child."

Mr Nair laughed. "Ah, but her father is an indulgent sultan, if he is letting her visit a Chinese house simply because she took a fancy to its owner. There is a great deal in a Chinese home that is haram to a devout Muslim, you know."

"I suppose she must not be particularly devout."

"Perhaps not. We will see. Meanwhile," he handed over a sheaf of papers to Miss Cassidy, "there are many instructions on how to prepare for her visit, and what she can and cannot eat, touch or do. I have translated them from the formal Malay to English for you, and you will have to do the final translation for the rest of the household, Miss Cassidy."

Miss Cassidy accepted the list grimly. Mui Ee was not going to be happy.

Indeed, Mui Ee's expression was a picture when Miss Cassidy showed her the list. "Is this a hotel?" she exclaimed. "And I suppose she will bring a huge retinue, and they must all be catered to. Wong Mi is still unwell, Yoke Jie must care for her, and of course a Muslim girl must be hosted only by women, which means Yeling and Yezi will have to do it, for they cannot be in charge of the kitchen. What am I to do about this princess's food? We do not have a halal kitchen, or halal utensils, or any of those things."

"Let us ask Mat," said Miss Cassidy, who entirely sympathised. "Perhaps he may suggest something."

It turned out to be a brilliant idea. Mat and his wife both came from a family of many women, all excellent cooks, and all excited at the prospect of cooking for royalty. They could provide the necessary utensils, and do all the cooking in their respective homes; Mat would put the motorcar to use for once, and ferry the food to Pandan Villa. Aminah, his wife, would set everything up, and remain on hand in case they needed help. Miss Cassidy and Mui Ee, much relieved, petitioned Mr Kay to compensate Mat and Aminah handsomely, which he did without a qualm.

179

"I confess, Miss Cassidy, I have no idea who the sultan's daughter is," said Mr Kay the night before her arrival.

Miss Cassidy looked blank. "But she is making a special effort just to see you, Mr Kay. Mr Nair tells me the sultan's letter was very specific."

"Yes, but I truly do not remember her. I have travelled quite widely, you know, Miss Cassidy; when I was younger and more robust, and still building up my business, I went all over British Malaya and Indochina. I learnt to speak Malay fluently, and a little Thai; I negotiated with many landowners and merchants, and a few tengkus. I am quite sure I never met a sultan, much less the daughter of one."

"Well, what are you going to do tomorrow when she comes?"

"Greet her formally, of course, and make sure she is well amused, and excuse myself. As a man, I am quite expected to do so, after all. I cannot sit in idle chatter with a virgin Muslim princess. That will be left to you."

"No, Mr Kay," said Miss Cassidy sharply, "this time, it really cannot be. Mui Ee will be perishing for help in the kitchens as it is. You will greet Her Royal Highness, introduce your daughters to her, and let them converse. You will sit and wait until she chooses to dismiss you, or be charming and polite till she leaves. If you need a translator, Aminah will be waiting in the corridor in her best dress, and she will be introduced as a friend of the family. Your daughters' governess has no business in an occasion like this, and I will take no part in it. And don't give me that look," she added in a huff as he smiled at her, "because you will not change my mind."

*

Although the princess was only expected after noon, the household woke at four in the morning to prepare for her arrival—as, no doubt, did the womenfolk of Mat's extended family. Every servant was set to work cleaning and scrubbing. Miss Cassidy drilled everyone on the instructions translated by Mr Nair. A large dining room—the same one used to host the Western dinner during Mui Ee's wedding—was cleaned and polished and brushed and set up almost as if it were a throne room, filled with flowers and fresh fruit. Dogs and pigs—of which the household had a number—were locked away in barns and huts.

The entire family was expected to welcome her, including Boon, Leong, Mui Ee and Wong Mi, though Wong Mi would be allowed to return to bed immediately afterwards. But the main job of hosting was to fall to Yeling and Yezi, who were very, very excited, and had been practising their Malay for days, schooled by their Papa, Mr Nair, Mat and Yoke Jie. They spent a long time choosing their clothes, and ended up picking the pink and blue outfits they had worn for their matchmaking.

"Do I look all right?" Mui Ee, in a frazzle, came running out of her quarters, patting her hair. Within the compound her children were wailing, outraged at being bathed in the middle of the day by Yoke Jie.

"You look very nice," said Miss Cassidy, and indeed she did. Mui Ee was not pretty, and quite plump, but she had the strong erect bearing of an energetic woman, and the healthy rosy complexion of one who was used to hard work. As the most senior woman in the house, although she was only in her mid-twenties, she wore an embroidered maroon velvet blouse meant for an older lady to signify her status. It had once belonged to Chen Choo, Mr Kay's wife, but Mui Ee had expertly altered it to fit herself, and she looked very smart indeed.

"My hair is dreadful," she sighed. "I wish it were not so wiry. It is from the heat in the kitchens, you know. I had lovely smooth hair once," she added enviously as the twins made their appearance, with their young bright faces framed by thick neat braids, gaily beribboned in pink and blue.

"Well, it will stay all right for the day," said Miss Cassidy, observing the merciless number of pins Mui Ee had stabbed into her coiffure to keep her bun-net in place.

"Dai-sou, you look so nice," chorused the twins brightly, and Mui Ee waved the compliment away with a "tsk" in the Chinese manner.

"Have you washed your faces?" she asked. "And your hair? Are you perfumed? Good. Now recite what you must say to the princess to Miss Cassidy."

The twins did so obediently. Then Yeling said, "Miss Cassidy, you have worn this same dress so many times. I think we must make you a new one."

Yezi, plucking at the grey poplin sleeve, added, "Yes, or make this one more fashionable. You look like one of Papa's old photographs, Miss Cassidy, from before we were born. There is one in the drawing room where he is with some Western couples. The ladies are all dressed like you."

"Girls, hush," said Mui Ee sharply. "You forget Miss Cassidy is not as frivolous as you, making new dresses every month. The rest of us economise. I never had a new dress except when I was married. I wore my mother's old clothes."

"Perhaps I should make a Chinese outfit," said Miss Cassidy, "I envy all of you your cotton trousers, Mui Ee."

Mui Ee laughed. "Oh, but the samfoo trousers are for working women, Miss Cassidy! That is why the twins do not wear them."

"I think I count as a working woman, don't you?"

Mui Ee laughed, then instantly sighed again as Wong Mi made her appearance, leaning heavily on her husband. She was in pale pink, which clearly annoyed Mui Ee. "That colour is for unmarried women. Good gracious, this child knows so little, I often want to shake her, Miss Cassidy."

Miss Cassidy agreed with her eyes but said with her mouth, "She is still learning, Mui Ee. Anyway, the princess will not know."

"Of course she will. Have you seen an older Muslim woman in this shade of pink? Of course not." With that, Mui Ee strode over to Wong Mi, spoke gently to her and then wrapped her firmly in her own dark maroon shawl.

"Are we all ready?" asked Mr Kay, coming to join them with a slightly ironic expression; Miss Cassidy suspected he had been listening to the women for a while before descending the stairs. "The great lady is on her way. Mr Nair has sent a boy with a message that she left the hotel about twenty minutes ago. I do wish I could remember who she is," he added aside to Miss Cassidy as he strode past.

"Gracious! He is wearing the exact same colour as you,

Miss Cassidy," murmured Mui Ee. "You had better stay well back, or it will look terribly peculiar."

Miss Cassidy, whose intention it was to stay well back in any case, fervently agreed. Of the servants, only Yoke Jie and Miss Cassidy were with the family to meet the princess, because an amah and a Western governess were status symbols. Both, however, would remain in the back and not speak unless spoken to.

The arrival of the princess was almost like a parade. First came some splendidly uniformed guards, tall and awe-inspiring. Then two more soldiers, mounted on horseback. Then a car containing three magnificently dressed women in brilliant silks, none of whom turned out to be the princess, only her ladies-in-waiting and chaperones. Then a male escort comprising two handsome and forbidding male cousins, and Haresh Nair in his best (and only) silk outfit, a brilliant ruby-red and white. Miss Cassidy had always thought Mr Nair was particularly tall and handsome, but he looked positively ordinary next to the magnificent guards and lesser Malay princes in all their finery. As if he had read her mind, Haresh Nair caught her eye and winked. Miss Cassidy had to stuff her fist in her mouth to keep from laughing.

Finally the princess arrived in a motorcar even more resplendent than Mat's. She was swathed head to toe in glorious blue and gold, with only her face and hands visible. As she was helped down from the vehicle, the household all bowed or curtseyed deeply, so that nobody could really look upon her face; but her footsteps could be heard, pat-pat-pat along the gravel. Then she laughed, and Miss Cassidy heard her exclaim in a voice both sweet and imperious, "Well, Kakak, do you remember me yet?"

They all looked up. The princess—who was very tiny, smaller even than the twins—had seized Mui Ee by the hands, and was beaming up at her with childlike triumph and glee.

Mui Ee stared at her. Then she said, "Nora?"

The princess pealed with laughter. "Yes!"

"It can't be," stammered Mui Ee. "It's not possible. Why, I used to give you red bean buns and make you pound rempah!"

"Yes, you did! And I was very upset when I went to find you, and your sister-in-law said you were married and moved to Singapore! I didn't go back after that," she added, making a face. "I don't like your sisters-in-law, nasty jealous spiteful things. No wonder you had to marry, to get away from them."

"I don't understand. This can't be. Why, you are just a little girl from the village—aren't you? Oh, my goodness," said Mui Ee faintly, "I must sit down."

The household was turned topsy-turvy. Without Mui Ee to take charge, nobody quite knew what to do, so Mr Nair and Miss Cassidy between them divided up the princess's grand escort, putting all men in the courtyard and all women in the drawing room. Mat and Aminah had already set out the food; with them were a bevy of brilliantly dressed female relatives, twittering like evening mynahs, trying to catch glimpses of the glittering event. They were put to good use as Mr Nair instructed them to entertain the ladies-in-waiting—who were, after all, quite important personages in their own right—while the princess was absorbed in explaining her delightful surprise.

The rest of the household quickly dismissed themselves after formal greetings were exchanged. "I am sorry for using your name, Mr Kay," added the princess, "the truth is that we have never met. I told my father you once cleared a path for me through a busy area—many kind gentlemen have done this, so it is quite believable. But once I found out where Kakak had gone"—using the familiar Malay word for "older sister"—"you understand, I had to find any means to see her."

"Of course you did," said Mr Kay, with a slightly wild-looking grin—the expression of a very busy man who has lost a day of work for a child's whim. "That is perfectly natural. Let us not delay your reunion any longer."

But the princess was not quite done. Her eye had ranged over the collection of people in the courtyard with speculative interest, dismissing all the men as unimportant, and fixing upon the twins (who were staring at her in awe), and Miss Cassidy and her flame-red hair. "You will all come with me," she commanded as she seized Mui Ee's arm. "We will all talk, and Kakak will tell me about her new life."

The twins squealed in unison, transported with excitement. Miss Cassidy, rather less enthusiastic, whispered hurried instructions to Yoke Jie and Mat, and scurried along after them.

The story was pieced together eventually. Mui Ee had one day come across a ragged-looking little girl in her chicken yard, shouting at and beating the chickens. Assuming Nora, as she said she was called, was a girl from the village, Mui Ee had boxed her ears, then felt sorry when she cried. She brought the child into the kitchen, fed her, gave her a task to do and chatted with her in Malay. Nora, taking a liking to her (probably because nobody had ever spoken to her that way before), returned to the kitchen a week later, and again and again over the course of about three years. Mui Ee fed her little treats and put her to use with easy tasks, like fetching water or pounding spices with a pestle and mortar.

But Nora was actually Princess Nur Sharifah Bismillah, sixth daughter of the Sultan of the State, and she was meant to be attending religious classes each time she turned up in Mui Ee's kitchen, dressed in the same grubby cotton smock she always hid in her bag. She had got away with it very easily. The maidservant who brought her had been meeting a lover, the first time she ran away. By threatening and blackmailing the maid, Nora got what she wanted and was never caught.

"The poor maid," said Mui Ee, aghast.

"Oh, don't waste pity on her! She was a sulky, naughty girl. She didn't like serving us. She ran away two years ago. I don't know where she has gone."

"But Nora, why did you never tell me who you were?" Mui Ee exclaimed. "I had you plucking chickens and washing rice! It is terrible," she added in despair. "I am so ashamed."

The princess spent a few minutes assuring Mui Ee that all was well, that her father had never found out, that it hardly mattered now she was grown up. "I am to be married soon," she added sadly.

"Oh! So are we," said Yezi, who, like Miss Cassidy, understood Malay but spoke it only haltingly. "Sama-sama."

It was more than two hours before Miss Cassidy was able to escape the room and the unrelenting chatter of the princess and the twins. Mui Ee could not leave, for besides wanting to talk to her, Princess Nora had brought a staggering amount of presents for her, from bolts of lush fabric to bejewelled hairpins to a big basket of rambutans, Mui Ee's favourite fruit. There was now nothing formal nor royal about the visit, as the girls sat and ate rambutans and admired dresses and jewellery and discussed the failings of boys—the eternal topic of teenaged girls everywhere, in all walks of life, through all time.

"Mr Nair, when will they leave?" Miss Cassidy hissed as the dashingly dressed clerk came over to help her with a tea tray.

"When the princess says so, I expect," he answered. "I have been asked, incidentally, to pass on compliments to the chef. The food is being thoroughly enjoyed."

"Chefs, plural," said Miss Cassidy, "a whole army of Malay ladies cooked this—are probably still cooking now, for I see them running about and the noise in the kitchens is unbelievable. Have you eaten, Mr Nair? I am very hungry, but I cannot swallow a bite in front of the princess."

"Mat has just ducked into that anteroom. I believe if we follow him, it will lead to good things."

Mr Nair was right. The "anteroom" was, in fact, the main dry kitchen. Aminah was refilling a large pot of biryani rice and mutton curry, and Mat was helping himself from it, along with Yoke Jie and a few of the other household servants. "Oh, bless you," cried Miss Cassidy, giving Aminah a hearty kiss on the cheek, which very much startled her.

Yoke Jie, looking towards the sun, said, "It is time for the Master's lunch, and the two Young Masters—what shall we do? We have prepared nothing. The kitchen is too busy."

"They will have to have mutton curry and like it," said Miss Cassidy decisively. "But let us eat first. The men can wait another ten minutes."

Miss Cassidy herself carried the tray to Mr Kay, with Mr Nair's help. "Skirts are a nuisance," she grumbled. "I cannot manage stairs alone while carrying so many things. And I only have one good dress, so it will not do to spill."

"I have noticed your one good dress, Miss Cassidy. Do you like my one good suit?"

"Yes, it is very festive, isn't it?"

"Because it is my Indian wedding guest outfit. I, too, cannot spill anything on it, or I will be shunned at family weddings for life."

Mr Kay and his sons were all hiding in his study, well away from the chaos, and were overjoyed to see their lunch being brought to them. "I thought we had been forgotten," said Mr Kay. "Leong was about to run down the back stairs and see if he could steal some scraps, like the tragic beggars we are today."

"Well, we have brought the scraps to you, and Yoke Jie has gone to bring some to Wong Mi and the two children," said Miss Cassidy. "I hope you like mutton curry."

"At this point, Miss Cassidy, we would settle for cardboard curry. When will the princess leave my house?" he added piteously. "If she intends to remain till sunset, I think we three mere men must abscond to the wharves."

"We should have absconded hours ago," murmured Boon, smiling faintly. "I think it will be hard to make an escape now, Father."

But luck was on their side. The sky began to darken shortly after lunchtime, and when the first rumble of thunder was heard, the princess' escorts began making polite indications that it was best they leave. Reluctantly, Nora submitted to being separated from poor Mui Ee, who was now hot, bothered and in a bit of a temper. It was clear that she could imagine the chaos the house was in, could hear the constant chatter of far more women in her kitchen than it should rightly hold, and had not seen her children since the early morning.

She kept her mouth fixedly smiling as they made slow progression to the exit. "I must come back," said Princess Nora eagerly. "I have not had a tour of the house, can you imagine? It is a beautiful home."

"Yes, you must come back," said Yezi excitedly.

"We will show you everything!" cried Yeling.

"Over there is Dai-sou's house, Prosperity Wing. She makes it very comfortable."

"And over there is Ee-sou's house, Longevity Wing. It is—"

They broke off. The twins were staring at a particular spot—and, indeed, so was the princess. "What is it?" asked Mui Ee, startled, looking and failing to see anything. "Is something wrong?"

Miss Cassidy, like Mui Ee, could see nothing. She looked around hurriedly, and seized an empty water glass left on a nearby table. She tapped it three times, lifted it, and looked through it.

She only just caught it—a flash of green, scrabbling at a small heap of rambutan stones set aside to be thrown away. It was there only for a moment, and then it was gone.

The princess, her face pale, stared up at Mui Ee. "Kakak," she said fearfully, "why is there a toyol in your house?"

XV

Miss Cassidy &
the Green Glass Bottle

"I THINK it is time you told me the truth, Miss Cassidy." Miss Cassidy, demure in her yard, plucking beansprout roots in a basket in her lap, asked with tinkling innocence, "To what do you refer, Mr Kay?"

The princess was now gone, the house was set to rights and Mui Ee had escaped to bed with a camphor footbath and a cold towel for her eyes. It was quite late, and Miss Cassidy had been about to retire indoors herself to escape the mosquitoes. It had rained quite heavily after the princess left, but now the storm had passed, and it was a delightful evening, the creamy scent of pandan wafting on the breeze. However, the damp always brought on mosquitoes.

Mr Kay never seemed much bothered by the insects. He sauntered into her yard, still in his grey Shantung silk jacket, which had matched so perfectly with Miss Cassidy's cheap poplin. He smoked his pipe in amicable silence for a few seconds, while Miss Cassidy continued plucking vegetables, before speaking again.

"You told the princess that she didn't see a toyol, but instead saw a green bottle rolling along the floor. You picked it up and showed her."

"Indeed I did. Here it is." Miss Cassidy tapped the small green bottle that stood by her elbow, glistening in the twilight.

"You may have convinced her, but you have not convinced Yeling and Yezi. They say they have seen this creature twice."

"I do not even know what a toyol is."

"The twins do. The princess has told them. It is a kind of imp, raised from the spirit of a stillborn or aborted child. It suckles blood from its mistress, but also demands milk, sweets and toys just like a child. In return, it will perform favours, steal money or torment an enemy, that sort of thing."

"It sounds dreadful."

"I have never seen such a thing," said Mr Kay, puffing on his pipe.

"Then perhaps that is not what the twins saw."

"You believe they saw this same green glass bottle, like you told the princess?"

"They saw something green," said Miss Cassidy, "and this bottle was there, in the correct place, catching the light."

"Mm. Where did this bottle come from, I wonder? It looks like the type used for medicated oil. I don't recall anyone in the family using medicated oil in a green bottle."

Miss Cassidy said nothing.

Mr Kay smoked a moment longer. "Miss Cassidy," he said seriously at last, "if something unpleasant was endangering my family, and you knew of it, you would tell me, wouldn't you?"

"Mr Kay, I am rather offended you even need to ask. Of course I would, if I could not deal with the situation myself."

He gave her a sharp glance, but Miss Cassidy's gaze was turned downwards upon the beansprouts in her lap.

He moved, and Miss Cassidy thought he was leaving in his usual abrupt manner; so she was very much startled to find that he had placed one knee on the ground, in order to be at eye level, and was gazing solemnly at her. He was very close—so close that Miss Cassidy clutched the basket of beansprouts to her, as a form of barricade.

"Miss Cassidy," he said, "I trust you. Entirely."

Without waiting for a response, he stood up, turned around, took another puff on his pipe and said quietly, "Goodnight."

And off he went.

Miss Cassidy let out the breath she had been holding. "Really, it is too hot outside," she muttered to herself, and accordingly went indoors.

"It is a good business," said Mui Ee approvingly.

It certainly was. The Tong brothers' Chinese medicine shop was so full of people that there were no more seats available at the counter, and Mui Ee and Miss Cassidy wandered about and looked around. The shop was on two levels; the ground floor sold Chinese herbs, powders and medicines, and the second floor housed the clinic, where patients could be seen to in private. There was an additional cost for such service, so most people contented themselves with purchasing one of the carefully labelled herb packets, and asking for instructions over the counter.

Miss Cassidy found it fascinating. There was a curious, herbaceous scent in the air, which also clung to the brothers wherever they went—not an unpleasant scent, but one that effectively advertised their occupation. Two glass counters were heavily stuffed with pink paper packets, Chinese lettering on them indicating they were for "cough", "diarrhoea", "wind in the body", "heatiness" and other ailments. Some packets were open, for customers to observe the mix of tangled roots, white seeds, red berries and various fluffy or twisted types of fungi.

More expensive items, like ginseng, bird's nest, deer antler and so forth, were displayed on their own, or in specially made boxes for gifts. There were great glass jars revealing inexplicable contents in preservative liquor, bottles of ointments and rubs, and commercially pre-packaged pills and oils, including a medicated oil which came in a green glass bottle. It was a distillation of aniseed, eucalyptus and camphor, and was Miss Cassidy's favourite headache remedy, so there was always a bottle in her pocket, the size of her littlest finger.

Miss Cassidy liked the shop very much. It felt both alien and familiar to her, with its jumble of powerful items and pointless nonsensical ones. Before the medicine women of Europe had been driven out as witches (or burned or drowned or killed in various other unpleasant, undeserved ways), there used to be a home like this near every village, a garden growing sound sensible herbs and cool dim rooms filled with bottles and jars, and a woman and her disciple pounding and grinding and boiling things.

Those women once had been regarded with a mix of fear and awe, but the Chinese medicine man was nothing more nor less than a respected tradesman, no different from a grocer or launderer, providing service in a particularly necessary field. The customers who came in requested medicines as one might ask for a bar of soap or tin of milk next door at the dry goods store.

It was a large, well-organised shop, if a little dusty. "But that cannot be helped," said practical Mui Ee. "The two men are alone, dealing with roots and fungi all day, making powders and pastes. I suppose they have someone in to clean. But they are quite right—they need wives, as soon as possible."

Miss Cassidy found she liked this view of the world, where a wife was a handy thing to have to run the store, manage the house, raise the children and keep one company, and not necessarily the receptacle of grand Shakespearean passion.

Yang was serving a customer at the counter, explaining the use of an ointment. When he opened the bottle and sprinkled two drops in his palm, the strong woody scent of it reached Miss Cassidy, who sniffed appreciatively. She watched Yang rub his palms together, and demonstrate a pressure-point massage on the customer's forearm. Yang's hands were large and strong, and the palms fleshy—prosperous hands, Madam Lim had called them.

He saw Miss Cassidy and Mui Ee when the customer had left, and beamed brightly, his good nature undimmed by a clearly busy day. "My brother is upstairs with a patient," he said in English, surprising Miss Cassidy with his fluency. "Acupuncture. Do go up to the waiting room so you may sit down, and help yourselves to tea! One of us will be with you shortly."

Miss Cassidy summoned the twins, who were waiting at the entrance outside. Yezi had been seized with a fit of nervousness and refused to go in, so they had both stayed on the threshold, making a bit of a nuisance of themselves in the narrow five-foot way, guarding the big basket of shopping Mui Ee had left at their feet.

Once in the shop, Yeling looked around in awe and grinned broadly at Yang at the counter; Yezi stayed behind her twin, gripping her hand, nervous and uncertain.

Upstairs was a short hallway leading to a small waiting room, and a closed door labelled "examination room" in Chinese. A low murmur of voices could be heard. At the end of the row of chairs was a locked grille-gate, which clearly led to the brothers' living quarters. Mui Ee walked straight up to it and looked in, unembarrassed. It was a clean, tidy living space with a dining area, a shelf filled with books and ledgers and some laundry by the windows. "I see at least four bedrooms," Mui Ee reported, peering, "and there is a dry kitchen and bathroom. The wet kitchen is downstairs, in the back. It is a good-sized house, girls. You will be very comfortable here."

Yeling giggled, and Yezi smiled wanly.

Just then, Wang's patient came out of the examination room—a heavily pregnant woman accompanied by her mother—followed by Wang, who smiled with pleasure when he saw who was waiting. Neither he nor Mui Ee seemed put out by her nosiness, as she stood with her face almost through the bars of the separating grille. "Ah, I will let you in," he said, immediately approaching with a large bundle of keys to unlock it. "Come inside, it is more comfortable."

Mui Ee looked pleased as they entered, and more furniture revealed itself, including a guest-set: a high-backed rosewood seat for four people and a marble-topped coffee table, both exquisitely carved. There was already a basket of tea; they always kept tea on, Wang explained, cooling tea for patients who needed it on hot days.

After some desultory chatter about the weather, Mui Ee presented the pretext for their visit. "I have come to ask your advice about my sister-in-law. She had an accident with her pregnancy," she said primly to the male physician, "and she needs strengthening up. It has been two weeks now and she is still too unwell to leave her bed. She is always pale and cold, and the pain in her belly is no better."

Wang looked rather grave. "Two weeks! That is a long time to be abed, even in such a case. Has a midwife been to examine her?"

"Yes. She says she needs blood, and heat—her body is too cold. But we try to give her liver and ginger soup, and she can barely eat it—or anything at all, really."

Yang came up the stairs just then, smiling. "I have shut up the shop a while," he said, "it is nearly time for our lunch, anyway. Will you ladies care to join us?"

"Ah, you are kind, but we have eaten," said Mui Ee politely. Her gaze had rested very quickly on the small meal of rice, meat and vegetables under a cotton cover on the dining table, probably left for them by the morning maid. If they all stayed, the brothers would have to cook for them.

Wang asked his brother's advice, and they conversed briefly before Yang said, "I will give you some herbs for your Ee-sou. Boil them with black chicken, and give her the broth. She should eat the chicken if she can."

"Is there," asked Miss Cassidy, "anything that might help her sleep deeply? She says she has bad dreams. She wakes exhausted, and of course she cannot get well."

"Hmm," said Yang slowly. "I can give you some laudanum. But you must be very careful with it. Are you familiar with laudanum?"

"I am a little, yes," said Miss Cassidy, "I have nursed a lady who relied on it."

"Then you know it would be unwise to allow a young woman to reach such a state. Do not leave the bottle by her bed; one of you should be in charge of dispensing it. One drop each time, and no more; only as needed."

When they left the shop, it was high noon and very hot. Mui Ee, fanning herself, instructed the twins: "Now check the list. What else do we need?"

They looked in the basket. It had been a busy day already; they had been up before dawn to go to the wet market for meat and vegetables, and had come home with four live chickens in straw baskets and several net bags of onions, carrots, kailan, bok choy and bean sprouts, and tiffins filled with tofu and fishcake. Mat had driven them then, because food for such a large household was heavy; however, for the afternoon shopping, Mui Ee wanted them to carry the basket and walk on their own, as she did every shopping day, usually with Miss Cassidy now that Yoke Jie was too old for such hot work.

"Dried shrimp, black mushroom, tins of tomato paste…"

"Cooking oil, candied plums, medicine for Ee-sou…"

And Yezi said, bashfully, "…cotton cloth."

"Indeed, the children need diapers," said Mui Ee blandly. "Let's go." Charles De Souza's fabric store was not where Mui Ee usually bought cloth; there was a fabric market in Telok Ayer that catered to the economical purse. The Far East & Indochina Trading Co Fine Fashion Emporium was meant for wealthy families and special occasion tailoring. It was three storeys high, and the second and third floors specifically catered to Chinese and Indian brides and bridegrooms, employing skilled tailors and dressmakers for that purpose. The first floor was for wealthy ladies of fashion, with very haughty sales clerks at high counters, and private rooms where one could make an appointment to have a live model demonstrate the latest fashions. Fashion plates imported from Paris were available for browsing to all ladies.

"Good gracious, there won't be cotton for diapers here," said Mui Ee with a chuckle, staring up at the grand shop, which looked almost like a hotel. "On the other hand, girls, at least your bridal outfit will be free."

"It is so grand," said Yezi in awe. "I am a little afraid of it."

"Nonsense, child. Your father is one of the richest men in Singapore. The silk he gave both me and Wong Mi for our wedding gifts came from here, and good silk it is too; I am keeping it for my children. You are the Kay daughters—you must act like it."

So the Kay daughters took a deep breath and marched in through the doors as fearlessly as they could manage. Behind them came Mui Ee, and then Miss Cassidy holding the shopping basket. Mui Ee had guessed—correctly—that if the sales clerks saw the twins with a white woman carrying their shopping for them, they would be accorded instant respect.

They were. A well-dressed, well-greased man greeted them as Young Mistresses—not Little Sister, as they were usually addressed—and asked how he could help them. From every wall, bolts of brilliant fabric gleamed in the soft light; two white women in magnificent outfits were choosing gloves in one corner, and a painfully modern-looking Chinese lady was selecting silk hose in another.

The twins hesitated. They did not actually know what to say. Mui Ee shot a slightly mischievous glance at Miss Cassidy, who was trying to look as subservient as possible, and not particularly succeeding.

Then Yezi announced, in ringing tones, "We want to see the manager."

"Yes," said Yeling, following suit, "the biggest manager. Mr De Souza."

The sales clerk looked startled. "The director? May I ask why?"

"We want to buy...cloth for..."

"...for something important..."

"For her!" said Yezi triumphantly, and pointed dramatically at Miss Cassidy, who blinked. "For a dress! A birthday gift from us," she added with great magnanimity, which made Mui Ee suppress a chuckle.

"For her excellent service," added Yeling.

"A reward."

"Yes, a reward. Bring us the director! We want him to choose the fabric for us."

"Ah," said the sales clerk, coughing politely. "Would it be all right if I—"

"We want Mr De Souza," both girls chorused.

"Very well," said the clerk, giving up. "What name shall I give him?"

They were shown into a waiting room, a little salon with tea and biscuits set out, a large comfortable sofa and a tall three-sided mirror. None of them had ever seen such a large mirror, and each took a moment to stare at their multiplied reflection in the glass, going on and on into infinity. "This must be where the model stands," said Mui Ee. "What a job it must be, standing about all day in beautiful dresses for other people to buy, then going home in your old samfoo."

With the twins present, Miss Cassidy did not explain that many fashion-plate models had other occupations, involving wealthy male protectors.

Mr De Souza appeared by and by, bringing with him an assistant laden with bolts of cloth. He laughed when he saw them all. "This is like a royal visit," he said. "The Portuguese ambassador's niece is in the next room, wondering why I have abandoned her."

"Oh! Then you must go back to her," said Yezi contritely. "It was only a bit of fun."

"In truth, I am glad to have an excuse to leave her. She

is very fussy, very skinny, very hard to dress, and very, very hard to please. It is why I must be there personally."

"Perhaps she comes so you can cheer her up," suggested Yezi.

"Perhaps," said Mr De Souza, amused. "Quite a lot of women come here to pass the time."

Yezi smiled. Yeling was looking at her twin with some dismay. It was beginning to dawn on her, Miss Cassidy realised, that marriage might separate them. "Loban, we need a dress for Miss Cassidy," said Yezi, "a nice, fashionable one, please."

"Girls, I really don't—" began Miss Cassidy, but Mui Ee interrupted her.

"Actually, it is a good idea, Miss Cassidy," she said. "That grey dress you have is outdated, and rather worn. You have turned it at least three times, I think."

"I have no need to be in fashion," said Miss Cassidy somewhat crossly. Mui Ee's eye was too good, sometimes.

"But you cannot start to look shabby. The grey dress must be your everyday dress now, Miss Cassidy. Let the twins give you a new dress—their allowance more than covers it, and then they will not waste it on unnecessary things for themselves."

The shop assistant, who was a prim little lady, was already waiting for her with measuring tape in hand, and an assessing look in her eye. "Hmm," she said, "red hair is difficult. Deep green, I think, medium neckline, loose fit on top, no puffs, no frills. Come, come."

Miss Cassidy, reassured by the decisive "no puffs, no frills", allowed herself to be hustled behind a screen to be measured thoroughly. She could hear the excited giggles and murmurs as Mr De Souza himself laid out fabrics for them to choose from. "Girls, nothing expensive, please," she shouted. "I couldn't bear the stress of an expensive dress."

"It is meant to be your best dress, Miss Cassidy," Mui Ee shouted back. "My best dress costs so much I shudder to wear it, but that is what a best dress is meant for. I like this one," she added. "Whisper the price in my ear, Mr De Souza."

By the time Miss Cassidy emerged from behind the screen, the evil deed was done. The twins had chosen a plain fabric of a very deep green, and a fine black lace to trim the collar. Yezi triumphantly showed her the pattern they had picked out, from a fashion plate sent from London. Miss Cassidy was relieved to see a simple dress with minimal embellishment, no sleeve puffs, and no ruffles. "I thought you would like this better than a pretty dress," Yezi said naïvely. "You see, you can put your brooch here, at the collar, like the picture."

"She has excellent taste," said Mr De Souza, with the approval of a businessman rather than of a gallant suitor. "The design will suit you well, do you not agree, Miss Cassidy?"

"I do indeed," agreed Miss Cassidy, warmly kissing each twin on the cheek, "and I thank you both from the bottom of my heart. Oh, and please, Mr De Souza, let me have a good, deep pocket sewn into this dress."

The twins were sober on the way home. Mat had come to collect them after all, in the motorcar. Four people were a squeeze in the jolting vehicle's single long passenger seat, but nobody minded very much. The twins spent the trip conversing in low tones, while Miss Cassidy and Mui Ee pretended to be engaged in other conversation.

"Poor girls," said Mui Ee when they were home and the twins had gone to change for dinner. "I think the reality of marriage is starting to sink in for them. By the way, did you buy glass buttons from the shop? I did not know you liked glass buttons. They are quite impractical."

"I don't, usually, but these were so very pretty. I will use them to trim a hat, I think."

It was a solemn sort of night at Pandan Villa. Miss Cassidy could see the lamp burning at the window of the twins' shared room till long past their bedtime. Mui Ee and Yoke Jie had prepared the tonic soup for Wong Mi, and put it to cook on a low steady heat overnight so Wong Mi could have it in the morning. This meant Yoke Jie would sleep in the kitchen to keep watch on the pot.

Miss Cassidy retired to bed early, but did not sleep. When it was dark, and the chirp of insects was loud outside her window, she sat up in bed and took out her jar of shiny things.

She had been collecting them for a while, and keeping them in a washed-out chilli paste jar. There were marbles of various sizes and colours, gathered from the Kay children's old toy chests, which Mui Ee's children were still too young to play with. There were a few shiny pebbles and seashells, cockle and mussel shells she had kept from their meals, and colourful bottlecaps. Now Miss Cassidy added the newest, prettiest addition—iridescent glass buttons in various colours from Mr De Souza's shop, beautiful things with an incised pattern of flowers and leaves in gold. And then, of course, her small, green glass bottle.

She had filled the green bottle with the sweetest liquid in the kitchen, pink rose syrup. Now she placed it carefully just within the threshold of her own door, and scattered salt around it. Then she stepped out, and looked up at the great glowing moon, full and swollen. "A little help today would be nice, Madam," she whispered pleasantly to it, "if you would be so kind."

Miss Cassidy began laying a trail from her door. She worked backwards in order of brightness, so the buttons were laid down first, glittering enticingly in the moonlight; then, in orderly paced-out steps, the marbles, the shells and the bottlecaps. Right at the door of Longevity Wing, however, Miss Cassidy placed the most tempting item of all—her own malachite brooch. The moon obligingly cast silver-blue beams upon it, so that it almost appeared to glow.

Miss Cassidy looked up at the silent and dark windows of Wong Mi's room. She would sleep, tonight, that absolute, laudanum-induced sleep Miss Cassidy had seen so many times—a stupor more than a restful slumber. Nothing would be able to wake her, and anything demanding her attention would be forced to seek amusement elsewhere.

Miss Cassidy returned to her room, and settled down to wait.

It was nearly three hours later when she heard the rattle of her iron key upon the hook on the wall, from which she had removed the wooden crucifix. She took it down—it was warm to the touch—and picked up the glass of water she had made ready beside her. Very slowly she raised it to her eye, and kept very, very still, as only Miss Cassidy could do.

The flash of green was, indeed, very much like the gleam of light off a green bottle. It was very difficult to see, unless one was concentrating on a specific spot. She could see the glittering buttons move, kicked about this way and that, as a very young baby might do, unable yet to understand how to close its fist properly. The buttons, originally in a widely spaced straight line, were now gathered together in a circle.

Then the moon peeked out from behind a drifting cloud and lit up the green glass bottle. It winked like an emerald.

Miss Cassidy watched a barely visible shadow of a creature making a cautious approach. It was so fast it was merely a blur, but she could see its footprints flashing over the salt as it went forwards, backwards, forwards, backwards. The bottle continued to gleam obligingly, and Miss Cassidy sent private thanks to every moon goddess she knew, not to mention the Chinese moon-fairy and moon-rabbit.

And finally, quite suddenly, the little bottle fell over. Rose syrup should have spilled out of it, but instead rapidly disappeared as if into thin air.

Miss Cassidy dropped the iron key over her threshold, and said triumphantly, "Got you."

There was a high-pitched, batlike shriek, a green flash and then a crackle, as if of electricity, and there it was—an ugly little green creature, like a very skinny baby, with beady red eyes and small black claws. It was scratching and pushing at an invisible barrier beyond the iron key, and screeched in fury as it found itself unable to leave.

"You have crossed my threshold," said Miss Cassidy, "and I have power over you now, wee beastie. If you will be good, I will not harm you."

But the toyol was in a temper. Up it leapt, and scratched Miss Cassidy's face; then it began to streak and hurtle through the air, slamming back and forth against the walls, trying to find a way out. It scratched at Miss Cassidy each time it passed by her, but she sat still and patiently waited.

Finally it stopped, landing on Miss Cassidy's bosom; with weakening limbs it clambered up and tried to bite her skin. Then it squealed in pain, and spat in disgust. Miss Cassidy's blood was no good to creatures of its sort.

At last it fell, unconscious, into Miss Cassidy's lap, undone by exhaustion, iron magic and an enormous dose of laudanum, which had been mixed with the pink rose syrup. Miss Cassidy took out the silk cord that Ah Nai had given her long ago, and carefully bound the creature up so that it could not move. Then she popped the toyol into the green glass medicine bottle, screwed the bottle tightly closed and dropped it into her pocket. With a "Hmm!" of satisfaction, she ventured back out into the night to gather all her pretty things back into their jar.

XVI

Miss Cassidy Takes a Holiday

"How did you do it?"

Wong Mi, clutching her bedclothes to her thin chest, stared tremulously at the green glass bottle, within which seemed to be nothing but a bit of silk cord, floating in translucent liquid. The bottle's colour masked the liquid effectively, so it was hard to tell if it was oil, water or alcohol.

"Never you mind how I did it. I want to know why it is here," said Miss Cassidy sharply.

Wong Mi had never looked worse. In the weeks since her "accident", despite the time and money spent on strengthening brews and tonic soups, despite the visits of midwives and physicians and masseuses, she had become thinner, paler and more fragile than ever. Her skin was sallow, her eyes looked bruised and even her hair seemed dried out and thin. A speckled red rash had broken out on her neck, and she was always cold and shivering.

"Your husband is very worried," added Miss Cassidy. "He and Mr Kay—I mean Kay Loban—are considering sending you away to a sanatorium. It will become impossible for you to hide this," she shook the bottle, "if you are sent away."

Wong Mi gingerly reached out and took hold of the glass bottle. It was warm in her hand. "My grandmother had it in a bottle also," she said faintly. "An old rice-wine bottle. It was bound with red cord. We found it hidden behind a cupboard when she died. We didn't know what it was. My uncle opened it and sniffed it and said it was just sugar water inside. He threw out the water and we put the bottle with the rubbish. After that..."

"After that," Miss Cassidy prompted as Wong Mi fell silent, "things started happening in your house?"

"Yes," she whispered. "Things would be moved from one place to another. Bright things, especially. Our jewellery, our silverware, they would go missing and turn up in strange places. Mother blamed the maids and fired them. But it went on. Then all the women started falling sick. And my brother's wife, she..."

"She had a miscarriage?"

"She had two. One after the other. And my sister, also, the year after."

"Hmm." Miss Cassidy tapped the bottle. "This creature is jealous. It wants no competition."

"Yes," Wong Mi murmured. "My father went to a tang kee and to a dukun. A...a spirit medium," she added by way of explanation. "A Chinese one and a Malay one. They both said that someone has brought forth a spirit, and it now belongs to our household. If we do not feed it and care for it, it will continue to cause mischief."

"A toyol."

"Yes, the dukun called it a toyol. We think my grandmother must have had it created," she added softly. "She was a fierce old lady, my grandmother. They say my grandfather wanted a second wife, and the wedding was all arranged, until my grandmother accused the woman of stealing her jade earrings. They found the earrings under the fiancée's pillow, and she was sent away in disgrace. And there were many other stories," she continued faintly. "Grandfather's mistresses, they all came to some grief. Two of them had miscarriages also. One gave birth to a child who mysteriously died."

"Hmm," said Miss Cassidy. "And now it has followed you here?"

"I thought I was rid of it, Miss Cassidy," cried poor Wong Mi. "I was so glad to escape that house. My mother did as the dukun instructed and left milk or sugar water for it every night, and it stopped moving and breaking things. But it was always jealous. My sister kept a pet bird once, and found it dead in its cage for no reason. My brother's baby son often cried in the night, and they would find bite marks on his legs in the morning."

"But was there nothing the dukun could do to help you?"

"Nothing. He said that the toyol can only be destroyed by the original bomoh who created it for my grandmother. We don't know who he is, or if he is even still alive. My brothers have all left the house with their wives, and it has not followed them. My little sister has been married out too, and it did not follow her. My mother said that since the creature does not much bother her, she would continue to feed it, and it would leave us alone. And when I first came to this house, it seemed I had escaped it. Then, last year I started to...to notice..."

"Something was happening in your kitchen?"

"Yes," whispered Wong Mi. "Things were moving around. Broken bottles on the floor in the morning. My jewellery would go missing. I stopped using the kitchens here," she said, "and made them as empty as possible. I tried to remember what my mother used to do, and I left out milk for it. It worked for a little while."

"Why did it come here, Wong Mi? Has something happened to your mother?"

Wong Mi nodded, tears filling her eyes. "She...she is ill. She cannot move or speak. I think she is dying, and the toyol knows it. So it has come to me, the next female in line. And I am so afraid...I am so afraid that..."

Miss Cassidy nodded, briskly. "Well, now it is bound, so it will do you no further harm."

"But I want to be rid of it," said Wong Mi passionately. "I do not want to give this burden to my own daughter. If the bottle is unsealed—if it breaks—it will all begin again. What should I do, Miss Cassidy? How can I destroy this thing?"

"You want a holiday?" Mr Kay looked sternly down at Miss Cassidy, who stood her ground quite firmly.

"Yes, I do, Mr Kay," she said. "I have not had a holiday since I first came to Singapore. That was four years ago, you know."

212

"Indeed! Two years with us, and two with Captain Bendemeer, yes? What slave drivers we are."

"Oh, well, remaining in the Captain's house was appropriate at the time," said Miss Cassidy vaguely. "And I enjoy being at Pandan Villa. But Christmas is coming," she added hastily as Mr Kay opened his mouth, on the verge of an observation Miss Cassidy preferred not to hear, "and at the turn of the new century too. You know it is important for my people, Mr Kay."

"Your people?" Mr Kay observed her quizzically. "What people might that be?"

"People who celebrate Christmas," she answered promptly.

"Or, specifically, people who celebrate the twenty-fifth of December?"

Miss Cassidy paused, nonplussed. "Yes," she said at last, as neutrally as possible. "So, may I have a Christmas holiday, Mr Kay?"

"And what will you do? Where will you go? You cannot travel all the way back to Scotland, surely."

"Gracious! No. I will spend the time among friends here."

"Among friends! What friends? Am I not also your friend?"

Miss Cassidy found herself unable to answer.

"And so," continued Mr Kay as if she had done so, "why do you propose to go away from me—from us—your friends?"

"Wong Mi is better and back in the kitchen, and the twins have become quite energetic little housekeepers, so I find I am less needed than before, Mr Kay. Apart from a few English lessons—which most of your household hardly need anymore—I have very little proper work. You know your girls will be married off soon," she added gently, "and you will no longer need me. I must start to think of the future."

"The future! Indeed you must," said Mr Kay, his eyes distant as he refilled his pipe. "We must all think of the future. I hope to have many, many grandchildren, Miss Cassidy, all of whom must have English lessons."

"Yes, but they can go to school. Times are different now, Mr Kay. Even Mui Ee has agreed not to bind her daughter's feet. She has seen that the twins can find good marriages and get comfortable husbands, without having to worry about the size of their feet. I think hers will be the last generation destroying their feet for beauty."

"Yes, well, in China they have been trying to outlaw it for decades. I have no doubt they will succeed. It is a ridiculous practice."

Miss Cassidy waited, stubbornly. It was nearly dinner-time. Mr Kay had been out all day at the wharves, and had returned to find Miss Cassidy waiting for him in his study—sitting in the same chair she had first been directed to with the statement that "the chair you sit in does not mind who you are"—patiently passing the time by elaborately weaving Chinese love-knots with red cord and iridescent beads. They were for the twins, she explained, a small marriage gift from her. She had little else to give but her blessing, so she wished to give it heartily.

They sat in her lap now, nearly completed, beautifully done. The beads were unusual, metallic and shining, instead of the green or brown jade normally used. "Hematite," she said, following his gaze. "Polished iron ore. I know it is not normally used for these knots, but I wanted them to be a little different. I should like them to look at these and think of their funny English teacher."

"I will tell them to hang them in a good place," he murmured. "By their mirrors, to remind them to grow old with grace and dignity."

"As I have?"

"As you have, indeed, Miss Cassidy," he said with a smile. "Age is distinction in Chinese culture, you know."

"Hmm," said Miss Cassidy.

"I notice you are wearing your good dress. Is this meeting so important to you?"

"Eh?" Miss Cassidy looked down at her grey poplin. "Ah! You have not kept up with developments, Mr Kay. This is now my day dress. The twins, bless them, have given me a new good dress, from Mr De Souza's shop. I received the finished product this morning, and it is absolutely lovely. We all admired it and then I put it away in my trunk, covered in pandan leaves to keep the insects out. Mr De Souza's people do excellent work."

"Mr De Souza made you a new dress, and the Tong brothers' mark is on Wong Mi's herb packets. You have been busy, you womenfolk."

"We have, Mr Kay, and that is why I would like a holiday, now all has been settled."

"Has all been settled, then?"

"Yes, Mr Kay," she said quietly. "You will find, tomorrow, that Madam Lim will be paying you a visit."

Mr Kay sat down, and drew a few more puffs from his

pipe. "Time is a brutal thing, Miss Cassidy," he said at last, quietly. "When you want to hold on to it, it hurries away from you; when you want it to move on, it lingers to torment you. Very well," he said at last, with a gesture that seemed to physically dissipate his melancholy, "you shall have a holiday, Miss Cassidy. One week, did you say?"

"Yes, please, if I may."

"You may. But will you tell me where you will be, and who you are with?"

"Mr Kay, that is hardly your concern," said Miss Cassidy rather crossly. "I am not a child—indeed, you have made it quite clear you think me a venerable old grandmother."

"Hardly that, Miss Cassidy, but as you are part of my household, I must be responsible for you, at least in part. If you are found cut to pieces in the jungles of Sumatra by the headhunters, it will be put to Kay Loban's bad fortune again, and I shall never find another English teacher."

"Well, if you must know, you must," she said in resignation. "My sister will soon be docking in Singapore."

"Your sister! I did not know you had a sister."

"Oh, we are quite a tribe of brothers and sisters, my family," she said, again rather vaguely. "But Anna's husband has been posted to Ceylon, and she has decided to make the trip here for Christmas to see me."

"That is a very dedicated sister—how many days is it between Ceylon and here? A week, I think."

"Yes, but she does not mind. She is a good sailor, and she will have her own cabin. She will be putting up in the Far Eastern Oriental Hotel, and I will share her room."

"My goodness," said Mr Kay mildly. "Well, Pandan Villa cannot compete with the Far Eastern Oriental Hotel, for certain."

"On the contrary, I think Mui Ee's cooking far outstrips any hotel chef's, but it will be nice to not have to kill the chicken myself for a few days."

"And you will join their annual Christmas party, I suppose, and attempt to drink hot mulled wine, with sweltering heat or pouring rain outside. In your lovely new dress," he added, grinning.

"Yes," she said primly, "in my lovely new dress, and I will send happy thoughts to all of you here."

Christmas was celebrated in Singapore in a somewhat bemused manner. There were many missionary-led schools in the colony, and each celebrated the holiday in its own particular manner, according to the dictates of each individual sect. Government houses put up Christmas decorations, holly and mistletoe made of paper, beads and wire; churches made similar efforts in varying degrees, depending on how well-blessed their coffers were. Children were taught carols and hymns with but half an idea of their meaning, and some school choirs wrote their own, in various languages. Here and there, a few even managed some form of Christmas tree.

The general intention of Christmas suited Miss Cassidy fine, as did similar festivals like Chinese New Year, Eid and Deepavali. They were, in their essentials, the same—a time for celebrating family and friends, and a good excuse for new clothes, good food and a little cheerful indulgence all round.

The details of why and how they were celebrated, to Miss Cassidy, were not important, and Christmas seemed largely unimportant to the rest of the populace, who regarded it as a kind of white man's family festival.

"Leda! Leda!"

Anna's unmistakable voice went ringing through the air, soaring even over the noise and chaos of the swarming coolies, disembarking passengers and rickshaw men shouting for customers. A moment later Leda was embracing her sister on the quay, and they were exclaiming in delight over the fact that neither of them was yet dead from cholera.

"What an irony that George has ended up in Ceylon," said Miss Cassidy. "You seemed quite settled in that Aberdeenshire village."

"Oh, Leda! I miss my lovely little cottage, I do indeed. And my horses, and my guns. In Ceylon I am expected to be a respectable lady—it is dreadfully dull. Are we to take one of these rickshaws?" she added, doubtfully. "My trunks are rather heavy."

"Ah, you underestimate the rickshaw men. But no, Mr Kay has lent us his automobile."

"His...his automobile? Gracious heavens, are we to ride in one of those?" exclaimed Anna, alarmed, as Mat pulled up to them in the vehicle. "What a sight we shall be!"

"Yes, we get a lot of stares, don't we, Mat? But once you get used to the rattle, it's rather jolly fun. Come along, then."

Fortunately, it was not very far to the hotel, for Anna did not enjoy the ride much, somewhat offending Mat, who was proud of the expensive contraption. Miss Cassidy thanked him, shooed Anna into the hotel, and was already halfway up the stairs before she had recovered her equanimity enough to look around.

The Far Eastern Oriental Hotel was one of the most famous in the region. A beautiful white building on two levels, it was staffed by grand Sikh men with imposing turbans and elegant ladies in sarong kebaya, and the bar and restaurant were famous for presenting a menu ranging all over Europe, from escargot to clootie dumpling to mutton chops in gravy. It had a famous marble stairway, magnificent red carpets and always seemed to smell of expensive whisky and lemon polish.

Miss Cassidy had been inside only once, to chaperone Sarah Jane Bendemeer for tea with some tremendously unpleasant ladies, but she had never had the chance to appreciate the brilliant draperies, filigreed chandeliers or, indeed, the top-of-the-line amenities such as running hot and cold water, electric lights and a telephone in every room.

All eyes seemed to be on the ladies as they ascended to their rooms. They likely made rather a sight, Miss Cassidy reflected. She herself was tall, broad and, of course, red-haired, but she absolutely paled in comparison to Anna, who was even taller, though a touch more slender. Anna's hair was dark, curly and splendid, and floated about her like an inky cloud; she had flashing black eyes and a commanding presence that belied her generous and affectionate nature. There was something about her that made men worship her (since, indeed, they literally had, thousands of years ago), as though her proper place was not here on a hotel carpet in her sensible travel tweeds and buttoned boots, but upon a marble pedestal, clasping folds of rippling drapery to her ripe bosom, about to bite into a blushing pomegranate with her lush crimson lips.

After the trunks were brought up, their room door was finally closed and Anna had triumphantly unhooked a tall trunk that turned out to be a travelling cocktail cabinet, the two ladies kicked off their shoes, unpinned their hats and settled down to make up for four years of gossip over crystal tumblers of whisky and vermouth (a cocktail that Anna was quick to point out was very fashionable in America).

"My dear, what a place you have holed up in," exclaimed Anna. "The air is like lemon drops, it is so full of sour and sweet all at the same time. Do you not get tired of it?"

"Not at all. I have not felt this alive for a long time. Let me tell you, my dear, what I have not been able to write in a letter."

Storytelling went on well into the evening, and seemed disposed to continue all the way into the night, except that both ladies abruptly realised that they had eaten nothing for hours. With exclamations of amazement at the time, both ladies set themselves to rights and descended to the restaurant, a little giddy and girlish, and ordered a great deal more food than two ladies could reasonably eat, except they finished it all.

"That is an excellent roast beef," said Anna, patting her stomach lovingly. "I wonder if they hired a chef from England?"

"The kitchen staff are Hainanese," said Miss Cassidy, sleepily chasing a blackcurrant doused in custard around her plate. "British food in Singapore is all cooked by Hainanese chefs."

"Perhaps British food in Britain ought to be cooked by Hainanese chefs then. Ooh," she burped, "pardon me."

This seemed very funny to them both, and they laughed and laughed, until Miss Cassidy became aware that a waiter was standing deferentially at her elbow, and had been for some time. "Miss Leda Cassidy?" he enquired politely. "There is a gentleman to see you."

"Oh," exclaimed Anna, "perhaps your Mr Kay has missed you so much that he has come for his evening chat."

"He is not *my* Mr Kay," said Miss Cassidy crossly.

"Not yet, perhaps," murmured Anna. "Who is it, then?"

It was Haresh Nair, and he looked so pale that Miss Cassidy instantly became sober. "What is it?" she exclaimed as she hurried across to the hotel reception desk where he stood. "What has happened?"

"I am so sorry, Miss Cassidy, I know you are on holiday. Mr Kay said to look for you here. He says to come at once... although I do not know what you could possibly do..."

"Mr Nair, speak plainly—has there been an accident?"

"We don't know. Perhaps." He ran his fingers through his hair. "It's the twins, Miss Cassidy. They have gone missing."

XVII

Miss Cassidy to the Rescue

"THEY were babysitting for me," said Mui Ee hoarsely. She was holding her children so tightly to her that both were crying in terror, unable to understand. "Yeling had Ah Boy and Yezi was carrying Ah Girl. I saw them playing five stones. I went into the kitchen to check on the porridge, and I heard my daughter scream. I thought she hurt herself. I came out and..."

She gestured. It was a very strange scene. The furniture in the courtyard was overturned, lying this way and that; it was all stone garden furniture, far too heavy for the twins to have knocked over by accident. The grass around the tumbled furniture was very wet, as were both the children—soaked through as though they had been in a thunderstorm, although it was a clear, dry evening.

Pandan Villa was in disarray. Every servant had been sent out to search, the men in the fields and undergrowth and the women out in the nearby streets, rousing neighbours, importuning passers-by. There was a tall Sikh police officer speaking to Boon; not far from him, a group of burly tattooed men were speaking to Leong, men Miss Cassidy recognised as belonging to the secret society 1416 that Mr Kay paid for protection on the wharves.

"Searchers have been sent out?" asked Miss Cassidy.

"Yes, everywhere," said Mui Ee tearfully. "Someone was sent to Mr Kay on the docks, and he asked men from 1416 to come, and called the police."

Anna, who had accompanied Miss Cassidy, partly to help and partly for the excitement, asked her in a language only they knew, "Where is the siofra?"

But Miss Cassidy did not have to look; Wong Mi had seen her, and was running towards her, face pale. Without preamble she took Miss Cassidy's hand and pressed the green glass bottle into it. It was empty, the top unscrewed. "I went to look for it the moment I could," she whispered. "I found it in our yard, like this. The toyol has escaped."

"Escaped? No," said Anna grimly, "it has been summoned—by its original master."

They were interrupted by a loud crash, the main door being shoved violently open, knocking over a tall plant pot. Mr Kay had arrived.

Miss Cassidy had never seen him so angry. Pale and furious, he turned instantly upon Mui Ee and demanded, "What has happened? Who has taken my daughters?"

"Mr Kay," began Miss Cassidy, whereupon he turned his wrath upon her.

"You! You and your holidays! If you had been here, if you had stayed within my doors—"

223

"It was not her fault," said Anna, laying a hand upon his arm.

Mr Kay stared at her, startled. "Who are you?"

"I am Leda's sister Anna, and I can help. Let this lady calm her children; they are cold and frightened."

"Cold? Why are they—"

He broke off as he finally noticed the state of the courtyard. Bewildered, exasperated, he exclaimed, "I...I don't understand. My house is always under guard. There are always men at my gates, and at my warehouses. The 1416 men say nobody who is not part of the household has come in or out. The police who patrol Pandan Villa Loop say the same. On three sides we have busy streets and neighbours, and behind us is an open field, all shrubs and low plants. There is nowhere to go, nowhere to not be seen. If someone has taken them, or..." he paused, pressed his lips together, and continued more quietly, "or brought harm upon them, they would have a hard time carrying away two grown girls with no one noticing."

Miss Cassidy said, "Mui Ee, ask Ah Boy what he saw."

Mui Ee, rocking her children, tried to coax a few words from her sobbing son. "He says," she said, rather confused, "a little boy came to play with them. Yeling and Yezi tried to ask who he was, but he couldn't speak. Then he tried to play with Ah Boy and Ah Girl, but the twins wouldn't let him. He tried to bite Yeling, and the girls said something like, 'We can see you, go away, don't touch the children.' They tried to grab him. And then they all—he says they fell through the ground."

Wong Mi bent to take the little boy's hands, and asked gently, "What did the little boy look like? Was he fat or skinny?"

"Skinny," said Ah Boy, sniffling, but rather liking the attention now that he was calm.

"Tall or short?"

"Short. Shorter than me."

"Did he have hair?"

"No, he was all bald and shiny," said Ah Boy after solemn consideration. "Like a fruit."

"And he was naked?"

"Yes. It was funny. His thing was dangling."

Wong Mi looked up at Miss Cassidy meaningfully. "He saw…it," she said, and Miss Cassidy's lips tightened.

Mr Kay took a step forward, as if he might seize and shake Wong Mi, so Miss Cassidy interposed herself between them and said sharply, "Kay Loban, I'm afraid your ill fortune has now caught up with you. Since you have already sent out as many people to search as is humanly possible, there is nothing else we can do. Let Yoke Jie and Mui Ee stay by the telephone for news. Your sons can stay with the police and the secret society men, and monitor their progress."

"Miss Cassidy," he said heavily, "what are they looking for? What will they…find?"

"They will find your daughters—lost in the jungle, but safe and sound," said Anna primly. "Leda," she added in their ancient tongue, "we must be quick now. What can we use?"

"I will get something from their rooms."

Mr Kay seized her by the arm as she turned. "Wherever you are going," he said ferociously, "and whatever you are doing, you are including me this time, Miss Cassidy."

"Mr Kay, please! There is no time to waste."

"Indeed. Let us not waste it then. Tell me what to do."

"Leda, don't argue," said Anna urgently, "let him come with us, if he must. We can always fix it later."

"Oh, very well," Miss Cassidy growled in exasperation, and seized Mr Kay's hand.

To Mr Kay it must have seemed like they were running at some inhuman speed, over the courtyard, up the stairs and through the halls to the twins' room, for it was hardly a breath later that they were there, and Miss Cassidy was rummaging through their drawers and cupboards, muttering to herself in that strange guttural language that made the hairs rise on his arms. "What are you looking for?" he asked. "Tell me what to do."

"I am looking for something the girls love, and have close to their skin. But it must belong specifically to each girl—it cannot be something they share."

"They share everything," Mr Kay said blankly. "They even still sleep in the same bed."

"You see why it is difficult. Ah!"

Miss Cassidy pulled out the two outfits made for their matchmaking, one pink and one blue. "They have never shared these," she said triumphantly. "They wore these so that the suitors would not mix them up. Give me scissors, Mr Kay—there, in their workbasket."

Miss Cassidy harvested a knot button from each blouse. It seemed again to Mr Kay that he only blinked and they were back in the courtyard, and Anna was removing her gloves to receive a blue button in her hands. "You seek the older girl,

Yeling," said Miss Cassidy. "Take Mr Kay with you, so she will not be frightened. I will find Yezi."

Anna did not stop to explain. She grabbed Mr Kay by the hand, and said, "Take a deep breath."

The ground suddenly fell out from beneath Mr Kay's feet. Pandan Villa's green walls flashed and swirled and disappeared. All the air seemed to get sucked out of his lungs, and there was a great intense darkness, a strange pressure and the scent of stone and earth and fire. The being holding his hand was, briefly, not a respectable woman in buttoned boots, but a creature ancient and dangerous and full of blood and flame.

And then she was again a respectable woman in buttoned boots, and she was looking at him with concern. "Bear up, Ah Tong," she said. "We must hurry."

She had used his old childhood name, which he had not heard since his father died and he became Kay Loban. It felt as if his mother were dragging him by the hand along the wet ground, a distant beautiful woman who had always overawed him with her glowing fragile smile.

He looked around, puzzled. "Why, we are at the seaside," he said, staring at the gravelly beach unfurling before them, bordered thickly with jungle and greenery. The night-time air was alive with insects and the howl and screech of predator birds in the trees. "What is this place?"

"It is an island," said Anna, still dragging him along with strides that were surely far too gigantic even for a woman of her stature. "It is called Death Comes from Behind You."

"That…that is an unusual translation for the name of this island."

"Is it? I have heard worse. But I only translate the gist of its meaning—I do not speak the language of those who named it. You would probably know its proper name better than I. Quickly, man!"

Mr Kay was already breathless, but he tried to quicken his steps nevertheless. "Are my daughters here?" he asked.

Anna looked at the small blue button in her palm. "Yes," she said, "at least, one of them is. But if you want to keep her safe, you must be quiet and let me do what is needed. Do you understand?"

"You are Miss Cassidy's sister?"

"Yes. I am one of her sisters."

"Then I trust you."

"How reassuring," said Anna coolly, and Mr Kay was torn between wanting to laugh and to box the lady's ears. But he obediently followed her, and when she said, "Shh," and pointed, he accordingly looked up and kept quiet.

It was hard not to cry out, though. Neatly arranged on a bed of seaweed, his unconscious daughter lay very blue and still; hovering over her was what appeared to be a man, naked, his skin a strange grey-green colour, slick and shining and dripping with dark oil.

"Orang minyak," said Mr Kay, amazed, and Anna shushed him too late. The orang minyak looked up.

"Stay here," she hissed, and stepped forward from the shrubbery, picking leaves off her clothes, shaking sand from her shoes. "Keep away," she said in disgust to the oily man, who was coming towards her curiously. "Where is your master? Or mistress? You are in thrall to someone, or you would have devoured this girl already."

"Siapa?" the slimy creature hissed.

"Who am I? My name is Anna. If you attack me, you will die," she added in a matter-of-fact way.

The monster bared all his teeth in a grin, and leapt at her.

Mr Kay did not manage to catch what happened next, or how it happened. All he saw was the orang minyak bursting suddenly into flame, head to toe, from no apparent source. The monster screeched and ran into the sea, but the flames continued to burn, and the creature continued to scream, and Anna stood on the beach and watched it, calmly, as it thrashed its way to a torturous end.

"What a very odd creature," she said. When the monster had fallen to ash, Anna looked around her and finally said, "Come, Mr Kay."

Yeling was waking up. She did not at first recognise her father; she was coughing, choking, gasping for air. Anna took hold of her head, turned her onto her side, and gave her back a great thump. Poor Yeling vomited out a copious amount of oily water, then sat limp and exhausted for a moment before crying out, "Papa!"

Mr Kay seized and soothed her, but she pushed him away very quickly and said, "Where is Yezi?"

"Yeling," said Anna, "can you first tell me what happened to you? What did you see?"

Yeling made a face. "A horrible little boy," she murmured. "We were minding the children. One of our five stones went into the bushes, and Ah Boy went to get it. And this dreadful, naked little boy came out of the bushes holding his hand. We could see it was unclean," she explained to Anna. "We see these things, you know, Yezi and I. It wouldn't speak to us, and it tried to hold Ah Girl's hand too. We pulled it away, and it attacked us. I heard a voice shouting for it—a woman's voice, a horrible, cold sort of voice. It shouted, 'Bring me the children, hurry, hurry!' But we grabbed it; I had its legs, Yezi had its arms, and it couldn't get free. And then all of a sudden we fell into water, and it was dark, and there was this...this lady there..."

"What did the lady look like?" asked Anna. "Think hard—it is important."

Yeling shuddered. "She...she had no legs, I think. Or maybe she had many legs, but they were soft, like a sotong. She was translucent like a sotong too, all white, and I could see her bones and blood underneath her skin. Her hair was like snakes, all moving around."

"Hah," said Anna triumphantly.

"She was angry when she saw us. She wanted Ah Boy and Ah Girl. She said...she said Yezi would have to do, since she is the younger of the two of us, and she gave me to this other thing, this oily man... He kissed me, it was horrible, I think he was going to drown me..."

"I had better hurry," said Anna. "If this lady is whom I suspect she is, Leda cannot deal with her alone. Mr Kay, take your daughter home—"

230

"I am coming with you for Yezi," said Mr Kay.

"So am I!" cried Yeling. "I cannot leave her alone!"

Anna sighed.

Miss Cassidy was in a pickle.

"Scylla," she said impatiently. "What on earth are you doing here?"

"Oh! *Scylla*, is it?" snapped the sea witch. "Are we friends, Lady of the Sidhe? I was ancient when your kind were living in mushroom fields and curdling milk. You will show me respect." Scylla clung to the rocks with her many tentacles, her purple blood pulsing through her body. Her eyes were great, large, inky globes that gleamed in the darkness.

Miss Cassidy sighed. They were in a cave, half-submerged in water, through which the sea was constantly rising and falling and pounding. The insufferable toyol was on her shoulder, nibbling at her hair, cutting it away from her head, the fiery strands falling into Scylla's slimy, waiting hands. It had already finished with Yezi, who had also been bound and laid out on a flat stone, her lovely black hair now shorn almost to the scalp, her eyes wide open in terror.

Miss Cassidy could not move, for all her many skills. Scylla was a monster more ancient and terrible than anything Miss Cassidy had ever faced, and she had been bound in place almost from the moment the creature had spotted her. Miss Cassidy had fought hard against her binding (and she could fight very hard indeed, when pressed) but had now decided it was best to save her energy, bide her time and hope Anna would arrive soon.

"I had lovely hair once," mourned the creature. "Golden hair. It will grow back again now—golden, as it once was, like the sun on the sea."

"Scylla—oh, very well, *Lady* Scylla," said Miss Cassidy, "you know that you do not belong here. You are halfway around the world from your home. What are you doing in these waters?"

"Easy enough for you to ask, Miiissss Leeeeda Cassideee," she snarled. "You frippery beasts, who may spend eternity jumping in and out of mortal form as you like, hobnobbing with goddesses and entertaining children with magic tricks! What do you know of the cursed beings? We, who must spend immortal lives in these foul, monstrous bodies, trapped forever in the dark forgotten places of the earth! Have I not power, magic and terrible might? Why should I not answer a summons, as much as you?"

"Who summoned you?"

Scylla laughed sibilantly. "Some foolish mortal woman. She wished to deal in the dark magic of her people, but did not know how. She went to the sea and sought to bargain with the sea gods. But she was neither sailor nor sailor's wife, and they all ignored her—the gods, the goddesses, the spirits, the selkies. So I answered her. Why should I not?"

"Hmm," said Miss Cassidy. "Did she offer you her unborn child?"

"Clever Lady of the Sidhe! Yes. She offered me the child she carried, and I took it, then and there. I tasted its blood—it had been many centuries since I'd had fresh blood—and I refashioned its empty body into the creature she wanted."

"The toyol."

"The imp upon your shoulder, yes. I like these oceans, Miss Leda Cassidy," said the sea witch broodingly, "there are many strange beasts and monsters in these waters that I had never seen before, which I have found useful pets. The magic here is different, dark, blood and meat and bone."

"But the toyol is not yours—it belongs to her family."

"Yes, and how have they treated the poor creature? He did what he was told, then spent sixty years in a bottle. And just as he was freed again, someone—you, Miss Cassidy—put him in an even smaller bottle! You see why he is a little put out, yes?"

"He is a vicious creature, and should never be free to roam and bite and kill," said Miss Cassidy sharply.

"Ah, dark magic has dark consequences, as you well know, fay. Speaking of which, I am glad you have come—I have need of your magic."

"Do you? Is that why you were waiting so patiently for me? I am glad I put on my party dress," said Miss Cassidy with a sigh, for the fine green silk was now soaked through and bedraggled.

"I cannot do it myself."

"Do what?"

"Inhabit a mortal body."

Miss Cassidy glared at Scylla. "Is this what you were trying to do? You wanted the toyol to bring you one of the children, so you could kill it and take its mortal form? What on earth for, Lady Scylla?"

"You dare ask?" the sea hag shrieked, whipping her great tentacles. "I was once beautiful. May I not seek to be beautiful again?"

"Beautiful! Why? What good does it do you?" demanded Miss Cassidy in vexation. "Honestly, you bloody nymphs and nereids and golden-apple goddesses! Is it so important to be beautiful, that you would give up the terror and awe of all mankind, and the magic and power of the ocean? You would sacrifice all this to be a simpering girl with golden hair?"

"Yes!" screamed Scylla. "Yes, yes, yes!"

Miss Cassidy tsked. "Well, I will not do it voluntarily, as you surely know," she said primly. "So you will have to kill me for my magic, and try to figure it out yourself afterwards. I warn you, it is very tricky with a full-grown adult. Changelings were only taken as babies, in our day. I do not know if you can even possess a full-grown body. We might all end up dead, if you don't know what you are doing."

Scylla brought her face close to Miss Cassidy's. "You smell of human," she snarled. "You have been with them too long."

"Since you propose to inhabit a human, I don't see why you should mind."

"I will kill you now," said Scylla, "and collect your magic. And then drown the girl. And then I will walk through the island and consume the men I find."

"Yezi's appetite is small. You will have some trouble, I fear, consuming a whole man, if you inhabit the body of a girl barely five feet tall."

Miss Cassidy tried to wriggle a finger, blink an eyelid—to no avail. Scylla knew well how to bind someone—had she not herself been bound for thousands of years?

Miss Cassidy thought hard. Anna was searching for her; Anna would find her. But she had to find her *in time*.

"I confess," she said at last, "you have conquered me, milady. But do you not feel that I would be more useful if I were in thrall to you? This mediocre child," Miss Cassidy tried to give the impression of waving dismissively, although she could not lift her arm, "surely she is not sufficient for your purposes. I could return to her household; I could bring you the one you really want, the baby girl."

"You are trying to trick me."

"That is sure and certain, as it always is of my kind, Lady Scylla, but I doubt you would be so easily fooled."

"I am not susceptible to your flattery."

"It is not flattery if it is true. Besides, you have power over me, as you have over the toyol—why should I not do your bidding, as it did?"

"I will not be fooled," snarled Scylla. "I will not be lied to, tricked, or treated like one of your gormless human pets. Do you think I have forgotten how you turned men into swine for your own amusement?"

Miss Cassidy started to answer, but could say no more. Scylla would not be stalled any longer; she swarmed over Miss Cassidy's trapped body, and the cold white tentacles were sliding down her throat, slime filling her nostrils, choking and suffocating her. Miss Cassidy could feel the world growing blank and dark, her body filling with ice...

...and then the pressure was ripped off her, and Miss Cassidy was on her knees, able to move once more, violently throwing up.

As though from a great distance, she heard the sound of running footsteps. A voice cried out, "Yezi! Yezi, are you all right?" The only answer was a series of painful gurgling coughs.

"Get up," exclaimed a familiar voice, "she needs help—get up, Miss Cassidy."

"Mr Kay?" she spluttered, but there was no time for more. Anna had seized Scylla in both arms, and was having a tremendously difficult time keeping hold of the thrashing, shrieking thing.

"No!" screamed the sea monster. "No, why are *you* here?"

"Why should I not be?" said Anna. "There are times, my dear, when I am everywhere you look."

To Mr Kay and the twins, what their eyes saw did not wholly make sense. Scylla's many tentacles from her head and her lower body were twining about Anna, thrashing, tugging and pulling, but she seemed unconcerned, only tightening her grip around the slippery body. It also seemed, strangely, that Anna was growing bigger, that her arms and legs were growing and rippling, that her long dark hair was tumbling into the water and becoming liquid.

"Miss Cassidy," cried Yezi hoarsely, "don't—don't!"

Mr Kay, clinging to his daughters, could see that Scylla's tentacles were still grabbing at Miss Cassidy, but in contrast to Anna, Miss Cassidy seemed to be growing smaller. Her green eyes appeared to be getting larger in her face, and her half-shorn red hair was drifting upwards, without wind.

The toyol ran shrieking at Miss Cassidy, who simply caught it, and held it dangling by one leg. "We cannot fight her here!" yelled Miss Cassidy. "Her power comes from the ocean. She must be separated from the water."

"Are we not ladies of fire and iron?" said Anna, and her voice was strange, ancient, guttural, echoing. "Come with me, sister. We shall get this done."

A great light was now blazing about Anna, as Scylla the sea monster screamed in rage. Miss Cassidy took a deep breath—then gathered up her skirts in her free hand (the other still gripped the outraged toyol) and ran towards them.

"Miss Cassidy!" shouted Mr Kay. "Miss Cassidy!"

She turned, at the very last moment, before she stopped looking at all like Miss Cassidy. And she shouted, "I'm sorry. Go home! Take a boat!"

The light became blinding. And then they were gone.

XVIII

Miss Cassidy Meets a Handsome Prince

I N the days when Miss Cassidy was young (although Anna was already old by then), the world was full of her kind. They flowed through the sap of every tree, and burned in the fires of every hearth. They were hidden but heard, soulless but seen, and in those days, those who knew how could trap one of the fay folk to do their bidding.

It was a time when the border between worlds was soft and permeable, and there was nothing especially unusual about ghosts, ghouls and gods living quite comfortably alongside human villages and cities. In those days, there was no need for Miss Cassidy's kind to hide behind a respectable—acceptable—conventional façade.

So there was nothing at all surprising about the fact that Anna was standing there chatting, quite matter-of-factly, to a beautiful young woman in gold-woven cloth, or that Anna was standing in a fire, or that she was nearly ten feet tall and made of stone.

Miss Cassidy was quite accustomed to seeing Anna in her traditional form (which, reproduced in various types of stone, stood in many museums around the world), but the same could not be said of Anna, who started when Miss Cassidy hovered over her shoulder. "Gracious," she said, "I'd forgotten what an odd little critter you are, little sister."

"Never mind that," said Miss Cassidy crossly, though her words emerged as a buzzy tinkle that only Anna could understand. "Where are we? What has happened to Scylla?"

"We are in the Golden Khersonese."

Miss Cassidy thought hard. "So," she said at last, "we are in the same place, but a different time. Which is why I cannot manifest properly. Why did you bring Scylla here?"

"Unfortunately, I did not intend to. I meant to bring her back to the place she is supposedly bound to—but she fought hard enough to pull us the wrong way."

"Where is she now?"

"I will find out," said Anna with stony patience, "if you give me half a chance to finish speaking to Naga Bari."

The beautiful Princess Naga Bari (for she was a princess, and did not look so very different from Princess Nora, either) smiled up at what appeared to her to be a cluster of glittering sparks, and waved a magnificent golden dagger.

"This little sister doesn't belong here," she said, not unkindly. "She cannot take form."

"Not yet—she is too young, in this place and time."

Naga Bari reached out and touched the shifting sparks that were now drifting down Anna's mighty, granite-hewed arm. "How fascinating she is," she murmured.

Miss Cassidy might have said the same, except Naga Bari would not have been able to understand her. The golden-garbed princess stood with bare feet on the banks of a gleaming green lake, lush with life—teeming with dragonflies, frogs, fish and flowers. Her long dark hair was unbound and trailed past her ankles into the water—indeed, it seemed as if the water was flowing from that sheet of glistening black hair.

"I saw the beast you are looking for, Great Lady," Naga Bari said at last to Anna. "She fell from the sky and tried to dive into my lake, but I cast her away. She would have poisoned my waters. I tried to bind her, but she is powerful—she broke free, and I think she is making her way to the sea."

"We cannot let her reach the ocean," said Miss Cassidy urgently.

"Indeed. Thank you, Naga Bari."

"Leave me a blessing, Great Lady, if you wish to thank me."

"Gladly. May your waters never run dry, as long as your people need them."

Naga Bari bowed. Anna folded her heavy fingers over Miss Cassidy, and in a whirl of heat and flame, they moved on.

It was becoming clear, however, that they would not make it in time. Storm clouds were already rolling in, blue and thick; the wind was up and thunder had begun to rumble. They raced past the villages—through the thick lashing forests—over the spiked roofs of glittering cities—across the sails of ships hurrying to harbour—to the island at the tip of the peninsula, disregarding the startled faces of hundreds of people, and the echoing shouts of sailors and traders and pirates and princes.

But Scylla was already in the sea.

The rain beat down. The sky hung low and ominous. The ocean, stirred by her rage, was heaving, churning, reaching up to seize and break ships, drag down and drown sailors. "Hold on," cried Anna, "we must catch her. Take good hold!"

And they plunged into the churning wine-dark sea, a trail of searing fire.

Miss Cassidy was not a creature of the sea; although Scylla had accused her of "turning men to swine", she was only a very distant relation to the ancient goddesses Scylla was familiar with. It was very hard to keep hold of Anna's shoulder, very hard to concentrate on keeping herself in one piece, as the heaving waters roiled and struck them.

They felt Scylla's tentacles before they saw her—indeed, it was nearly impossible to "see" her, for she had grown. Enormously.

The power of the ocean had fed her fury, and she had ballooned to monstrous proportions. Her voice was the clamour of thunder, her mouth a gaping maw of churning brine, her every thrashing tentacle sending waves surging and crashing, smashing poor souls into the sharp rocks.

"*YOU WILL NOT TAKE ME!*" she roared, and the immensity of her voice turned the cry into a thundercrack that shook the heavens.

"We'll see about that," said Anna crisply, and she lunged forward and plunged directly...down Scylla's throat.

Scylla shrieked. Lightning crashed. Miss Cassidy was thrown off from the sheer speed of Anna's attack, and decided she had best get out of the way and help the poor humans thrashing about on the waves. After a few wild, panicky transmutations, she decided on the form of a large dolphin, and began to swim with all her might towards the nearest kicking legs.

She could not do much more than shove floating debris towards flailing fishermen, in a valiant effort to keep them at least afloat, but she did her best. The waves continued to heave and the sky continued to hurl lightning, as Anna battled the sea monster in a building maelstrom of heat and flame. Miss Cassidy could see the blossoms of golden fire down below in the murk as she leapt, gasping, through the battering water.

Leda!

Panting, Miss Cassidy paused a moment in the water. "What do you need?"

I need metal. I must bind her.

"Metal! Where am I to find metal?"

Find it, Leda! Or she will escape again!

Desperately, Miss Cassidy leapt through the waves. There was no metal to be had, not in sufficient amounts—a nail here or there would not do. She spied a single ship, what must have been the very last boat still in one piece on the sea—a beautiful, strongly built, slim-bowed vessel, cutting neatly through the thrashing waves. But the men aboard were clearly struggling, and among them, Miss Cassidy saw it.

A crown. One of them was wearing a crown.

She raced towards it. The men saw her, but they were too busy fighting to stay upright to take heed of her, though she jumped furiously around them to get their attention. Besides, they could not understand her. "Prince," she cried, "Prince!" But all they heard was frantic squeaking.

She had to make him look at her. But how?

Leda, if you don't hurry, we are done for!

Miss Cassidy leapt as high as she could into the air, and halfway through the leap, she transformed into a white lion.

It was the only thing she could think of. She knew Singapore meant Lion City, although she did not know why; the only time she had asked, Sarah Jane Bendemeer did not know. But there must have been a reason the place was named as such even though lions were not native to the region. Lions must have a meaning, and surely a lion's sudden appearance would make the prince look up...*and he did.*

He stared. What he saw must have been perplexing—a white, glittering, male lion (Miss Cassidy judged, rightly, that it was a proud male lion with a flowing mane that the city was probably named after, not the female lions who actually did all the grunt work), half-transformed out of the gleaming blue body of a dolphin. But the prince was looking, and that was all Miss Cassidy needed.

"I need your crown!" shouted Miss Cassidy, and it came out as an echoing roar.

In a different time, in a different place, nothing would have happened. But this was a world where the boundaries between realms were soft, and human eyes could see through them more often than they can now. The prince did not question what he saw, and though he did not understand what she said, he knew what she wanted.

He took off his crown and flung it into the sea.

It all happened in but a split-second—this prince clearly was good at snap decisions. Miss Cassidy, returning to dolphin form, seized the crown by looping it around her nose, and plunged into a dizzying dive. So rapid was her descent that she became lightheaded, though she quickly reached the place where Anna—terrible Anna, fury and flame and molten stone—held Scylla gripped in her great arms. Anna looked up, and her eyes were burning pits, and her hair was spitting snakes.

This metal is powerful. It has meaning. Thank you.

"You're welcome," said Miss Cassidy.

Anna gripped the golden crown, and with powerful fingers as mighty as mountains, *bent it into shape...*

...and Scylla began to scream, and shrink, and struggle, and fall into her new golden prison...

...while the seas started to calm and the storm to abate...

...while the young prince raised his uncrowned head and looked up in wonder...

...and Miss Cassidy lost consciousness, and knew nothing more.

PART THREE

1904

THE SCHOOLHOUSE SEANCE

XIX

Miss Cassidy Gets a Letter

"A ND he fastened the demon to a rock by tying down its hair with his fishing net," said Miss Cassidy, demonstrating the tying of a large invisible knot with her hands, "and when the demon asked, 'What do you want?' Badang wished for great strength."

The children gathered in the pretty little schoolroom were of various ages, sizes and states of untidiness, but all were now sitting still—a very rare phenomenon—and gazing rapt at Miss Cassidy. There was a chilly breeze in the air, but inside, clustered together around the cheerful pot-bellied stove, and around their fascinating instructress, all were warm and comfortable.

"Miss Cassidy, why did he not ask for great wealth?" asked one child.

"Or to become king?" asked another.

"Or to be handsome so he could have a beautiful wife?" asked a third.

Miss Cassidy pondered the question. The children liked her

because she always took their questions seriously, and never answered, as other adults did, "Because I say so." "Well," she said at last, "I think because the strength of his body would belong to him alone. Wealth can be stolen, power can be usurped, and beauty—well, beauty is nice to have, but it has not got much practical value, has it?"

The children thought about this deeply. "It would still be nice to be beautiful," said one of the older girls at last, wistfully. "I hope I am beautiful, when I grow up."

"A very natural hope, Charlotte, as long as it is not your only one."

The boy at the next desk, scoffing at the nonsense girls say, asked eagerly, "Then what happened, Miss Cassidy?"

"Well! The demon said, 'I can give you great strength, but you must eat whatever I give you from my mouth.'"

"And what was it?"

"What did he give him?"

"Well, children," Miss Cassidy said, drawing out the moment, "what comes out of your mouth?"

"Teeth!"

"Saliva!"

"Ugh!"

"Sick!"

"Alas, James is right," said Miss Cassidy, shaking her head mournfully. "The demon, ahem, 'sicked' up all the fish it had stolen from Badang, and Badang had to eat it all to gain great strength!"

"Ooh, that's horrible!" cried the children in delight, though Charlotte looked a little green. "Did he do it?"

"Yes, he did, and it was much worse than the spinach you never eat, James," said Miss Cassidy with mock severity, and little James made a face. "And Badang became very mighty. He could uproot trees with just his arms, and fling great boulders many miles—"

Miss Cassidy was interrupted by the peal of the church bells. The children looked disappointed as she clapped her hands and announced, "Very well, that's all for today! I will see you all tomorrow. Remember to bring me your ciphering books. And James and Charles, do not tease the cat."

"Will you finish the story tomorrow, Miss Cassidy?" asked James eagerly.

"Yes, I will, if you are good. Now go on, your mother is waiting."

The children burst out of the little schoolhouse like devils set free. It was a glorious spring day, and Miss Cassidy did not bother telling them not to run, not even the older girls. The cat was well out of their way, snoozing in the rain gutter.

James' mother had come to meet him, a slender fair-haired lady, neatly and modestly dressed, carrying a covered straw basket. After kissing her son on the top of his head, she smiled at Miss Cassidy, and took her hand.

"Mrs Weston, how do you do?"

"Miss Cassidy, really! I know you keep trying in front of the children, but it is just too odd for you to call me Mrs Weston."

"Very well, Sarah Jane," said Miss Cassidy, smiling. "I must say, I find it unnatural myself. Is the curate well?"

"Yes, he will be home today. I have an ulterior motive related to that, Miss Cassidy—I have tried a new recipe for currant buns, and I want your opinion of them first. You know how Edward likes currant buns."

"I do, and so do I," said Miss Cassidy, beaming. "Come in, Sarah Jane—I have tea already on. James, will you have some milk?" But James preferred to take a currant bun out of the straw basket and run about the yard holding it in his mouth, trying to rouse the cat.

The village schoolmistress' home was two rooms attached to the back of the school itself—generous lodgings considering both the size of the school and the size of the village. Miss Cassidy had planted a garden in the backyard, reminiscent of the vegetable garden in Pandan Villa that her little priest's hut used to overlook more than four years ago, except here she grew sweet peas and potatoes instead of yams and cabbage. The sweet pea seeds had been given to her by Anna, and always blossomed profusely in season, covering her little green patch with a riot of pinks and purples. "Your flowers always look so lovely," said Sarah Jane. "My geraniums have been looking very seedy."

Miss Cassidy smiled. Sarah Jane Weston was, quite literally, a world away from Sarah Jane Bendemeer. She had married Edward Weston, a poor curate, two years after returning to England. She'd sent a letter, written with kindness and affection, to Haresh Nair, who had then returned her locket by post with his congratulations and good wishes. Miss Cassidy herself now possessed this locket, and the silver bangles Haresh had given Sarah Jane as a parting gift—mementos Mrs Weston felt were best not kept in her own jewellery box, with their weight of memory.

Captain Bendemeer had died only two months after seeing his first grandson christened after him, leaving Sarah Jane a wisely hoarded fortune that had, after all, been meant to support a much larger family. Sarah Jane Weston and her curate had therefore become not so poor, and the village school's extension was a donation made in Captain Bendemeer's name.

Sarah Jane was now an active curate's wife. Ah Nai had passed on not long after the Captain, and her brother had chosen to return to their family in China, feeling lost without his sister's sharp tongue to guide him. So Sarah Jane now managed her household alone, with a husband and three small children, along with the needs of the parish, the women's church organisation, the village school, Sunday school and all the various unending work required of a curate's wife in a small isolated village. She had put on weight, become strong, wise and cheerful—blossomed, in short, with hard work and purpose.

As they ate fresh hot currant buns with new butter, Sarah Jane said softly, "Miss Cassidy, I have never asked you how you came to be on the path to our church that day, wet through and with nothing but the clothes on your back. I am glad you did, for you came at just the right time, but it is still a remarkably strange coincidence, is it not?"

"Hmm. I suppose it is."

"Especially considering how far we are from everything on this island, and the last letter Papa had from you was still sent from Singapore."

"Indeed. I had to leave quite suddenly, you see."

"I have noticed, Miss Cassidy, that people hardly ever do ask you important questions. It is most remarkable."

"What sort of questions do you mean, my dear?"

"Oh, I don't know, like, 'Where did you come from? Why are you here? How do you know the things you know, and do the things you do?' Who are you, really, Miss Cassidy?"

Miss Cassidy smiled. "For the moment, I am Miss Leda Cassidy, village schoolmistress, and friend and protector of the curate's wife."

Sarah Jane smiled faintly. "Thank you, Miss Cassidy. I should rather have you on my side than all the armies of Christendom. But I have a specific question today, that you will not mind answering—have you heard, lately, from Haresh?"

"Lately? Mr Nair's last letter to me was, I think, four months ago. If he has written again, the letter is probably still on its way to me."

"Well, I have heard from him. A wife has been arranged for him, and he will be married soon. Indeed, he probably already has been, since he went to the post. Here is the letter—he has asked me to show it to you."

Miss Cassidy licked the butter from her fingers, and accepted the letter with great curiosity, written and crossed in Haresh Nair's precise, businesslike script.

Dear Mrs Weston,

I hope this letter finds you and your husband well, and your children thriving.

I considered a long time before deciding to write to you, for it is perhaps not appropriate that we should be in regular correspondence, but I think on the whole it is best. My mother has spent a year trying to arrange a marriage for me, for I am "growing old", she says (I am thirty this past April), and I am her only unmarried son, it is most disgraceful, etc. As I no longer have poverty as an excuse, having now a perfectly adequate salary to raise a troop of children, I have finally agreed to it. I have been writing to the lady in question for a few months, and as she seems a lovely, sensible, warm-hearted sort—well, in short, she is already on a ship en route, with an assortment of cousins as chaperones, and a dowry of tea and sugar, and we will be married when she arrives. There is a nice house for her to be married into, and even a servant to help her. I wish your father were still alive, so I could show him that his advice was sound, even though the end result of it is a bit different than we first planned on.

Once we are settled, out of respect to Shadha (my new wife), and indeed to you, I will write no more letters to other ladies of my acquaintance. But if you would like, write to her as my sisters might; I should like us all to remain friends, in some small way.

Now, there is also the matter of Miss Cassidy.

Miss Cassidy is a dear friend, and I trust and hope she regards me with the same affection. To this day I have kept her secret—none of the Kay family knows where she is, nor are they aware that we are in correspondence. Once I am married, however, again I cannot be writing to unmarried ladies without disrespect to my wife.

Indeed, it has been difficult to keep this secret. The ladies of the house were very much distressed in the beginning, when the message from Miss Cassidy's sister came, saying they were both obliged to go away immediately, with Miss Cassidy's great love and sorrow. That "great love and sorrow" drove Mr Kay into quite a rage, for some reason. Well, I know the reason, but I must pretend I don't.

If not for his oldest daughter-in-law, Mr Kay would still be raging now. The woman is a gem. Everybody is all right, she said: his grandchildren are all right, his daughters are all right (and Yezi's hair grew back very quickly, besides), his family is all right. Even the second daughter-in-law seemed more cheerful than usual. And they all know that no harm came to Miss Cassidy; she left suddenly, as employees sometimes do, but she did not steal, lie or cheat, and that should be enough. Of course, it was not, but life had to go on, and it did. Mr Kay has an army of grandchildren now, two each from his daughters-in-law, twins from Yeling in Mr Tong's household, and one more on the way from Yezi, in Mr De Souza's household. I think Mr Kay finds great joy in this, but nevertheless he broods when no one is around to keep him occupied.

In short, Mrs Weston, since I must reluctantly give up Miss Cassidy as a penfriend, I wish she would choose one of the Kay family to write to, one whom she feels would keep her secret, if she chooses to continue keeping it.

Miss Cassidy has never told me, but I still want to know what happened the day the twins went missing. It was all quite mysterious. The girls and Mr Kay arrived at the docks in a bumboat from Pulau Blakang Mati, an island with nothing but jungle and a few fishermen's families. Everyone was wet through, Yezi's hair was cut off, and nobody could remember anything. Mr Kay does not recall how he reached the island, but he says he found the girls standing in the jungle, lost and confused, and they too did not know how they came to be there. They luckily found a fisherman willing to take them back to shore, and we all had a most confusing time afterwards trying to make sense of it all to the police.

The girls were married not long after, in quite a merry double-wedding. I got the sense that Mr Kay wanted them safe, and thought them safer with their respective new husbands than in Pandan Villa.

Now, as to my last bit of news, and it pertains directly to Miss Cassidy. Pandan Villa is to be sold. The senior Mr Kay is retiring. His business, and most of the servants of the household, go largely to his older son, who has decided to purchase a smaller home closer to town. The new Kay Loban has kept on all his father's staff, including myself, but he has discontinued the paying of protection money to the secret societies. In truth, there is nothing they can do about it—their time is over.

The younger son, Kay Leong, has started his own business, and he and his family intend to move to Penang. The twin girls, of course, each have their own household. Their father has not yet decided whether he will live with one of them or alone, but I think he inclines towards living alone, probably with old Yoke Jie and Mat to help him.

255

I believe, personally, that the fate of Miss Cassidy still weighs heavily on his mind. Now that he is growing older, and giving up his business, I think it will do so more than ever. Mrs Weston, please show Miss Cassidy my letter, and may it convince her to pen a few kind words to make an old man happy.

My great affection, respect, and admiration are yours always,

Haresh Nair

"Hmm," said Miss Cassidy.

"I know that 'Hmm'," said Sarah Jane, buttering another currant bun. "Come, Miss Cassidy—Haresh and I both know you too well. You wish to write to Mr Kay, but you feel you should not."

"I absolutely should not," said Miss Cassidy stoutly. "There are many reasons I should not. For one, Anna would think me mad."

"Well," said Sarah Jane mildly, "keep the letter, and think it over. Haresh meant it more for you, anyway. Gracious, the bells—is that the time? I must go now; the ladies' auxiliary club is meeting with me in half an hour. Good day, Miss Cassidy."

That night was a brisk one. It was a cold she had missed while she lived in India and in Singapore, that sharp freshness in the air. Miss Cassidy could not sleep, so at around midnight, she got out of bed and sat by her window, dreamily watching the wind stir the leaves outside. Night in the village was very dark, very silent; it had been difficult to get used to it, after the noise and bustle, the crickets and critters, of a tropical colonial night.

She did not think she would ever go back to the colonies. She had been fortunate in Singapore, to avoid most of the worst of it—the opium dens, the race riots, the pirates who brought down ships on the open sea, the secret society dealings. She had witnessed worse in India, seen the British rob the Maharajahs of the very jewels from their crowns, seen a despicable trade in slavery far worse than she had ever known, from days when slaves had been conquered in war, not snatched wholesale like beasts herded from a field. Miss Cassidy had lived in brutal worlds and was used to them, but she was, for now, tired of them. For the moment, anyway, she wished to remain in a world run by women, where the food was better, the washing was thorough, a stitch was always done in time, and one never wasted energy and breath on trying to save the world, merely on keeping one's children safe from the world's dangers.

Miss Cassidy twiddled and twiddled her fingers. "She'll think me mad," she repeated to herself, now and then. And then, "It will make things worse." And then, "I really shouldn't, I really should not."

And then, with a kind of despair, Miss Cassidy gave up the fight.

It only took a moment to fill a saucer with water and place it by the window, under the light of the waning moon. It took a little longer for Miss Cassidy to calm herself enough to actually begin, but when she did, everything was crystal clear.

The first image that came was of Yezi. She clearly had a large mirror in her bedroom, from which hung the Chinese knot with the hematite bead that Miss Cassidy had made for the twins before her unexpected departure. She was not asleep with her husband; she sat in a large easy chair in the gentle morning light, patting her very pregnant belly, softly humming.

Though her face was still sweet and pretty, she looked quite different from the little schoolgirl Miss Cassidy had last seen. She wore a lovely pale-green dressing down and beaded bedroom slippers, her hair now fashionably short and her nails varnished a deep red. It was clear that Charles De Souza had found himself the perfect wife for the business in which he was engaged. Miss Cassidy smiled, sent Yezi a blessing for her baby, and moved on.

Yeling was still asleep. She too had the Chinese knot hanging off her mirror; her small son slept between her and her husband Yang in the same bed, clearly refusing to remain in the nearby cot. Yeling's hair was still long, now neatly bound in a single braid; the hand resting on her son's back was slightly ink-stained. The room was made pretty by her touch: gossamer curtains, flowers in familiar-looking vases, a scattering of homemade children's toys. Miss Cassidy blessed her as well, and moved on.

Wong Mi was drowsily awake with her baby at her breast, seated in a comfortable rocking chair, while Leong snored lightly in bed. Longevity Wing looked a bit different, toys and children's clothes scattered here and there, crumbs on the tables, unwashed cutlery in the kitchen. Altogether, it was an improvement, thought Miss Cassidy as she left her blessing.

Mui Ee was wide awake when Miss Cassidy peeped in at her, putting on her slippers in readiness to head to the kitchen to start the fire. She looked the same: ageless, eternal, more absolutely immortal in her place and role in the world than Miss Cassidy or Anna could ever be. She yawned widely, surprised at the suddenness of it, as she clump-clump-clumped down the stairs and shooed pigeons from her yard. Miss Cassidy offered her such a hearty blessing that Mui Ee actually turned and frowned, as if she had heard it, and Miss Cassidy hurried quickly away.

Miss Cassidy paused. "Well," she muttered to herself, "now it has begun, it must be finished."

Mr Kay was in his study. It was hard to tell if he had even been to bed or not. A tray of tea and biscuits was at his elbow, but the tea was cold; papers and ledgers were spread out all over the desk, weighed down by a heavy abacus, but the ink was dry. A little greyer, a little older—indeed, older-looking than he should have been, for not so very long a time had passed—he sat with his sleeves rolled up to his elbows, his pipe in his hand, and his gaze out the window, chin resting on one fist.

Miss Cassidy gave herself the luxury of gazing long and hard at him, at the severe mouth and jaw, at the eyes that could flash with fire or twinkle with mischief. He seemed more tired than she remembered. Miss Cassidy did not flatter herself by thinking this had anything to do with her. More likely it was the result of his beloved twin girls leaving home, and perhaps the realisation that this great household he had put together, like a modern-age palace, was not to last beyond one generation. But Mr Kay never did things by halves. If he had decided his sons were in charge, their decisions would be final and inarguable. If he disagreed with the sale of their family home, he would not express it more than mildly, as his sons were sensible, practical young men, who probably had compelling reasons to do so.

Insubstantial and invisible, Miss Cassidy sat down directly across from Mr Kay, and smiled warmly at him.

"Bless you, Mr Kay," she said gently. "Bless you for your kindness, your generosity, your good humour, your courage and your open, loving heart. Bless you for being a great solid rock in a shifting sea, a safe shady spot under a fiery sky, a simple soul in a complicated world. May you find joy, love and comfort all the days of your life, till a gentle and noble rest comes upon you. May all who bear your blood be blessed also, with the same tranquil mind and affectionate soul you carry, from here on till the end of all worlds. As Lady of the Sidhe, so do I give my blessing."

As she spoke, though Mr Kay did not notice it, the lines of his palms were changing. It was subtle; some faded, some grew deeper, some retreated to the edges, some advanced to the centre. By the time she had finished speaking, Mr Kay's ill-omened hand was ill-omened no longer, and the stars had changed around him.

Miss Cassidy knew she should not linger. The spell had gone on too long; there were those who would notice. She stood up, and stepped back.

Mr Kay started suddenly, looked straight at her and said in shock, "Miss Cassidy?"

"Good gracious!" she exclaimed, aghast...

...and then she was gone again, and Mr Kay stood staring wildly about him, his pipe lying broken upon the floor.

XX

Miss Cassidy Is Summoned Again

"WELL, that is an unusual way to kill a chicken," said the butcher's wife, her tone caught somewhere between disapproval and astonishment.

"Isn't it?" said Miss Cassidy mildly, as she slapped the unfortunate hen onto the chopping block. "I learnt it from an excellent lady in Singapore, several years ago. She was good with pigs too, so fast with her knife they had no time to squeal, and all the blood collected neatly in a bucket, not a drop spilt."

Miss Cassidy enjoyed being in a busy kitchen again. It was a beautiful day, and though everyone seemed to be in everyone else's way, and there was far too much high-pitched, childish squealing, everyone was mostly in good spirits, and this made the occasional elbow in the ribs and spilt drop of cream quite all right.

The annual church fête was a jolly affair, an excuse for chickens and geese to be roasted, cakes and pies to be baked, and homemade jam and cheese and sweet wine to be put out in competition with one's neighbours'. Several women were bustling about—Sarah Jane, Miss Cassidy, the wives of the butcher, the baker, the grocer and the surrounding farmers, all aprons and flour and feathers and breadcrumbs. Heavenly smells filled the air, and the women shared thimblefuls of blackcurrant or elderflower wine while constantly exclaiming, "I really shouldn't."

The ladies of the village had by now grown accustomed to Miss Cassidy. Some still looked askance at her, for there was no denying she was well-bred and well-spoken, and had a great deal of learning, and it made her an oddity in a distant northern village. However, as time passed, they came to accept her simply as someone whom God had brought to them, for unknown reasons; besides which, her seemingly endless fount of useful knowledge and surprising skills gave her a certain cachet.

A general atmosphere of goodwill prevailed this day, in any case. The children were running about the yard, being as noisy as they possibly could, kicking cans and flying kites and looking for early conkers. The men were with their livestock, prize bulls, cows, pigs and sheep, good-naturedly shouting insults. Those who could play the fiddle or carry a tune were warming up in the cemetery among the gravestones of their forebears. The anticipation of cake and meat and revelry was keeping all squabbling at bay.

"Miss Cassidy! Someone wants you," shouted a small blond head through the doorway.

"Who is it?" she asked, but the head disappeared too rapidly. Miss Cassidy sighed, wiped her hands on her apron and ventured out. Around her, children swarmed and laughed, and she wound her way through them, puzzled. Nobody seemed to be waiting for her.

And then the world changed around her.

It did not take Miss Cassidy long to recognise the scrubby backyard, the chickens in their pen, the fire crackling and sputtering under a steely sky. Pak Labah smiled at her—rather cheekily, she thought crossly—and spat betel juice on the ground at his feet. He looked no older than he had when she first met him; though, then again, neither did she.

"You are a formidable old man," she said in vexation. "I can't imagine anyone could summon me from halfway around the world with an old banana peel and a handful of coins."

A familiar voice said, "He had something rather better than that."

Miss Cassidy whirled around, and was confronted with... her grey poplin dress, draped over a low rattan stool.

She had left the old dress behind, of course, for she'd been wearing her new best dress, the green silk, at the Far Eastern Oriental Hotel, and this was all she possessed when she turned up at Sarah Jane Weston's gate. It was just as well she'd had it on, for the fine material and beautiful tailoring, not to mention her malachite brooch, indicated that she was a lady of decent means, and the other village folk did not have to take Sarah Jane's plain word for it.

"Well?" said the voice. "I have come a long way, and went through quite a lot of trouble, to find out how to do this. I even asked the advice of the sultan's daughter, you know, for it seems this trick is so difficult that only the most powerful of bomohs can perform it. And truly powerful bomohs like to remain hidden, known only to special clients. As all powerful beings do, I suppose."

Miss Cassidy stood very still, and continued to stare fixedly at her old grey poplin dress, now faded, every stitch and seam familiar and distant.

"Miss Cassidy, turn and face me."

Miss Cassidy shook her head firmly.

"I warn you, if you do not face me, I will leave your dress with Pak Labah, and he will have the power to summon you willy-nilly, and pass that power on to his disciple, and you will be their pet hantu air till the end of time."

"I am not a water spirit," said Miss Cassidy, offended; and when she turned, Mr Kay was there.

Though it had been less than a year since her "visitation", his hair was now almost completely grey, except for a few black streaks here and there, and his eyes were traced with laugh lines. Apparently the effort of gathering the knowledge and resources to summon her had taken a toll, ageing him prematurely. He was still very tall, and wore his grey Shantung silk jacket, smoking what looked like a new pipe with a beautifully patterned bowl. He was smiling the same smile he always kept for Miss Cassidy.

"Do you like it?" he said, lifting the pipe after following her gaze. "A birthday gift from Yeling and Yezi. They had it specially made. I broke the old one, you know, when you startled me that day, and I dropped it."

"I don't know what you are talking about," said Miss Cassidy; at least, she tried to say it, but the words seemed to get stuck in her throat.

"You should have seen them, Miss Cassidy, my two little girls, their own little girls with them. Nobody mistakes which twin is which anymore, you know. Yezi is thin, thinner than I like, but they tell me it is the fashion these days. She wears beautiful dresses, of course, Shanghainese-style chongsams with all these sparkling things on them, whatever they're called, and keeps her hair so short. Yeling is different, plump with good food, her hair in a hair net with a jade pin, a busy little laoban-niang, a boss lady. So different! But they gave this pipe to me for my birthday," he added, smiling faintly in the direction of his feet, "just as they used to when they were children—hiding behind my door, you know, whispering and giggling. They sent their children in first, and while I was distracted they produced this lovely Japanese lacquer box, and showed me this terribly expensive pipe, with all these dragons and whatnot carved into the bowl, and this part here made of brown jade, and this here of gold, and I don't know what else. I have never seen such a ridiculous thing. It is the only pipe I use, now."

He puffed it, eloquently, and stepped neatly into her eye-line, whereupon she hurriedly dropped her gaze to the ground. "Miss Cassidy," he said, "you never gave us the chance to thank you for what you did."

"And what did I do?"

"I don't know, for I don't remember. Neither do the twins. I think Wong Mi has a clue, but even then, it is vague. I suspected she knew something, from the way she goes to the temple every New Year, lighting joss sticks and asking for blessings for Miss Cassidy."

"How is Wong Mi?"

"Very well, I would say. Leong and Wong Mi live in Penang now. He trades in antiques. Beautiful home. They came back on Chinese New Year. And Mui Ee, if you are wondering, is exactly the same as she has always been; when you watch Mui Ee in the kitchen, it is as if time never passed, and she is still teaching Wong Mi to steam dumplings and you to kill chickens and the twins to scrub pans."

Miss Cassidy finally looked up. "Why have you summoned me?"

"To explain this." And he held up his hand.

Miss Cassidy smiled again when she saw his altered palm, and its clean, smooth, clear lines, unbroken in their uncomplicated passage across his skin. "What ever do you mean?"

"Ah, don't give me that look," he said, "not before we are done speaking."

"What look?"

"This one, this one! This face that says, 'I know what you are asking, Mr Kay, but I will pretend not to on purpose in order to vex you.'"

"I don't have any such look on my face."

"Indeed you do. Wipe it off, and tell me what this means." And he brandished his hand again. "Madam Lim nearly had a heart attack. She told me my fortune had changed in a most unlikely manner. Now I seem to have a bright and successful career, a long life, many children and general prosperity."

"You had all that before your palm changed, Mr Kay. What does it matter what the lines are?"

"You tell me, Miss Cassidy! How would I know? My third eye, as you call it, does not give me knowledge, only vision. I know what I see," he added, "but I cannot always explain it."

"I am afraid I cannot explain it either," she said primly.

"There is that damned look again. What happened on Pulau Blakang Mati, Miss Cassidy?"

"I have no idea."

"Something came for my girls. They no longer remember, but I know they did not wander off by themselves, leaving Mui Ee's two little children crying behind them. What came for them? How? Why?"

"I know the how," said Miss Cassidy, relenting slightly, "but it would make no sense to you. And I imagine the why was simply...the opportunity arose. Your ill fortune, Mr Kay, was unique to you, you see. It did not mean you would fail in business, or die young, or all those other things the fortune tellers thought they saw. It meant that you and your household were vulnerable to...to certain influences, that there were weak spots in your world, where those unpleasant influences could leak through. It meant some things had a level of power over you and your kin that they would not have over another family, and that power would be hard to shake off. Your bloodline carried a curse, Mr Kay, of which the third eye was only a small part."

"And so...something came through, and took my daughters?"

"In a manner of speaking. She had been waiting a long time. She would have taken anyone she could have reached, but it was your family that fell into her influence, and your family that was vulnerable. It would have been Mui Ee's children, if the twins had not been there, if they had not been able to see what they saw."

"And I would have lost them, if not for you."

"If not for my sister, Anna, in fact. Whatever you think I am, Mr Kay, you have no concept of how much more Anna is."

"More...what?"

"More everything." She smiled faintly. "We are quite a tribe, my brothers and sisters."

"Mm." Mr Kay puffed on his pipe again. "I hope Anna is well?"

"She thrives. She always does. Her business is to thrive."

"It has been nine months."

Miss Cassidy was silent.

"Nine months since my fortune changed. Nine months since I saw you before me like a shadow made of light. I called to you, and you said, 'Good gracious,' and went away, just like that. Was 'good gracious' the last thing on earth you wanted me to hear of your voice, Miss Cassidy?"

"Well, I—"

"You owe an apology to Haresh Nair, for I demanded he track you down, and he was forced to go to the immigration offices and the placement agency that facilitated your post with the Bendemeers, and find an address and a family member and...and...oh, I do not remember, everything he could possibly find. Do you know what he found?"

She did, but again, she did not answer.

"Nothing. Your listed next of kin was Anna Clodagh O'Shea, wife of a British officer posted to Ceylon, but George

O'Shea had taken his orders and left Ceylon and our letter never reached him, and no one knew where he had gone. Letters sent to your last known address came back 'undeliverable', and the actual spot was described to me as, and I quote, 'a field of mushrooms and cow dung'. Using the name Leda Cassidy led me as far as your last known posting in India, to the unfortunate Randall family, all of whom perished, and therefore could be of no help. So what was I to do, Miss Cassidy? How was I to trace you?"

"But why did you..." Miss Cassidy decided not to finish the question.

"And so, in despair, I asked Wong Mi what she knew," he said at last. "Quiet, quiet girl, Wong Mi. She keeps secrets well, you know. She pretended to know nothing for a long time. But eventually she told me what you did for her. And then I understood. Or at least, I think I did." He gestured dismissively. "In any case, I decided that I needed a different sort of help. I asked Mui Ee to write to her friend, Princess Nora, and Princess Nora gave me a very, very secret list of all the dukuns attached to various members of the royal family. None of them could help me—they sent me to this person, then the next, then the next. Then Pak Labah heard of this whole matter, and I think he recognised your unique description, Miss Cassidy," Mr Kay smiled, "and it was he who then came to me, and said he would help me, for a price."

"Oh dear. What price is that, Mr Kay?"

"You left a few things behind, Miss Cassidy. One of them was a green glass bottle, and another was an iron key."

"The bottle was empty," she said. "The thing inside died with its mistress."

"I presume Pak Labah will use it to hold something else. It seems it can hold all manner of things, now it has passed through your hands."

"Well, yes, but…" She sighed. "Oh, very well. I hope it is never misused, that's all."

"If it is, it is your own fault, for being so hard to find."

"That is the *purpose* of hiding," murmured Miss Cassidy.

It was then that Miss Cassidy experienced a new sensation—a rare thing for one of her many years—that of being firmly taken by both arms and shaken like a rag doll. For a man of gentle temperament, Mr Kay's grip was remarkably strong, and he was clearly not short of energy, as he punctuated every word of his next sentence with a vigorous shake that made Miss Cassidy's head rattle.

"Why"—*shake*—"were"—*shake*—"you"—*shake*—"hiding?!" And a double-shake for good measure, to emphasise the point, before he released her, leaving Miss Cassidy breathless and outraged and all bits and pieces. Her dress was still covered with chicken feathers, and they flew about Pak Labah's yard now like an agitated snowfall.

"Why?" he demanded again. "Answer me, Miss Cassidy. It had better be a good answer, to make up for the nine months I have spent seeking you."

"Why, Mr Kay, have you spent nine months seeking me?" she retorted, now well put-out. "What on earth possessed you to do so? I was only your daughters' English teacher, and Anna sent a message—"

"Indeed! How magnanimous of Anna!"

"There was no reason for you to look for me!"

"For my daughters' English teacher? Well, for one thing, I owed her a quarter's salary, and I have it here." He reached into his jacket and pulled out a yellowing envelope of banknotes, which still had written on it in Haresh Nair's neat hand, *Salary for English Teacher*, the amount and the date. "It is still an open column in Mr Nair's ledger, unpaid for nearly five years. I have, besides, a poplar-wood trunk full of a Western woman's clothes and things, which my daughter-in-law had to clear out and store away in secret because she knew I would be angry they were touched. I do not know what to do with these things, which nobody in my household has any use for, this collection of bizarre items I do not understand—a jar full of marbles, and a sewing kit with an inordinate number of needles and scissors, and iron nails and keys, and a paper bag of salt, and...and... this dress with its pocket full of beads and bones—this *dress*!"

He stabbed an accusing finger at the shabby grey dress, as if it might speak to defend itself. "Say something, Miss Cassidy," he demanded. "Explain."

Miss Cassidy found she had stopped breathing. She took a moment to begin again, and drew a few more breaths of the damp, balmy air she remembered well, the scent of frangipani and pandan carried on the breeze.

"Well, Mr Kay, Anna and I had to...put someone back where she belonged. To keep her from doing further harm, she has been bound to her place for a hundred years. But she has something of mine, you see, Mr Kay. She took some of my hair. It does not matter much for humans," she explained

272

gently. "She took Yezi's hair too, but it is now useless to her—human hair is a dead thing when it is cut. But it is not so with us. Whatever is part of us, whatever we touch or use, we leave a trace on it. If the trace is strong enough, those who know how to find us can do so. As you yourself have now discovered," she added, gesturing at the grey dress.

"So you see, I could not come back, Mr Kay," she continued as he began to pace the ground. "Not to your family, who are already vulnerable to her. If she breaks her bonds again, and comes for me, I will have placed your entire family in danger. Do you understand?"

Mr Kay continued to smoke his pipe, and said nothing.

"Mr Kay, I am sorry you have wasted nine months in tracking me down," she said quietly. "If I had known it was important to you..." He spun on his heel and glared at her, but she continued adamantly on, "I might have left you a better message, but it seemed safest to let things be. Where I am now, there is nobody with me who is vulnerable to these influences, and it is a place I can leave easily if I must."

"The place you are now. Do you like it?" he asked abruptly.

"Yes, Mr Kay. I do."

"Would I know this place if you showed me on a map?"

"No, I'm afraid not. It is an island of no particular importance, with a scattering of villages, and a great many more sheep than people."

"Would I like it if I were there?"

"No, Mr Kay, and you will not be coming here."

"Mm. Well. Firstly, take your wages. I have had them converted to British currency, which I presume will be more useful to you now." Not knowing what else to do, Miss Cassidy accepted the envelope of notes and coins, and put it in her pocket.

"Secondly," he said, "whatever you are, Miss Cassidy, and I honestly do not care, tell me—can you summon things as well?"

"Summon things?" she repeated blankly.

"Yes, summon things," he said, waving his pipe in a vague manner. "For I must presume that however powerful old Pak Labah is, you are surely more so."

"My folk do not...'summon things' offhand, Mr Kay," she said disapprovingly. "You never get what you bargain for, when you go about seeking the attention of creatures you do not understand, often very dangerous ones, and requesting favours from them."

"But you would not be requesting a favour. Well, you would be requesting the favour of my company, perhaps. That is all."

Miss Cassidy was silent for a moment, as she processed this remarkable sentence. "Mr Kay," she said slowly, "are you suggesting that I...summon you to me?"

"Yes." He did not elaborate, merely put his pipe in his mouth.

"I....but...for what purpose?"

"Conversation."

"Mr Kay, be serious," she exclaimed.

"I am serious. I cannot summon you to me, clearly—I am not a bomoh. But I am quite certain you can bring me to you."

"Not...not substantially, no. You are...well, you are physically very heavy, you know."

"Am I? I must eat fewer lotus paste buns."

"No, no, I mean…there is… Mr Kay, you are not of my world, and you cannot be summoned," she said at last, briskly. "And that is that. If you like, I will write letters—"

"Oho, *now* she speaks of letters!" he cried, making a wild and furious gesture that sent tobacco ash tumbling. "She could have sent a letter any time these past five years, but we come to the point of sorcery and black magic, and she proposes, now, to send a letter! The time is past for letters, Miss Cassidy."

"Mr Kay—"

But he had taken her hand, and was gripping it so tightly she gasped a little. He grinned down at her, a little mad and mischievous, and strange and wild.

Then, very quickly, he opened her palm and pressed a kiss into her hand.

It was too late to stop it. Miss Cassidy blushed like fire.

Before she could snatch her hand away, he put his pipe into it, and firmly wrapped her fingers around it. "Leda Cassidy," he said, "I wish to remind you that you never formally left my employ. If creatures like yourself must obey those whom they are bound to, you are most certainly bound to me, and you are to do my bidding. The fire is almost out," he added, "I have used up all of Pak Labah's firewood, and I am not yet done talking to you. Find a way, Miss Cassidy! I trust you."

"Mr Kay, don't—" she began…and the fire went out.

XXI

Miss Cassidy Has
a Tea Party

"I BROUGHT a seed cake," said Anna chirpily, and took from her basket the biggest, most luscious-looking seed cake Miss Cassidy had ever seen, and placed it on the table in the centre of the schoolhouse.

Miss Cassidy sighed. "I wish you would be earnest, Anna."

"Oh, but I am in deadly earnest! Summonings make me hungry—they work me up so, that afterwards I must have cake. Do you not get that feeling?"

"I do not perform summonings, as a rule," said Miss Cassidy coldly.

"Well, I suppose not; you are of the ilk that others try to summon."

"I am not a demon," said Miss Cassidy in a huff.

"Come now, Leda. I'll wager you have led a few unwary travellers astray in your day, because they could not solve your riddles."

Miss Cassidy did not deign to answer, instead pouring the tea while Anna shook out a new packet of salt from her purse. "Have you ever summoned a human, Anna?" Miss Cassidy asked as she counted the sugar lumps.

"Oh yes. But you know, those were different days. They understood the division between the ka and the ha, you see. In those days, humans valued their mortal flesh less."

"Well, they were apt to lose it much sooner."

"I suppose so, especially with folk like yourself wandering about!"

"When you are done teasing me, tell me what I should do."

"Give me his totem, and let us see if this will work."

Mr Kay could not sleep, so he poured himself some cold tea and took his favourite seat by the window.

It was a stormy night, with rain lashing off the rooftops and the trees bent half over from the roaring wind. Mr Kay sometimes remembered the sea passages he had taken in his youth, when storms like these bubbled up across the world, and they would all be tossed about and sliding around, and he would remember his ill-omened hand and think, *Well, I have nothing to lose.*

He sometimes thought of Chen Choo, as well, who had been afraid of thunder, but who found her own fear amusing. When lightning struck she would scream, clap her hands to her ears and then laugh at her own reaction. He used to see her ghost around the twins when they were very young, and they would reach out to her from old Yoke Jie's arms and gurgle, and she would smile. She never seemed to see Mr Kay, or anyone else; only her daughters, whom she had never had the chance to meet. And then as they grew, she faded, and he saw her less and less, until finally she was no longer there.

Yoke Jie herself would likely be the next to go. She was quite old now, and though she was supposedly "taking care" of Mr Kay, in truth his only working servants were Mat and the daily scrub maid. Yoke Jie was no longer allowed to sew or boil water, but to keep her from feeling her infirmity, Mr Kay let her have a broom and feather duster, and totter about the house at her own pace, doing her small bit to keep things tidy. In the evenings he would sit with her and read the newspaper aloud so she would not be lonely, even though she seldom understood what it said. Yoke Jie would not linger, Mr Kay knew. She had lived her life to its natural completion, nothing left undone; she would leave no uneasy ghost behind.

In the initial years after Chen Choo died, Madam Lim had pressed upon him the need to take another wife. To raise his children, she insisted, to manage his household, and to keep him company in old age. She had made many suggestions, and Mr Kay, lacking the courage to turn her down flat, simply smiled and nodded and said he would think about it, and the years had passed and passed until Boon came of age, and Madam Lim gave up and turned to the younger man.

Mr Kay had never thought of himself as a lonely man— there was no time to be lonely, no space to be lonely, with a thriving business to run and a large noisy household to take care of. And even now, in solitude, he did not feel lonely. Silence was comforting to him.

What he did miss, however, was the laughter. Chen Choo had stolen his heart because she knew how to laugh. His daughters had stolen it again because they too were full of laughter and mischief, and had never really outgrown their childlike humour. And then, of course, there was Miss Cassidy.

"Is it working? I can't tell."

"Hush, Leda, for heaven's sake. I am trying to concentrate."

"The pipe appears to be smoking. Should it be smoking?"

"Is there tobacco in it?"

"No."

"Well, put some in it, my dear! The pipe is not complete without tobacco—how will he smoke it?"

"Is he meant to?"

"Yes! It is an offering to tempt his spirit! Who is tempted by an empty pipe?"

Mr Kay tapped his pipe on the windowsill. It was an old pipe, an unfussy, ugly black thing that served its purpose well enough for him. When the girls, pouting, asked what had happened to their present, he'd said he had accidentally broken it and sent it off to be repaired.

Tobacco was his only real vice. He disliked drunkenness so never drank to excess, he had always been too busy to gourmandise, and now he was too old to care for fancy food, being quite happy with rice and tofu. He had never bothered much with women, because he had seen how complicated one's life could become with the wrong kind. All these luxuries had never had much appeal for him, but at the end of a long day, he used to like to stroll about his own compound, listening with satisfaction to the hum of voices within the walls, while smoking his pipe. It had never been the pipe in itself; it was merely a good excuse to be outside.

Mr Kay never forgot the feeling of great satisfaction that had come over him the first evening he saw Miss Cassidy in the small, scrubby yard of the humble priest's hut, tucked away among the sweet potato plants. She had not appeared to materially change anything in that bare little accommodation, yet it had seemed brighter for her presence in some indefinable way. Of course, if he asked the womenfolk, they would have pointed out that Miss Cassidy had cleared the yard of weeds and rubbish, swept the floor, put in fresh sheets, and polished the window-grilles and fixtures till they shone, so what he thought of as a mysterious aura of crisp goodwill was merely the result of efficient housekeeping. Still, it did not change the fact that seeing her there for the first time, seated primly in the yard with her flame-red hair over her shoulder, had given him a strange sense of the rightness of things.

She had been sewing, he remembered, and smiling to herself. It was the smile, a funny secret sort of smile, that had made him drift towards her and start a rather out-of-the-blue sort of conversation. And somehow that had become a habit, taking a walk to Miss Cassidy every other evening, even if only to exchange two sentences.

Mr Kay had not thought very deeply about what he was doing. He simply enjoyed her company—she was unique, invigorating and amusing. He came to like the faint smile that crept over her face when the scent of his pipe announced his approach, and the determined way she demurely refrained from looking up at him, so that he sometimes had to say outrageous things to force her to react naturally. He had not realised how much he soon came to rely on Miss Cassidy for company, until the time came when she was no longer there.

"Anna, this is not working."

"You must be patient, my dear. A summoning is a complicated thing, and you forget that he is mortal and substantial."

"I never forget he is mortal and substantial. It was you who said this could be done. I never entertained any such thought."

"But you hoped, when you asked me, that it could be done somehow. And I assure you it can. But you cannot get frustrated. Remember, when the old priestesses summoned your folk, they were willing to wait many hours in salt circles, in damp mouldy forests full of insects."

"We are not going to sit at this table for many hours. I haven't the time. I promised Sarah Jane I would help her with the cheese today."

"The cheese be damned, Leda! Something is missing. What do you think of, when you bring Mr Kay to mind?"

"I...well. I don't know. A pipe."

"We have a pipe. And it is lit. What else about the pipe?"

"Oh dear."

"What?"

"I think...I think I shall have to smoke it."

*

Mr Kay was not sure what made him decide to venture out into the garden. The rain had abated somewhat, certainly, and the air was cool and fresh. Perhaps it was just too hot and quiet in the little house. In any case, he stepped into his slippers, refilled his pipe and ambled out.

The sky was full of stars—indeed, it seemed the stars were brighter than he had ever seen them. The air was crisp, almost cold.

There was a light in the distance, winking oddly, like a candle flame. Mr Kay stared at it, puzzled. There were not many houses around his; certainly there should be none in that particular spot. For no reason he could fathom, he started to move towards it.

As he approached, he seemed to recognise the scent of another pipe. The outline of a small house began to take shape in the shadows: a narrow, high-roofed house with a yard in front of it. There was a tree there that was unlike any tree he had ever seen in the tropics; it looked suspiciously like an oak tree. The winking light came from one of the small narrow windows. Shadows moved within; faint voices carried on the still air.

Mr Kay paused. Then he began to walk towards it more quickly than ever, with determined strides. The house seemed to fade and retreat, then return and advance; Mr Kay did not stop. Faster and faster he went, till he was almost running; and then he really was running, throwing the old brown pipe over his shoulder, running as hard as he could manage, towards the scent of his own tobacco smoke.

*

"Oh! This is foul. Why do men use these things?"

"Why do men do anything, I ask you, Leda? But I think this is better. The scent of it is a stronger pull to his spirit than merely the flame."

"Is it? Oh dear." Miss Cassidy coughed and coughed, and put the pipe down in despair. "Oh, Anna, really, this is too ridiculous. Let us think of something else. I will put more tea on, and we shall have some cake. I will need to get to the cheese in about twenty minutes."

There was a knock on the door. Miss Cassidy, her knife poised to slice the enormous seed cake, sighed. "That is probably Sarah Jane now. Put those things away, will you, Anna? They will look most peculiar to her."

"Leda," said Anna slowly, "just…just open the door, will you?"

Miss Cassidy stared at her. Then, in a kind of stupor, still holding the cake knife, she went to the door, took a deep breath and threw it open.

Mr Kay smiled. "Hello, Miss Cassidy," he said. "I believe you have my pipe."

ACKNOWLEDGEMENTS

The Formidable Miss Cassidy owes its existence to more people than I can easily enumerate, from its illustrious inspirations (Neil Gaiman, Charlotte Brontë) to the ones who put in the hard work and elbow grease to get it into the shape you see here—most notably the Epigram Books team: editor Jason Erik Lundberg (whom I have to single out for ardently encouraging me to enter the Epigram Books Fiction Prize after receiving the manuscript through the regular submissions portal), designer Syafiqah Binte Rosman, Chris and Doretta in marketing, and of course the invincible publisher Edmund Wee—all while surviving a global pandemic! Grateful thanks also to the jury of the 2021 EBFP for judging the novel worthy of co-winning; especially Monica Lim, whose enthusiasm gave me the first glimmer of hope.

This book started as a short story, written as a Circuit Breaker hobby and sent off on a whim to a small indie horror press in Canada. I am deeply indebted to editor Selene MacLeod, who liked Miss Cassidy enough, in her original and rather raw iteration, to suggest she should have her own novel. Needless to say, I'm glad I listened to her!

My research into the world of Miss Cassidy runs the gamut, from trekking through every museum in Singapore to taking up online certificates in fairy magic (yes, really, I can now tell your fortune in tarot cards and tea leaves). I also had the privilege of speaking to many amazing ladies (and one gentleman) whose spirituality inspired much of Miss Cassidy's paraphernalia. They are too many to list here, but in particular, I'd like to thank Amelia Kang and Serene from Ame de Lumière, who always make exploring your spiritual (and maybe psychic!) side a fun and fabulous journey.

I'd also like to honour my family: I am descended on my father's side from an actual fortune teller, a truly formidable lady who lived in a three-storey shophouse on Club Street, where my paternal grandmother was still living well into the nineties as one of the last original residents of Chinatown; and on my mother's side from a great-grandmother whose feet were, indeed, bound, and who didn't let that stop her from being absolutely fearsome.

Love and thanks, always, to my supportive husband Steven, whose Scottish heritage is heavily referenced in *Miss Cassidy* (although he is not red-haired, and most assuredly does not sound like Gimli from *The Lord of the Rings*).